DIZZY DUKE BROTHER RAY AND FRIENDS

DIZZY DUKE BROTHER RAY AND FRIENDS

ON AND OFF THE RECORD WITH JAZZ GREATS

LILIAN TERRY

P 5 4 3 2 1
∞ This book is printed on acid-free paper.

Library of Congress Cataloging-in-Publication Data
Names: Terry, Lilian, author.
Title: Dizzy, Duke, Brother Ray, and friends : on and off the record with jazz greats / Lilian Terry.
Description: Champaign, IL: University of Illinois Press, 2017. | Includes index. |
Identifiers: LCCN 2017024540 (print) | LCCN 2017025737 (ebook) | ISBN 9780252050176 (ebook) | ISBN 9780252083167 (pbk. : alk. paper)
Subjects: LCSH: Jazz musicians—Interviews. | Gillespie, Dizzy, 1917–1993—Interviews. | Ellington, Duke, 1899–1974—Interviews. | Charles, Ray, 1930–2004—Interviews. | Lincoln, Abbey—Interviews. | Roach, Max, 1924–2007—Interviews. | Silver, Horace, 1928–2014—Interviews. | Evans, Bill, 1929–1980—Interviews.
Classification: LCC ML394 (ebook) | LCC ML394 .T46 2017 (print) | DDC 781.65092/2—dc23
LC record available at https://lccn.loc.gov/2017024540

CONTENTS

PREFACE

I was born in Cairo, Egypt, in a household where music was constantly in the background. Father and mother were opera buffs. Aunt Tina was a piano teacher and uncle René an avid collector of jazz records and faithful listener to the American Forces Network radio station during World War II. My attention was definitely caught by jazz, and by the time I was thirteen years old I was singing more blues and jazz songs than playing Chopin on the piano. My formal schooling entailed English-Italian-French studies mainly at The English School in Heliopolis, Cairo, then in Florence, Italy.

Residing in Italy from the early 1950s, I discovered that the nation of the "bel canto" had no real knowledge of what jazz music was about. I also had my difficulties in being accepted in a male society: I was a woman and a foreigner with better knowledge of jazz history than most of my colleagues. Fortunately, I emerged.

By the 1960s I was active in the European jazz field, singing at concerts, festivals, radio, and TV productions in Europe (Eastern and Western), and later in the United States. I also recorded with Dizzy Gillespie, Kenny Drew, Tommy Flanagan, Ed Thigpen, and Von Freeman, among others.

Lyric writer in English and Italian, I was also a journalist and producer of jazz shows with RAI, the national Italian radio and TV network, conducting live interviews with special guests. In October 1967 I represented Italy at the Warsaw Jazz Jamboree attending the creation of the European Jazz Federation, where I was elected vice president of the Division of Education.

During the 1970s and 1980s I represented RAI at the yearly EBU (European Broadcasting Union) International Jazz Quiz, broadcast live by all member countries. I would translate simultaneously from English or French into Italian. I also translated into Italian Dizzy Gillespie's autobiography, *To Be or Not to Bop*, as well as various Duke Ellington writings.

During the 1980s and 1990s the Italian educational authorities requested I hold lecture/concerts for high school students across Italy, illustrating the cultural, political, and social history of Afro-American music.

In September 1983, I created with Dizzy the "Dizzy Gillespie Popular School of Music" in Bassano del Grappa, Italy. In 1987, celebrating Gillespie's seventieth birthday, the school inaugurated a section dedicated to blind students. The school closed its activities in 1997, three years after Dizzy's passing away. I handed the students over to the music teachers and in September 2000 retired to Nice, France, with time to write my jazz memoirs.

Dizzy, Duke, Brother Ray, and Friends covers my relationship with historical jazz icons with whom I had the privilege of maintaining close friendships. My purpose is not to dissert on their artistic worth, composition, and performance skills—or other technicalities that you will find better analyzed elsewhere—but to share with all jazz lovers some of those unique, unrepeatable, close encounters offering direct insight on the human being behind the musician. Why did all these important American jazz artists decide I was worthy of their confidence and trust? I must refer you to the particular relationship between American musicians and Europe.

Historically, the first impact between jazz musicians arriving in Europe and the friendly welcome they were greeted with took place in the early 1900s, when black dance bands were hired to entertain the elite tourist patrons of famous cruise ships crossing the Atlantic. Upon landing in Europe, mostly in France and the U.K., the artists were soon befriended by the local musicians, delighted with this exciting new music and creating occasions where they could learn to play it with their American guests. From then on, through the U.S. Army bands of World War I and World War II, jazz music was to become a solid part of European entertainment, recognized everywhere as the most respected and original form of North American culture.

Thus began the migration of American artists who decided to remain in Europe, going back to the international black dancer Josephine Baker who became an honored French citizen earning the Légion d'Honneur. By the middle of the twentieth century, Europe had attracted many famous musicians who elected final residence mostly in Paris and Denmark, such as Sidney Bechet, Kenny Clarke, Bud Powell, Johnny Griffin, Ed Thigpen, Kenny Drew, and Dexter Gordon. Many others would choose to reside in Europe for long periods at a time, such as Chet Baker, Randy Weston, and Tony Scott.

Incidentally, it should be noted that during the Cold War years (1947–1991) the American State Department, thanks to the "Voice of America," was very successful in permeating most communist countries in Eastern Europe with the very popular jazz radio programs presented by the famous voice of Willis Conover.

In closing this preface I wish to thank my friends—Italian, American, French, and Egyptian—for urging me to put down on paper these memoirs; a heartfelt "grazie" to my son, Francesco, and daughter-in-law, Julia, for their active collaboration in checking the various interviews and presentations, as well as curbing my impulsive and impatient writings. A final and huge thank you I owe to Laurie Matheson for believing in this project.

DIZZY DUKE BROTHER RAY AND FRIENDS

INTRODUCTION

One day I discover, with amazement rather than dismay, that I have passed the birthday sign marked "80." I sit on my terrace in Nice, enjoying the view that embraces the Mediterranean from Cap Ferrat to Cap d'Antibes, and I count my blessings. I sigh my thanks from a Latin "Deo Gratias" to an Oriental "al hamdul'Allah" in homage to the land of Egypt, where I was born and given my first fourteen years of multiethnic education. I felt neither a British subject, as had been my Maltese father, nor a maternal Italian one, considering myself simply a "bent el Nil," a "daughter of the Nile," as did most of us European schoolgirls in Cairo.

I realize how incredibly blessed I have been in my career dedicated to the diffusion of jazz music, and feel I should put down on paper all those unique "Close Encounters in the Jazz Dimension" experienced in the first person right in the midst of the truly innovative, historic, and magical jazz years. Although this text is written in the first-person singular, I consider myself but a witness to lead you through all of the happenings—conversations, interviews, and anecdotes—drawing a unique picture of the following artists as I have known them.

I was warmly accepted by a giant such as Duke Ellington during his last seven years. He chose to be my friend, demanding my annual presence during his concert tours in Europe as his "good-luck charm" and as his sounding board for all the phrases he would dictate to me, to be used later in his own writings. Our relationship was an unbelievable and precious experience.

Ray Charles and I were close for more than ten years, as the many taped interviews will prove. His initial interest in me as a young woman soon developed into an affectionate, protective relationship where he organized our yearly meetings with almost secretive discretion. He not only let me tape our long talks concerning music, segregation, health, and religion, but he also enjoyed being my technician, handling the tape recorder most efficiently.

Abbey Lincoln and Max Roach entered my family life in 1967 in Italy, charming my mother and young son and establishing an immediate trusting relationship between all of us that lasted strongly through the years till their passing away: Max in 2007 and Abbey in 2010.

Also, Dizzy Gillespie chose to become a most welcome member of my family. Involved with us during the last twenty years of his life, he chose to participate actively in my most important educational projects in Italy and in general became a beloved member of our community, becoming officially elected Honorary Citizen of Bassano del Grappa, where we had founded the "Dizzy Gillespie Popular School of Music."

Horace Silver was irresistible with his sharp sense of humor and brilliant music. He possessed also a special kindness toward his fellowmen, starting with a total dedication to his family. We could spend hours in serious discussion about religions and history, yet such moments were always interspersed with laughter. Our friendship, born in 1968, lasted through all his years.

Mentioning Bill Evans gives me a feeling of deep regret for the loss of such a unique artist and surprising human being. For some odd, fortunate reason he chose to spend one full day with me, in Bologna, Italy. We walked and talked; we stopped for cappuccinos and talked. To my joy, he was willing to share his thoughts on music, education, and politics, with a few smiles added. I felt grateful for his friendly attention, and that single day was worth a lifetime for me.

Each of these great artists had a very different, well-defined personality. They opened their inner doors, generously allowing me to enter and witness their private lives. You are welcome to join us.

EDWARD KENNEDY ELLINGTON

"Uncle Eddie"

Act I—Juan-les-Pins, France: The 1966 Jazz Festival. I am "adopted" by Duke Ellington and Billy Strayhorn.

Act II—Milano, Italy: Entrance of Herbert von Karajan in Ellington's dressing room.

Act III—Star-Crossed Lovers: After the passing away of both Strayhorn and Hodges I honor their memory by recording "Star-Crossed Lovers" with the Tommy Flanagan Trio.

Act IV—Christmas in New York 1967/68: New Year at the Ellington mansion on Riverside Drive. Giancarlo Menotti asks to be put in touch with Ellington.

Act V—Newport 1968: Ellington gives me a taped "interview-conversation" explaining the history of his Sacred Concerts. He also sings to me in Anglo-Italian.

Act VI—What is Jazz? New York 1968: Ellington accepts to write an article on jazz for Italian publishers Fratelli Fabbri Editori. His outlook on jazz is fascinating.

Act VII—Evelyn Ellington: Ellington introduces me to Evelyn, first wife of Mercer Ellington, and a warm friendship results. When my young son and I visit New York, we join Ellington in the basement recording studio of the Edison Hotel, where Ellington seats my son next to him on the piano bench to "assist him."

Act VIII—The Vatican: In the early 1970s RAI, the Italian National Radio, asks me if Ellington would perform a Sacred Concert in the Vatican for the Holy Father.

Act IX—Final Interview: The Italian Television asks me to tape a very special interview with Ellington. He talks freely about his whole life story. That is our last meeting.

Act X—"Fare thee well!" On May 24, 1974, he says goodbye.

ACT I—JUAN-LES-PINS, FRANCE

The most precious and amazing memory I treasure—of the many historical artists I had the privilege of meeting—is the unique world of Edward Kennedy Ellington.

From early childhood, during the Second World War years, I had been a constant radio listener, especially to the American Forces Network, enjoying artists called Frank Sinatra, Ella Fitzgerald, Benny Goodman, Bing Crosby, Glenn Miller, Dinah Shore, the Dorsey Brothers, not to forget Dame Vera Lynn . . . and, way above them, was the Duke Ellington Orchestra.

Through the many years that followed I had learned the names of the soloists who gave us that special Ellington sound. Although I admired them all, Johnny Hodges was my favorite. Especially when the famous Ellington repertoire offered the heartbreaking ballad from the *Romeo and Juliet* suite "Such Sweet Thunder" called "Star-Crossed Lovers," performed by Hodges with that sensuous, almost physically caressing voice of his alto saxophone. From the late 1950s, that ballad had become the showcase of his magic.

As my singing career progressed, I found myself performing at various International Festivals in Europe. One of the most prestigious being the Antibes–Juan-les-Pins festival, on the French Riviera, I was thrilled to appear there especially, as their greatest guest star was Duke Ellington, whose orchestra would also accompany Ella Fitzgerald, with Jimmy Jones at the piano.

On Tuesday, July 26, 1966, backstage at the Pinède Gould, I noticed Johnny Hodges standing by the stage steps. On an impulse I approached him: "Mr. Hodges, my name is Lilian Terry. I'm a singer. But above all I'm a passionate fan of your rendition of 'Star-Crossed Lovers.' I have attended most of your concerts in Italy these past fifteen years, always looking forward to hearing you play it. Recently, though, it's no longer in your repertoire, to my great disappointment. Is there any chance that you could play it tonight?"

Listening in silence, while inspecting me from head to toe, he shook his head: "Nope, sorry, we haven't played it in years. We've got a whole new book tonight, but . . ."

He hesitated, and then made up his mind. "Come on, let's go ask him . . ."

He guided me backstage to the beach cabins used as dressing rooms during the festival. He knocked, opened the door and, thrusting me in, he growled: "She wants me to play 'Star-Crossed Lovers.' Before you say no, take a look at her." Then he stepped back by the door.

To my amazement I recognized "the great Ellington" stretched on a beach deck-chair, wearing a short blue bathrobe, bare legs resting on a pillow on a chair in front of him. On his head was a hairdresser net to keep his locks in place. His eyes were closed and I just stood there, speechless. He turned his head and gave a close scrutiny to my whole appearance, from my short haircut to the white and gold sandals. His gaze rested on them as he pointed and asked: "Italy?"

"Yes, Positano." I whispered.

Always looking at them, he answered Hodges:

"'Star-Crossed Lovers,' huh? Well, if you want to play it for her, go talk to Norman, and tell him it's OK with me."

And, closing his eyes, he resumed his meditation, dismissing us.

So Hodges went looking for Norman Granz, dragging me along. He explained the subject. Granz looked at me, raising his accented eyebrows: "Well, if Edward agrees . . ." he shrugged and walked away from us.

For the first time, Hodges gave me a large, satisfied grin and patted my shoulder: "Well, we're on, kid. I'll play it just for you tonight. What did you say your name was?"

"Lilian. And thank you so much!"

"My pleasure. I'll go tell Ellington, he'll want to tell the guys . . ." then a bigger grin as he added ". . . but then again he might not. . . . See you later."

When they began preparing the open-air stage for the orchestra's performance, I joined my friends of the French TV crew. As I perched beside them on the railing in the open wings, I informed them that there might be a surprise that night.

The band walked onstage among enthusiastic shouts of welcome and applause from the public: There was Sam Woodyard fiddling with his drum set, joined by bassist John Lamb. Followed the four trumpets of Herbie Jones, Cootie Williams, Cat Anderson, and Mercer Ellington. The middle row featured the trombones of Lawrence Brown, Buster Cooper, and Chuck Connors. Finally, the reeds with Jimmy Hamilton, Harry Carney, Russell Procope, Paul Gonsalves, and last . . . Johnny Hodges reached his chair nonchalantly. As he turned around to sit down, he noticed me in the wings and gave me a curt nod, then proceeded to ignore me throughout the concert.

It was now practically over. The last performance had been a very long exploit by my favorite soloist, and Ellington kept shouting his name repeatedly, "Johnny Hodges!" while the audience sent wave after wave of enthusiastic applause. Hodges, standing in front of the orchestra, turned to Ellington and then motioned with his head toward me.

With an amused smile Ellington went to the microphone, announcing formally: "Thank you very much for Johnny Hodges. We do have another request. A lady has come all the way from Rome and she's asked for a couple of numbers from our Shakespearean Suite "Such Sweet Thunder." We'd like to do the title number for you now . . . oh no, Johnny Hodges is here, so let's do the other one, let's do the one which is *Romeo and Juliet.* And the Bard called them the 'star-crossed lovers'!"

Walking back to the piano Ellington gave me a long look, satisfied with my obvious emotion; then, motioning with his arm toward Hodges, he announced in his famous hyperbolic style: "Johnny Hodges! 'Star-Crossed Lovers'! Johnny Hodges!"

The whole band was searching for the music through their chart sheets—obviously unprepared for this surprise—while Hodges attached his instrument to his neck ribbon, stood by the central microphone, and practically turned his side to the public in order to face me in the wings. Ellington began the introductory arpeggios while nodding imperiously at his musicians, who began playing by memory. With evident emotion, I received the compliments of my French TV colleagues and settled to listen to the greatest gift Ellington and Hodges could have given anyone.

At the end of the concert I waited at the foot of the stage steps for Ellington to descend so as to thank him properly.

"My God! What an experience, Maestro Ellington! I shall never forget your kindness! But how did you know that I live in Rome?"

"My dear, I always find out who is the prettiest girl in town, especially if she becomes a member of my family. You are joining us for a 'coupe de champagne,' aren't you?"

As he spoke he slipped his arm through mine and led me firmly to where the rest of his "family" awaited him: his son Mercer, his nephew Stevie James, his hairdresser/valet Ronnie Smith, his musical assistant Herbie Jones, then a couple of old friends from London, Renée and Leslie Diamond . . . and on he went with the introductions till there were about a dozen people around us. I was presented as "Lilian, my Roman niece from Egypt" and obviously scrutinized by all of them. Which fact amused Ellington no end, as we entered the Provencal Hotel and went up to his suite.

When Billy Strayhorn joined the reception, Ellington led me to him: "This is our Lil from Rome, who loves 'Star-Crossed Lovers' madly."

I noticed the white bandage around Billy's throat and recalled hearing about his serious health problems, possibly terminal. However, he was smiling cheerfully at me, offering his hand, so I introduced myself properly and expressed my admiration for all of his ballads, which I sang with great pleasure, especially "Lush Life."

"Now that's really sweet of you, come and sit down. So you're a singer?"

He was extremely kind as he sat me next to him and we spoke of his music. Of course I confirmed my passion for "Star-Crossed Lovers."

He smiled: "Ah, I see now why Edward decided to play it, just out of the blue. The guys in the band had a little problem, having to play it by memory, hah, hah. . . . However, I'm glad you asked for it; it's one of my favorites too."

"I'm only sorry that it has no lyrics, I would love to sing it. And I would try to have that special sensuous 'Hodges sound.' Heavens, when he blows those long, languid notes . . . it's an actual caress!"

"Yes, it's very . . . physical, isn't it? And you would like to sing it?"

I nodded, and he patted my hand.

"Tell you what I'll do. Write me down your home address . . . you live in Rome, don't you? OK, I promise I'll send you some lyrics as soon as I get back to New York."

I thanked him, though telling myself not to hope too much. I then expressed my admiration for another extraordinary composition of his, the suite "A Drum Is a Woman," which I had often presented on my Italian radio programs.

"Really? I didn't know it was popular in Italy . . ."

"And I also sang one of the tunes, 'You Better Know It,' during a concert with the Kurt Edelhagen Orchestra in Cologne. They didn't know the suite, but they got the music from the States and Dusko Gojkovic wrote the arrangement for voice and orchestra."

"Why then, you really are a member of the family!"

During the days that followed, Billy and I had the opportunity to spend more time together. His kindness touched me deeply, and on the day he was leaving for Paris we hugged each other as he was entering the limousine: "You know, Lil, if I'd had a daughter, she would probably have been like you. Take good care of yourself now, and I'll be sure to send you those lyrics. Bye . . ."

Going back to that first evening, at the reception, when I rose wishing everybody a good night, Ellington walked me out of the suite to the elevators.

"Ah, Maestro! What an unforgettable evening. You know, as a rule, when great and famous artists, such as yourself, are approached privately, they are often a dreadful disappointment. But with you . . . the essential human being is even more fascinating . . ."

With that special cool-amused smile of his he grabbed me by the shoulders: "Now that is the sort of phrase I adore. May I use it myself, on some other appropriate occasion?"

My sense of humor emerged through all the emotions experienced that night, and I promised very formally to put at his disposal my whole repertoire of the kind.

He looked closer and asked if I did not wish to "forget" my jacket and perhaps come back for it when the other guests had gone?

I looked him in the eye and shook my head. "No sir. Fortunately, my sense of preservation is stronger than my attraction for you. You would discard me tomorrow morning with your breakfast tray and without a backward glance. This way you might remember me at least till lunchtime."

Still holding me at arm's length, he was grinning while scrutinizing me.

"Oh, I think I'll remember you long after that! As you wish, my dear. Tomorrow Norman has organized one of his fancy PRs. I am meeting Joan Miró at the Maeght Foundation, then there's the lunch at the Colombe d'Or at Saint Paul . . . the whole Granz production, so I won't be able to see you. But I want to see you the following morning. Stevie will come for you before midday, and we'll have breakfast here, at my suite. Remember, no food before then! Breakfast is a very important moment for the body!"

"Yes Sir! As you say, sir!"

"Now I'll give you four kisses for your four cheeks, and wish you goodnight."

Two mornings later, at twenty to midday, Stevie James was banging on my door: "Hey, Lilian! We've got to move. Uncle Eddie said you were to wake him up at midday sharp. Hurry up!"

From that moment everything was rushed: washing, dressing, a brush through my hair, no time for makeup, hurry! Laughing and moving at a trot, Stevie and I discovered we had a similar sense of humor, and by the time we had entered Ellington's suite our friendship had been established.

"Wow, it's five to twelve. Wake him up Lilian, while I run his bath . . ."

There I was, alone in a darkened room with a naked jazz icon barely covered by a white sheet, snoring, face down in a huge bed. Why not? So what? Laughing silently to myself I sat by his side, laid both hands on the bed sheet and, starting with his lower back, began a massage moving up toward his neck and shoulders. At every move forward he would give a satisfied grunt as I asked a different question:

". . . Who is the greatest American composer of all time?"

". . . And who brings joy to millions of fans throughout the world?"

". . . And who is admired and befriended universally, including by crowned heads of state?"

". . . And who is an irresistible heartbreaker?"

By then I had reached his shoulders, so I paused as he turned his head toward me and sighed:

"Who?"

"Who else but you?"

Stevie called out that the bath was ready, and I moved rapidly to the living room.

Punctually, the room-service attendant rolled in the breakfast trolley as Ellington appeared—wearing his short blue bathrobe and hair net—to sit in his armchair, settling his bare feet on the usual raised pillow. Strayhorn entered the suite. He sat next to me on one side of the sofa while Stevie chose the other side. Seated opposite us, Ellington stared at my sandals and pointed accusingly: "That's a different pair from the other night. Always your Positano man?"

"Yes, he's a real magician, makes them in all shapes and sizes."

"How many pairs do you have?"

"Well, I've been collecting them through many years, so . . . about fifteen?"

"Fifteen different shapes and colors? Hum . . . however, I like the white ones you wore the other night."

"I'll be happy to have a pair made for you. It's quite simple: I'll draw the outline of your feet on a piece of paper and he'll create the sole exactly to your size, then he'll fit my white pattern on top of the soles and there you are."

"We'll see. But let's not leave the water to cool now!"

Very formally he explained what his important breakfast ceremony entailed: To begin with, we were all to down two large glasses of hot water, one right after the other, to wash away the poison from our "insides." At that point we were allowed the choice either of a continental breakfast with croissants, brioches, toast with bitter marmalade, or a tray of French cheeses, various breads, and a ham omelette. But he was adamant concerning the two large glasses of hot water to start with.

While still juggling with them, we were joined by trumpeter/assistant Herbie Jones carrying a large portfolio of paper music. He reminded Ellington that on that day they were to film "Duke Ellington at the Côte d'Azur," organized by Norman Granz. He asked Ellington for instructions, but the Maestro was not in a mood for work; he replied that it all depended on the wishes of "la plus belle Lil." Herbie asked: "Who?" and the three of them—Ellington, Strayhorn, and Stevie—pointed their fingers at me. Herbie lifted his faithful camera, always hanging from his neck, and while he asked them to hold the pose, he clicked one of my most precious pictures, as seen on the back cover of my record with Tommy Flanagan.

At that point the rhythm of the day was set for us by the Maestro, obviously in no hurry to comply with Granz's plans. He dressed and made his way downstairs, the four of us trailing as his retinue. The other guests of the Hotel Provencal, recognizing him, murmured their greetings with smiles of admiration as he made his way toward the main entrance. Suddenly, he stopped us in our tracks as he discovered the piano bar of the hotel, where the personnel were in the midst of cleaning up. He turned to me.

"Ah, a piano! Now you will sing for me!"

"Right now? I can't!"

Ignoring my protest Ellington walked into the room while the personnel faded into the background.

Stevie dragged me to the piano where his uncle, with an amused smile, began a musical introduction, saying simply: "You will sing this specially for me . . . with meaning!"

Fortunately, my spinning head recognized the melody and there I was, singing "Loverman" with Edward Kennedy Ellington at the piano and a group of surprised bystanders growing ever larger.

I sang the last phrase, "Loverman, oh, where can you be?" ready to make an escape, but Ellington rose and stopped me, smiling at the applause we had earned. He kissed my cheeks four times and we emerged from the hotel.

Once outside, he was recognized, and a wave of waiting fans came rushing up the steps clamoring for his autograph. He complied, while thanking them for their compliments, then he suddenly turned to me: "You see how very nice they are to me, just because I'm with a pretty girl like you?"

"Wow! That phrase is worth two of mine!"

"Now you're coming with me to my special underwear place. Underwear for me," he specified, when he saw my alarmed look.

We went into a gentlemen's boutique where they had obviously been expecting him, for they had prepared a series of Eminence items. Ellington, amused, would ask for my advice, giving the impression that I must be very familiar with his underwear. I played along, advising him with obvious intimacy and then moved away to look at some handsome belts. I drew his attention to them.

"Look, isn't this belt rather elegant? It's slender and in this 'English school tie' silk, in blue and silver-grey. It would look very good with your 'Ellington blue' trousers, don't you think?"

He examined it; then, turning to the clerk, he asked for two of them, identical. He requested a pen and wrote something on the suede leather lining of one of them before handing it to me.

"Here, this way you'll remember me every time you wear it and I will do the same with mine."

I read the message he had written: "A la plus belle Lil, wear this in good health. Love, Duke."

"Good grief, you are really set on turning my head, aren't you? However, I promise not only to think of you each time I wear it, but that I shall keep it forever. [NB I still do to this day.] Thank you very much."

Outside, with the crowd of fans surging around, Herbie reminded him of the filmed rehearsals that could no longer be postponed, and I took the opportunity to ask to be excused. He told me to be at his suite for dinner that evening, at eight sharp. We would then cross to the Pinède Gould in time for the orchestra's performance. He did not wait for my answer.

However, as one of my main activities was a weekly jazz program with the Italian radio network, my presence at Juan-les-Pins—apart from my singing appearance—entailed also various interviews with the artists attending the Jazz Festival. So with my faithful recorder I went to the appointments previously made and by late afternoon called the Ellington suite to excuse myself for not being able to join them for dinner. Stevie came to the phone: "Lilian? Uncle Eddie wants to know why!"

"It's his fault. In his overpowering presence I completely forgot that I am here as a working girl. I have a series of interviews to make and I promised Anita O'Day, who is using my rhythm section, to be there for the sound check and her performance this evening. So he must forgive me and I'll see him tomorrow, whenever he wishes."

I could hear the long mumble of Stevie's explanation and a pause of silence. Then Ellington's sharp tone reached me over Stevie's voice: "Tomorrow morning! Before mid-day. Breakfast!"

I smiled, answering Stevie, "Yes, but on condition that I do NOT have to drink all that hot water!"

More mumbling and then Stevie's laughter as he talked to me. "You win! No hot water . . . but two large glasses of hot green tea instead. Good enough?"

"Good enough. Will you come for me tomorrow morning?"

"You bet!"

During those special festival days my whole life seemed to rise in a new direction. I struck friendships with well-known artists like Charles Lloyd as well as his young—then unknown—sidemen Keith Jarrett and Jack DeJohnette. Famous Jazz producer George Avakian, as charming as Ellington himself, accompanied them. Of course, during those days there grew a special friendship with Johnny Hodges, Paul Gonsalves, and Herbie Jones. In truth, through the years, I always received a friendly welcome from the Ellington band members, with knowing smiles in my direction as they played "Star-Crossed Lovers" whenever I attended their concerts.

At Juan-les-Pins a special friendship grew with Stevie James, who gradually told me about himself. He was the youngest son of Ellington's sister Ruth, who had married a handsome Englishman, which explained Stevie's striking looks with his honey-colored skin, blue eyes, and curly blond hair, and who was obviously spoiled by his uncle.

Once again it was almost midday and there I was, seated on Ellington's bed, pressing his back with both palms, working gently up to his neck. Once again I would ask him his "ego" questions while he appreciated the massage with soft grunts:

"Who is that most elegant orchestra conductor, so admired wherever he appears on stage?"

"And who is mostly dressed in royal blue trousers . . . the world famous Ellington blue . . . ?"

"And who wears Ellington blue trousers that are a little bit too short for my taste?"

A movement under the white bed sheet proved he was reacting to my criticism.

". . . On the other hand, who has the handsomest legs—which he shows off when he wears his short bathrobe—and who can therefore wear shorter trousers than usual?"

He was well awake now, as Stevie came in to announce that the bath was ready. I made a swift exit before Ellington could turn around.

So there we were, his faithful subjects: Strayhorn, Stevie, Herbie, Ronnie, Mercer . . .

While he poured out the glasses of hot green tea and Stevie distributed them, the conversation concentrated on that night's concert, the last one at Juan-les-Pins. With Mercer and Herbie they went through the program, which would include the two outstanding ex-Ellingtonian guests who would join the orchestra that evening: Ben Webster and Ray Nance. At the choice of the last song, Herbie grinned at me while asking Ellington: "Always 'Star-Crossed Lovers'?"

"Every time we have 'la plus belle Lil' with us."

Having dispatched the operation "last concert," he turned his attention on me. "Now this is your third pair of Positano sandals . . . You'll have to take me to this man of yours. I want a pair just like the ones on that first night. White and gold."

"By all means. To begin with, you will now stand on these two pieces of paper while I draw the outline of your feet. And you'll have the sandals when next we meet . . ."

He complied with curiosity, standing still while I marked the outline of both feet, then he asked, pointing at the papers, "He'll make a pair of sandals just from that?"

"He will. My friend Costanzo Avitabile is a magician and I promise you they'll be perfect."

"Ah! Very good. And I'll pay for them."

"Absolutely not! They would be my way of saying thank you for 'Star-Crossed Lovers.'"

At that point Stevie explained that Ellington was very superstitious and believed that if a gift of shoes was made between two persons, then the shoes would walk away from the donor, causing a definite separation. Therefore, Ellington wanted to pay for the sandals. The argument was closed when we finally agreed—after much haggling where Ellington began by offering at least one hundred dollars—on the sum of one dollar.

The next day, when Ellington and the orchestra were leaving for Paris, he asked me to ride along in his limousine, with Stevie. Driving to the Nice airport we enjoyed the beautiful coastline on a perfect sunny day and somehow ended talking about poetry, discovering our mutual taste for it. He mentioned having studied Shakespeare while composing the music for the Stratford, Ontario, musical festival and quoted a piece of poetry from *The Merchant of Venice*:

> The man that hath no music in himself,
> Nor is not moved with concord of sweet sounds,
> Is fit for treasons, stratagems, and spoils.

Came my turn to offer a poem and I chose my favorite:

> The moving finger writes: and, having writ
> Moves on: nor all thy Piety nor Wit
> Shall lure it back to cancel half a Line
> Nor all thy Tears wash out a Word of it.

"Ah, yes, good old Omar Khayyám." He approved.

"Actually, we have a saying in Egypt regarding whatever happens to you. It's 'Kullu Maktoob,' meaning that it's all written down in your Destiny, just as my passion for 'Star-Crossed Lovers' had to lead me to you." I teased him.

He then began inquiring about Egypt and gradually wanted to learn more about me, my family, my broken marriage, and my musical career. I was amused at the serious way he listened to my answers to his very specific questions, such as the cost of raising a six-year-old son. I asked him if he was an Internal Revenue investigator, but I was touched to note that his flirting attitude held now a certain paternal kindness. He was particularly pleased to learn that my son had been born on the 13th of September. Wonderful! For that was indeed a very lucky number!

As we reached the Nice terminal, Stevie informed his uncle that he was driving back with me to remain in Juan-les-Pins to the end of the festival. Ellington gave both of us a piercing look.

"I see . . . Well, I want you to do your utmost to entertain our Lil as lavishly as I would have done. Here." And he passed a large wad of money to his grinning nephew.

Came the moment to say "au revoir" and, while I expected a hug, Ellington extended his arm, offering his hand which I took, nonplussed, only to discover that he was trying to hand a huge wad of dollars to me as well. I recoiled, closing his hand over the money.

"What on earth are you doing?"

He was embarrassed: "I want you to have it . . . just like the rest of the family. I'm sure you'd make better use of it than they do. Please take it . . ."

"I can't, honestly. But I am very touched, and I promise that if I ever need help . . . it's you I'll turn to. Cross my heart."

He shook his head, putting away the money.

They were calling him to board the plane. He gave me his "total embrace" and murmured, "Fare thee well!"

I completed the famous phrase: "And if for ever, still for ever, fare thee well."

"No, not for ever, Lil . . . I'll see to that!"

A month later, back in Rome, I received a large envelope from New York with the music sheet and lyrics for "Star-Crossed Lovers" enclosing a little note of friendship from Billy Strayhorn. When I phoned to thank him he said he had done it willingly—wasn't I his adopted daughter? He was looking forward to hearing me sing it.

Once again, I relived the Juan-les-Pins extraordinary adventure that had brought me into the fascinating Ellington "family." It was unbelievable and most extraordinary. What had prompted their adoption of one more anonymous admirer? Would they really remember me by next year?

ACT II—MILANO, ITALY

Six months later, in early January, I received a large envelope from New York and extracted a very large piece of paper, folded in four, which proved to be Ellington's special Christmas card, bearing his short poem of good wishes. So I was still a member of his "family" circle, although I wondered at the lateness of his Christmas wishes. I learned that he always sent them at a later date so that his wishes would not be "mixed up with the rest" of the season's greetings. I noticed a small message attached, handwritten. It said very briefly that they would be in Milano on Saturday, January 14, and I would be receiving an air ticket to join him at their hotel. If it was an invitation of sorts, it obviously accepted no refusal. I checked, and in fact the Ellington Orchestra was to appear at the Teatro Lirico on Sunday, January 15, 1967.

So on Saturday, January 14, I was dutifully carrying a brand-new pair of sandals for the maestro, created in my presence by Costanzo in Positano. Entering the hotel, I ran into Johnny Hodges and Paul Gonsalves. We made a big fuss of each other and I promised to accompany them for some special shopping for their ladies. Ella Fitzgerald smiled by and waved at me, saying, "No red roses, please!" remembering our first meeting, a year earlier, at the Rome airport of Ciampino, when I had offered her a bouquet of red roses with thorns piercing us both as we embraced. Herbie Jones came by and told me he had special pictures to give me from the Juan-les-Pins days. Harry Carney and other members of the band waved by, Cat Anderson calling out: "There we go again . . . star-crossed lovers, I bet!"

Among a group of men I recognized Arrigo Polillo, our leading Italian jazz critic, standing in friendly discussion with Ellington, who had his back to me as I approached. When Polillo spied me and began saying "Maestro, I would like you to meet . . . ," the Maestro turned around and, before Polillo could finish his phrase, had grabbed me without a word, planting his "four kisses" on my cheeks.

I had to burst out laughing, on the one hand for a most theatrical greeting but, above all, for the look of total amazement on the faces of my Italian friends, who obviously wondered at an unsuspected passionate affair between the Duke and their own Lilian Terry.

He looked at their bewildered faces and explained, very seriously: "This is 'la plus belle Lil'; she's my niece, from Cairo."

No other explanation given. He motioned to Ronnie Smith and asked him to show me to my room, saying he would call me as soon as the interview was over.

So there we were later, in his suite, reunited once more with Mercer, Herbie, Ronnie, the singer Tony Watkins, but sadly without Billy Strayhorn or Stevie James.

I handed Ellington the package, which he opened very carefully. He was a little boy examining a new toy. Yes, they were the true replicas of the white and gold sandals I had worn on the first evening we had met. And yes, they had been created on the shape of his feet drawn out on paper. He tried gingerly one of them but quickly removed it: "No. Before I can try them on, I must give you some money."

"OK, you owe me one dollar. But do you like them, at least?"

He was still concentrating on his superstitious thoughts as he pushed the sandals back into my hands saying he could not keep them—not before his money had passed into my own hands. I could only take the sandals back, according to his wishes.

That evening we were all bundled in a large bus and driven out of Milano to a recording studio where the orchestra rehearsed some new items Ellington intended to perform the next evening. I discovered him to be rather cool and uncompromising as he worked his musicians until he had obtained the exact results he desired.

Typical of him, he decided he had to have the sandals at three in the morning, when we had all retired to bed. There was a discreet knock at my door and Ronnie's voice calling me softly. He apologized profusely, but Ellington had decided he couldn't wait to get his sandals, so here was some money and would I please hand them over? I did so, and Ronnie pressed into my hand the usual Ellington wad of dollars, which I tried to hand back to Ronnie, who shook his head, distressed. No, he could not take the money back, and Ellington wanted the sandals NOW! So PLEASE no problems at that very moment; I could always give the money back tomorrow.

"Very well, Ronnie, here you are. Hope they fit well."

The next day I led Gonsalves and Hodges rapidly through the meanders of fashionable Milano, and then we rushed back to the hotel, as they had two performances that day and the bus would soon be there to drive the orchestra to the afternoon concert.

Ellington complained about my desertion in favor of "a star-crossed lover" as we were driven to the theater in a limousine. However, he also expressed his pleasure for the sandals, which reminded me that I had a wad of dollars to return to him.

He finally accepted the money back, minus one dollar, but very reluctantly and adding that it was the first time he had ever been handed any money by a lady!

We occupied his dressing room, where I helped him set the usual cushion for his tender feet on a chair in front of his armchair. We sat and talked of friends and family; he asked about my "lucky number" son and my singing career, then he gave me news of Stevie and his mother Ruth. He informed me that on his next tour I would be meeting his daughter-in-law Evelyn, who was sure to become a good friend of mine, as we had many points in common. When I asked after Strayhorn, I was very sad to hear that he was again in hospital, his terminal illness advancing rapidly. I mentioned the letter and lyrics to "Star-Crossed Lovers" that he had sent me, adding that one day I hoped to sing it in memory of him.

Then it was time for the afternoon concert to take place, and the Teatro Lirico was already packed. Shoes on, coat jacket hanging perfectly, Ellington-blue trousers a little short . . . he stepped out of the dressing room and was greeted by fans and friends as we went on backstage. As usual, the musicians filed in nonchalantly, and when they were all set in their place and Ellington was about to enter the stage, we realized that Paul Gonsalves was missing. No one had noticed his absence until then. The performance was about to begin, and I admired Ellington's cool reaction as—just before he stepped out in front of his public—he turned to ask me to take the limousine back to the hotel and drag that man from his bed and onto the stage. Please.

At the hotel I phoned Paul's room, and some minutes later his dreamy voice answered my urgent plea to wake up, get dressed, grab his horn, and come downstairs quickly, for the concert had already started. Hurry, please!

"Hey, Lil. . . . What? OK, OK . . . I'll be right there in a few minutes. Love you madly." But his few minutes were endless, and by the time we did reach the theater, the orchestra was playing its fourth number. Paul grabbed his tenor and—smiling mildly at Duke and at his fellow musicians—he joined in the playing while walking in and sitting down.

When the concert was over, Ellington thanked me; I replied that he was very welcome as long as he remembered to play "Star-Crossed Lovers" that night.

While we relaxed in his dressing room before the second performance, he settled himself comfortably, resting his feet on the usual pillow. He was in a mood for chatting, expressing his thoughts and trying out on me what would be included in his future book. I sat at a small table with notebook and pen, and whenever he would say something funny, or special, I would write it down with the pledge to give him a copy for his personal use. Here are some of his favorite expressions, considerations, and advice: "Repeated listening makes for enjoyment of music. Jazz needs also understanding and an intelligent appreciation, although what counts is the emotional effect on the listener."

"Good luck is being at the right place, doing the right thing with the right people, at the right time. When those four things converge, then it is good luck."

"Anyone who loves to make music knows that study is necessary. Music can be a lucrative pursuit, but it must not be the only reason for participating in it. Then money can be a distraction more than anything else. Music . . . you either love it or leave it; in fact, what has money got to do with music?"

"How do you know if you're playing the right thing? When it sounds good, then it is good!"

At one point we were back to quoting poetry when I asked him if he had ever written any himself. To my surprise he seemed almost bashful, hesitant, and then admitted that he had written a poem, and Billy had created the music for it. I begged him to recite it to me as I scribbled the words:

> Love came as a dulcet tone,
> Humming up above, suspended.
> To one who had been so much alone
> It said "your doldrums blues are ended."
> Petals of red roses rare
> Strewn along the path to guide me
> The breath of spring had filled the air
> Love of my life was there beside me . . .

At that very moment there was a peremptory knock at the dressing room door and Ellington asked if I would please . . . ?

I opened the door and there stood, in all his handsome charm . . . Herbert von Karajan!

I stared in admiration as he smiled at me, amused: "Good evening. I have come to present my homage to Maestro Ellington . . ."

"Good evening. By all means, do come in, sir!"

He entered as Ellington got up from his armchair, and there was a friendly greeting between "Herbert" and "Edward."

I stepped quietly outside, on a cloud. One of the greatest classical directors had asked to "present his homage" to the greatest jazz director, and I had been a witness to it!

My only regret was that I was not given the rest of Ellington's poem to jot down.

The evening concert was excellent, with very wide-awake musicians who played long solos for an enthusiastic public. Ellington was enjoying himself, smiling at me from time to time as I stood in the wings, waiting for the moment when Hodges would play for me. Suddenly I realized they were actually playing the closing signature tune! I whispered to Ellington as he sat at the piano:

"If there's no 'Star-Crossed Lovers,' then I'll take my sandals back!"

He threw his head back, grinning, and nodded. The very moment the signature tune ended he went to the microphone and informed the public: "We have a request from Miss Lilian Terry, the greatest singer in Italy. She would like to hear the Romeo and Juliet theme from 'Star-Crossed Lovers,' the melody played by Johnny Hodges!"

Then he sat at the piano and began the introductory arpeggios.

Hodges got up with his alto sax and smiled at me, going to the microphone.

Once again, the orchestra performed my beloved ballad with my beloved soloist.

ACT III—STAR-CROSSED LOVERS

To my deep sadness, I was informed that Billy Strayhorn had passed away on May 31, 1967. His funeral would take place in Harlem on June 5.

Three years later came the sudden, unexpected passing away of Johnny Hodges. It happened on May 11, 1970, in the office of his dentist. The news was unbelievable, and I felt bereaved, remembering the way he would play "Star-Crossed Lovers" with that lazy smile, as if we shared a secret. First Swee'Pea and now Hodges. I drew out the lyrics to their magic ballad and promised myself that one day I would record it to honor them.

As always, Fate took things in hand at its own pace and in its unfathomable way.

It was twelve years later that, at the end of a Jazz Festival at the Rome Opera House, a group of us went to a late dinner and I was seated between Max Roach and Ran Blake. Opposite me sat Tommy Flanagan, whom I admired immensely, especially for his art in accompanying singers. He asked me about my activities, and I mentioned my work with RAI radio and TV, the annual concert season I was producing for the city of Bassano del Grappa . . . then Max spoke up: "Yes, but she's not telling you what a good singer she is!"

Tommy seemed curious. "Is that so? And which is your latest recording?"

"Oh, that was ages ago."

"And why is that?"

"I decided years ago that I would not enter a recording studio again, unless it was with Tommy Flanagan. You are the only asset I truly envied Ella for."

"I see. . . . And what kind of repertoire did you have in mind?"

"Ah, very special songs that have a personal meaning for me."

"Such as?"

"Well, I recall singing 'Loverman' at Juan-les-Pins one afternoon in 1966, accompanied by Duke Ellington at the piano."

"Ellington?"

"Yes."

"OK, 'Loverman.' Next?"

"Well, Ellington means Strayhorn, who means 'Lush Life.'"

"Very good . . . next?"

"Ellington plus Strayhorn brings to mind Johnny Hodges and his sensuous way of playing a particular ballad that has never been sung before. I told Billy of my disappointment that it had no lyrics; he promised to send me a text, and a month later . . . there it was!"

Tommy was becoming very attentive.

"And what song was that?"

"It's from the suite 'Such Sweet Thunder . . .'"

I leaned over the table toward him and he met me halfway to say in unison:

"Star-Crossed Lovers!"

He exclaimed, "I knew it! Why, do you know that's my very favorite ballad and hardly anybody plays it? And Swee'Pea gave you the words himself? OK. Let's do it. Now which recording date would you have in mind?"

He was drawing out his agenda and turning the pages. I looked at Max Roach, who nodded; this was really happening—Tommy Flanagan was willing to go into a recording studio with me. We exchanged addresses and phone numbers, and I said I would speak to my producer in Milano.

Of course, Giovanni Bonandrini was delighted to add such an LP to his "Soul Note" production list, which had already earned him the approval of the jazz press worldwide. We contacted Danish contrabassist Jesper Lundgaard and Ed Thigpen,

"Mr. Magic Brushes," who also lived in Denmark. Tommy approved, and we set a date.

So, on April 17, 1982, we were entering the Barigozzi Studio in Milano, where Bonandrini and Giancarlo Barigozzi, saxophone player and excellent recording technician, were waiting for us.

The first step was a "cappuccino and cookies" work meeting with Tommy and Diane Flanagan, Lundgaard, Thigpen, Bonandrini, and Barigozzi. Incidentally, that was the first of many snacks wherein we discovered that Tommy had a certain weakness for cookies. From that day, he was "the Cookie Monster."

Each song was recorded and then approved by all of us together.

Tommy was in command of the trio with a touch that was masterful yet gentle. From his introduction to the first song "Loverman"—so logical and so thoughtful—we went on to the sophisticated "Lush Life," then to the magic duet he and I enjoyed with "Star-Crossed Lovers." Followed "Black Coffee" with a grateful bow to Peggy Lee; "I Remember Clifford" to thank Benny Golson, and naturally for Brownie. We then chose Mr. Monk's "'Round about Midnight," closing inevitably with Lady Day by choosing "You've Changed."

As we listened to the playback I was ever more aware of how, throughout the whole record, Tommy had enhanced my performance with his unique phrasing and what I called his "languorous touch."

The brief Italian tour that followed was a continuation of the magical "together" feeling with the trio. When, upon saying goodbye, Tommy asked me what would be the title of the album, I replied on the spur of the moment: "Lilian Terry Meets Tommy Flanagan—A Dream Comes True."

He gave me his "chinaman" smile of approval, a big hug, and off they all went.

Good friend George Avakian, pleasantly surprised that I had recorded after ten years of silence, and in such good company, wrote very flattering liner notes. The recording was an immediate success, especially in Japan but also in the United States.

The ballad that surprised—and therefore was most played on the air—was "Star-Crossed Lovers." I had recorded it with a saddened heart, remembering Johnny Hodges and Billy Strayhorn, yet filled with gratitude that two such huge artists should have given me their friendship. Thanks to Tommy Flanagan, the dream of honoring them had really come true. Alas, today also Tommy Flanagan has gone, adding his shining star to the musical heavens.

ACT IV—CHRISTMAS IN NEW YORK 1967/68

I spent the 1967 Christmas holidays with my friend Jan Olson and her husband in a fascinating but freezing New York. Soon after Christmas Day I met with Stevie James for an elegant lunch where he introduced me to his girlfriend of the moment. He also gave me Ellington's personal phone number with firm instructions to call him the next day, at midday.

I complied, and we had a long chat where he informed me that they were rehearsing his Second Sacred Concert, to be performed on January 19 (1968) at the Cathedral of St. John the Divine. Ah, what a pity, I was due back in Rome before then! However, we made an appointment for "breakfast at twelve" the next day at his apartment on Riverside Drive.

Arriving punctually, I admired the exceptional view on Central Park from his elegant suite and met his sister Ruth, who, upon learning I lived in Europe, told me about her early studies in Paris. She then added how much her son Stevie had enjoyed visiting France with his uncle, the previous year, and especially his holiday in Juan-les-Pins. Stevie sat grinning while his amused uncle offered us some more green tea.

I was also invited to Ellington's New Year's Eve party, where I met a great number of interesting people from various milieus: theater, film and Broadway stars mainly, but also a good sprinkling of fashionable personalities. They were all very elegant and obviously successful. Ellington received them graciously, accepted their flattering compliments and seemed to be on rather intimate terms with all of them, especially the ladies. It was an extremely interesting experience, and I loved watching him move from group to group.

At midnight, everybody was kissing everybody else. When he came over to where I stood talking to Don George, Duke warned him to stop flirting with his niece. He then kissed me his Happy New Year wishes, and I pleased him with one of our exaggerated compliments: "Ah, have I told you how extremely handsome you look tonight? The whole room is full of beautiful people, but they really shine through your own reflection upon them."

He motioned toward me, asking Don, "See what I mean? Could I ever let her go?"

"Yes; however, right now I really have to be going as I promised to drop in on another party. Could I call a cab . . . ?"

But Don George insisted on accompanying me instead. As Ellington saw us to his door, he gave me the usual four kisses on the cheeks and his "total embrace."

A few days later I received a phone call from Italy at Jan's home informing me that Maestro Gian Carlo Menotti was asking me for Ellington's private phone number, as he wished to speak to him directly about a possible performance at his "Festival dei Due Mondi" at Spoleto the next year. He had been told, in Italy, that I had a direct link to Ellington. Surprised, I explained that all I could do was give Ellington whatever phone number Maestro Menotti wished to be reached at, and they could take it from there. When Ellington took note of the message, he was amused: "Ah, Lil! You see? They all know about us."

"So it would seem."

"When are you flying back to Rome?"

"Tomorrow afternoon. But I'll be at the Newport Jazz Festival this summer—will you be there?"

"Yes, briefly. I'll write you a poem."

"I'm sure you will . . . ! Ciao bell'uomo! Success for your new Sacred Concert!"

Christmas poems

Ellington's pleasure in writing poetic messages emerged every Christmas in the shape of his huge paper, folded in four. Having managed to save four of them, through all these years, I'm happy to offer you their texts.

The first one read:

You've been such good girls and boys
Every day of the year
Let me tell you of the joys
You'll be very glad to hear
There's a day known as Christmas
December Twenty-Fifth
Santa Claus comes visiting
And that is not a myth
Santa Claus is good-natured
And likes a Christmas tree
He wears a handsome smile
And he's as stylish as can be
Santa's sleigh is packed, complete
Santa's in the driver's seat
Bringing every good boy and girl
Something nice and pretty and sweet
Signed: Duke Ellington

The next Christmas wishes were briefer but in a large classic Grecian setting:

The first spring blossoms in the tree
The soft, warm summer breeze
Expectant autumn on her knees
Winter and
A boy
Christmas Joy

Also signed Duke Ellington.

The third huge Christmas card had the poem zigzagging white on deep pink:

The echo of that
First Christmas day
Is still here and it's bright and gay
Ringing clear
And bringing cheer
Year after year
And it's here
To stay

Usual signature: Duke Ellington.

The last greeting in my possession is actually half the size of the former sheets and with a totally different personality as far as the poem and the picture, both being in a very modern style.

Life is—love is
Sweet is—right is
Beauty is endless life
And love—and light
And sweet—and beautiful
Endless Christmases
And Happy New Years
And Ash Wednesdays
And Joyous Easters
To come—to past
To future—to you
To yours—to ours
To us

Below the signature of Duke Ellington you can read, in a corner, a very tiny piece of information: Design by Stephen James.

ACT V—NEWPORT 1968

I spent four extraordinary days at George Wein's 1968 Jazz Festival at Newport, under the brotherly supervision of Max Roach and Papa Jo Jones. I was meeting and interviewing jazz icons such as Nina Simone, Ray Charles, Cannonball Adderley, when, finally, Ellington made an appearance on the fifth of July.

He told me he was leaving Newport soon after the orchestra's performance. However, he had time to chat with me and, as we relaxed in a quiet corner, he consented that I tape our talks.

I hoped to obtain some answers from him regarding his decision to turn to religion for his musical inspiration, as shown by his First Sacred Concert followed by his Second Sacred Concert, performed a few months earlier, on January 19 at the Cathedral of St. John the Divine. Hereunder you will find the essence of that long conversation with a very relaxed, reminiscing, amused, and amusing Ellington.

The first question was: "How did you happen to write sacred music and what are the feelings that you are trying to express through your sacred music?"

"I did my first sacred concert because I was invited to do a sacred concert at Grace Cathedral in San Francisco. They had heard some of the things I had done before, which were spiritual and gospel flavored . . . so they invited me to do a whole concert. Such an invitation as this, going into this beautiful cathedral . . . was quite a bit of a shock, and I said, "Wait just a minute. I have to get myself together and bolster up my eligibility, this that and the other, you know? So I got organized . . . and about a year later we did it! It was September 16, 1965. We took it on the road in America and Europe."

"Where in Europe?"

"Coventry Cathedral and Great St. Mary's at Cambridge."

"Then the Second Sacred Concert . . ."

"The Second Sacred concert was much bigger than the other one. It was over two hours long without an intermission; we employed the entire band, four choirs, and twenty-two dancers."

"Now, what are the feelings that you are trying to express through the sacred music?"

"Well . . . first of all, when you get the invitation, you have to decide whether you're going to do it . . . or regret. Then you go back to when you used to go to church every Sunday . . . first to my mother's family church, then to my father's family church. One was a Methodist and the other a Baptist, so I went to two churches a day . . . then later, after I came out of school, I read the Bible completely through, about four times, and I found out in reading the Bible that I actually understood what I had learnt in school. It adjusts your perspective, your scale of appraisal in life and so forth and a very valuable contribution, cause there's nothing new. . . . So what we do in our concerts is to preach, with our music. We do fire and brimstone 'sermonettes' with titles like 'Don't get down on your knees to pray until you have forgiven everybody . . .' and the freedom things: 'Freedom to be the contented prisoner of love,' 'Reach beyond your reach, to reach for a star,' or 'To go about the business of becoming what you already are.'

"Then we have the Billy Strayhorn freedoms of course, which were the serious things. Billy lived with these major freedoms: Freedom from hate unconditionally; freedom from self-pity; freedom from fear of possibly doing something that may help someone else more than it would him; and freedom from the kind of pride that would make him feel he is better than his brother.

"Then there's the thing about Heaven, like the phrase 'Heaven to be is the ultimate degree to be,' and these lines I tested with my theologian friends, you know? I got the greatest response; a reverend in Connecticut wanted to record that phrase to study it, and also other theology experts were consulted, then I recall Rabbi Shapiro who went back to the ancient Bible. . . . So you get associated with these people, you see? And we feel like we are a kind of messenger. We are talking to people . . . but we are not missionaries, of course."

"Tell me, is this a field that you wish to really enter into and widen?"

"This is not 'career'; I don't 'work' at this. . . . This is a thing where you make observations; these are arguments, like you present a case. You go to court and you present the good guys and you say, 'These thousands of people have dedicated their life to it; after all, they're not suckers. Just because you've got a million dollars, so what? One day you're not going to have it.' It's a great form of security for anybody who can understand it. I mean, understanding is one of the . . . I mean, wisdom is valueless without understanding (*pause*). Did I say something profound?" he asked, grinning.

"What will you do now, in the near future? Are you going to take a rest?"

"Rest? No! Rest! I never rest, I'm scared to rest!" he laughed, then went on.

"I'm writing a work for the Los Angeles Philharmonic which I'm supposed to do on the third of August"

"That's very good!"

"It's not very good because this is now the fifth of July!"

"Will you be using the Philharmonic Orchestra and your band?"

"No, just the orchestra"

"Just the orchestra and yourself on piano?"

"No, no piano"

"So you'll be composing for the Philharmonic and directing it?"

"Yes. You know, one of the greatest thrills I had with a Symphony Orchestra is when we did the 'Symphonic Ellington' album . . . did you hear it?"

"Yes! I have it!"

"Yeah, you know, we'd planned to record these four orchestras in Europe: the Hamburg symphony, the Stockholm symphony . . ."

"The Scala . . ."

"The Paris Opera Orchestra and then La Scala Orchestra. And when I get to Milano, of course, the orchestra has got a rehearsal that afternoon, and then they've got to go back and play 'La Bohème' that night. So, in other words, I can only have them for two hours, and you cannot do a rehearsal and record within two hours, so at ten o'clock in the morning I start writing a new number . . . and I do the thing called———"

I interrupted him, naming the number in unison with him:

"La Scala, she too pretty to be blue . . ."

He was pleasantly surprised: "Oh, you know it?"

"Of course I know it!"

"Say that in Italian," he asked me.

"E' troppo bella per essere malinconica."

He listened, delighted, and approved in Italian:

"Molto bello, molto bello! Grazie mille!" he laughed.

This brought us to his promise that he would sing a special ditty of his own invention, in Italian, for me.

"And now, as a gift, I want you to sing your Italian song for our radio listeners, as you promised."

"Well, you have to understand now: this is a song I first wrote in 1950, on my first visit to Italy. In Milano, Maestro Rizzo was sort of guiding me around and I was learning Italian. And naturally the first thing you learn to do is to count. And I was combining, you know . . . it was a real quick thing 'cause I was only there a little while. Did you ever know a gypsy violinist . . . Nino?"

"In Milano?"

"Yes, he used to play at a Piccolo . . ."

"He has a Hungarian restaurant?"

"No, not now, he died . . ."

"Oh, then no."

"Oh, listen, I started to tell you about the La Scala Orchestra . . . when I heard those violins . . . I almost flipped! It was the greatest thing in the world! Absolutely!"

"Thank you, thank you very much."

"Too much!"

"So, would you be happy to compose something for the La Scala Orchestra?"

"Oh, I'd love it! I mean, well. . . . You know, my imagination normally doesn't run in that direction and . . . but I mean it would be a gas . . . to do it."

"All right, I'll see if there is anything I can do about that, but first . . . you must sing the song."

"Which song is that?"

"The 'Uno, due, tre' song."

"Uno, due, tre . . . sing it?!" he was alarmed.

"Sing it!" I confirmed.

"You're going to record it, eh?"

"Yes!"

Obviously amused, he surrendered and sang—to the various bystanders' surprise—the following opus:

> Uno, due, tre.
> Quattro, cinque, sei.
> Sette, otto, nove . . .
> Won't you come over?

Nove, otto, sette, sei, cinque, quattro, tre
Do you know that you're the "uno per me?"
Such a bellissimo "due" are we
And we'll be "bella, bella, bella" when we're three!
Uno, due, tre, quattro, cinque . . . say you'll name the day
"per voi e per me" [pronounced "may"]

We laughed together as he accepted my very formal compliments.

"Thank you very much, Maestro. And when are you coming to Italy?"

"Well, I'm supposed to come after the first of the year, sometime."

"After the first . . . in 1969? All right then, we'll say "arrivederci in Italia."

"Arrivederci . . . how do you say 'I love you madly' in Italian?"

"Vi amo follemente!"

"Vi amo . . . follemente. Vi amo?"

"Yes, when it's general. For one person it's 'ti amo.' Vi amo is for everyone."

He then repeated it to me in perfect and passionate Italian style, hand on his heart:

"Vi amo follemente!"

"Grazie! We hope so . . ."

"Prego!"

With his amused smile he had stood up as he was being called away, and then turned at the door to remind me that I would be receiving an air ticket at my home in Rome, to join him in Milano in October. We would celebrate his seventieth birthday.

He added: "You know what kind of birthday gift I'd love from you . . . don't you?"

With a wave of his hand and an amused-wicked grin he walked away.

ACT VI—WHAT IS JAZZ? NEW YORK 1968

I had just returned to New York City from the Newport 1968 Festival when I was requested to join Ellington at his house rather urgently.

He introduced me to a representative of the Italian publishers Fratelli Fabbri Editori; famous for their popular editions on most subjects, they had now decided to tackle the musical world. They had produced an excellent series regarding the various forms of music, presented with a booklet plus an EP recording. When they had come to the music called jazz, they had decided to obtain a long preface by the greatest jazz personality alive. "Il grande Ellington!"

As usual, Ellington was amused to present me as his niece, and he declared that he would write the preface on condition that I should be the translator into Italian. At his worried look I reassured the Italian gentleman that I had been an official Italian-French-English translator-interpreter at FAO of the UN, in Rome, for seven years. And no, I was not really Ellington's niece, but yes, I was that Lilian Terry with the RAI radio program on jazz music that was aired every week from Rome. Reassured, the gentleman accepted Ellington's conditions as well as the choice of the music that would be used for the EP: "Rockin' in Rhythm," "In a Sentimental Mood," and the "Black and Tan Fantasy." He left for Milano hoping to receive the papers at our "very earliest opportunity."

I was due back in Rome myself, so Ellington agreed to prepare his papers and send them on to me. Knowing his reputation for procrastination till the very last minute, I gave him a definite time limit, which he noted down, protesting for my doubting his word.

The papers arrived, and I was fascinated by yet another facet of Duke Ellington's personality: very serious, scholarly, something of the sociologist, giving his precise judgement on jazz history as it spread worldwide. I translated the papers faithfully and forwarded them to Fratelli Fabbri in Milano, who proceeded to publish the booklet and EP recording, as agreed. It came out in 1969.

Being the property of the editors, I will not write down the original Ellington papers, but I can give you the general gist of it according to the various interviews I recorded with him through the years. These interviews were, as always, faithfully typed out and handed over to him for his own future use.

To begin with, his reaction to the word "jazz" itself was definitely and surprisingly negative. He would enounce, a shade snobbishly: "We stopped using the word 'jazz' in 1943."

"And what is it called now?"

"The American idiom. Or else music of freedom of expression. Definitely not jazz."

"Does the word 'jazz' have a racial connotation for you?"

"It's not a matter of color, but it does enclose our music within a ghetto, which causes various problems. But I would not say it's racial. The problem is rather economical."

"Such as?"

"Well, when you enter the world of music, you must seek your rewards through living it, experiencing it. Now, music can also be lucrative, and of course you do have to make a living through your music. But it becomes a matter of how much money you are determined to make and on what terms. It can distract you from the reason why you chose to be a musician in the first place. I always say: 'Music, love it or leave it'. Actually, what does money have to do with music?"

I considered the large amount of money his worldwide musical empire brought to him through his records, printed music, the annual world tours, and I decided to move on to another subject.

"Would you say that the roots of this American idiom music emerged spontaneously? Through the specially gifted artists who could not read a note of music, like Buddy Bolden or Armstrong and all the way to Errol Garner today . . . ?"

"Quite true. I myself, after a few useless piano lessons in my childhood, began playing exclusively by ear. I even composed my first tune called the 'Soda Fountain Rag' during my high-school years. It was a big hit with the students, but I soon realized I needed to study music seriously."

"So today you would advise young people interested in becoming jazz musicians to take music lessons?"

"Although for many years I prided myself for creating my music successfully with hardly any real classical music studies, today anyone who loves to play any kind of music discovers very soon that study is necessary. I would add it's essential."

"What other advice would you give to a music student?"

"Another important aspect of their education is that they must also take time to listen to the music, carefully and repeatedly. That's what makes you really enjoy the music, whether you're a musician or a listener. The more you listen, the better you understand and appreciate intelligently the music."

"And what should the musician aim at, when he performs?"

"Above all you're aiming at the emotional effect of your music on the public. You can always tell when that link has been established, and do you know how you can tell? Because you are playing a musical statement which you can feel is important not only to you but also to the listener. When it really sounds good . . . then you just know it is good. And the public's ovation confirms it."

"There is a special, unique quality in the sound of your orchestra that makes it recognizable with eyes closed. What is your secret?"

"Well, first of all, you must know that the music that is written for my orchestra takes into consideration each of their outstanding qualities as musicians but also whatever limitation they might have. Of course, specific instrumentalists with their own musical personality get special compositions particularly suited to them, like your Hodges with 'Star-Crossed Lovers.' When he died I declared officially, 'Because of this great loss the band will never sound the same again,' and it has not."

ACT VII—EVELYN ELLINGTON

From October 1969 I would accept invitations to join Ellington on his annual Italian concerts if and when I was free, which meant hopping from Rome to Milano, to Bologna and all the way down to Bari.

Sometimes, to my great amusement, Ellington would be in an unusual state of embarrassment in greeting me, and I would know he had been joined, unexpectedly, by his semi-official companion whom everyone referred to as "the contessa" and who was supposedly jealous enough to carry a gun in her purse. On those occasions I would reassure him, mock seriously, that I had accepted his invitation mainly to hear my good friend Hodges play his ballad for me and that I had no problem in keeping well away from him.

In Rome I finally met his daughter-in-law Evelyn Ellington, not to be confused with his other official companion Evie. Evelyn was an extraordinary woman who combined kindness and strength, along with a delightful sense of humor. As Ellington had foreseen, we were soon at ease with each other.

Evelyn was Mercer's wife and the mother of three handsome youths. I believe Mercedes was on her way to becoming an affirmed stage dancer; Gaye was a young lady who studied art; Edward—the tall elegant replica of his namesake grandfather—was studying to become a sound engineer.

Through the years, Evelyn and I kept in contact, and I could well understand Ellington's total trust in this straightforward lady, wholly dedicated to her family.

In 1971 my son Francesco was about to enter sixth grade and, as had been promised him, he was now to make his first grand tour of the United States.

Evelyn informed me that she would pick us up at the airport in New York and added that Ellington had booked a room for us at the Edison Hotel, where he was rehearsing a new album in the Edison Recording Studios. He wanted us within his reach.

My son was totally excited during the long plane trip, and finally there it was: the amazing view of the Big Apple from the skies. Then he passed through the airport gate and there was this lovely, elegant black lady who welcomed him to New York with an embrace.

"Francesco! There you are at last, welcome to the United States! I'm Evelyn, a friend of your mother's. We have a car waiting for you outside."

She led us to a huge white limousine with chauffeur, and Francesco was completely bowled over. While he took in the bewildering magic that is New York, Evelyn explained that Ellington's orders were "that we should take possession, briefly, of our room to then join him, rapidly, at the Edison Studio in the basement of the hotel, where he would give us a proper welcome."

Yes, sir!

We settled "briefly" in our room, made ourselves presentable, and then followed Evelyn "rapidly" down to the studio.

The orchestra was spread in a semi-circle around a grand piano where Ellington sat playing some notes and, from time to time, correcting the music displayed on the sheet in front of him. Raising his head, he saw us standing discreetly to the side. He rose from the piano and came directly to my son who was kissed soundly on the cheeks four times.

"So there you are, Francesco! Is it true you were born on September 13th? Now that is a very lucky number, did you know? I'll tell you a secret of mine that will help you all your life: Good luck comes to you when you're at the right place, doing the right thing with the right people and at the right time; always remember that and you'll be just fine."

Francesco had been mesmerized from the first kiss on the cheek, listening intensely and nodding. Ellington went on: "I hear you are entering the Rome Conservatory this fall? You will study the piano?"

My son finally found his voice and replied shyly, "Yes, and also harmony."

"Why, then we are compatible! Know what? I want you to come and sit next to me at the piano and to be my assistant while I resume working with the band. Will you do that for me? I'm sure your mother will allow you. Now come along, we have work to do."

They sat side by side on the long piano bench, and Ellington handed Francesco a container with a dozen pencils and a sharpener, explaining, "You see, I need these pencils to correct my music and they have to be extremely sharp. So each time I shall use a pencil and then set it down, you will take it, sharpen it, and put it in this jar, ready for use."

They nodded at each other. For the next magic half-hour Francesco was Duke Ellington's "special assistant." That was the only time they were together. Yet the clear memory of every moment, and every word spoken, remained embedded forever with my musician son.

Obviously, my affection for Ellington was becoming deeper as he revealed more hidden aspects of his kindness, thoughtfulness, understanding, and patience with the persons he chose to allow into his privacy.

His behavior with me was familiar and relaxed; he often teased me with the amused, flirting attitude of the frustrated lover he would put on, while I told him that his attraction would only last as long as I would say "no thank you," His embraces were always "total," from shoulders to lower back, yet never disrespectful.

There was also the verbal game between us that we both enjoyed. One day, as we were parting with the usual embrace, he asked me suddenly: "You know what attracted me about you in the first place? It's that mixture of girl and boy in you; your short haircut with your frivolous sandals. You walk like a girl but move swiftly like a boy."

"Girl and boy? Am I to take this as a compliment?"

He smiled, sphinxlike, as he let me go, obviously satisfied with my wondering reaction to his comment.

ACT VIII—THE VATICAN

In the early 1970s, I was introduced to an RAI National Network high official, usually a politically assigned post, who sat me in his handsome office and asked point-blank: "You are a . . . very close friend of Maestro Ellington, I am told?"

Surprised, yet amused, I explained: "You could say that we are very good friends but not 'very close' the way you mean . . ."

Taken aback, he fidgeted with his Montblanc pen. "Ah, I had been told . . . but no matter, if you are good friends then you will no doubt obtain for us that he comes to play his Sacred Concert for the Holy Father?"

This time I was the one to be taken aback. "Perform a concert in the Vatican for the Holy Father?"

"Yes. You must know that each year RAI offers the Holy Father a special concert. As a rule, it would be in the realm of classic music, with some prominent artists. However, we have heard some very interesting comments regarding Ellington's sacred music coming from the classic milieu itself."

"Ah, well for that matter I myself have witnessed a very brotherly greeting between Ellington and Herbert von Karajan . . ."

"Exactly. Therefore, we have decided that a performance of Ellington's Sacred Concert would be most appropriate."

"Actually, he has composed two Sacred Concerts, and I do believe he is working on a third one. Would that be of interest? I mean, a command performance of his Third Sacred Concert?"

I could tell the man was extremely interested and kept scribbling on a piece of paper. I went on, musing aloud. "Of course, it depends on various aspects. On how soon the third concert will be ready to go on the road. On what former engagements his agent has already accepted. As well, of course, as the possible date of the Vatican concert?"

A phone call was made and he obtained an appointment with the Vatican authorities.

A few days later I was walking alongside the director, enjoying the architectural beauty of the Vatican. When we reached the doors of the office in question, I was kindly asked to sit in a handsome armchair and wait. As I sat there, I thought of Ellington's recent interview where the journalist had asked him if—having, at his age, been blessed by all sorts of honors, fortune, wealth, and success—there was yet one more gift that he wished to receive from life? Ellington had considered the question and then answered that perhaps the most important moment of his life would be . . . to be allowed to present his last Sacred Concert to the Holy Father, within the Vatican walls.

Eventually the RAI director reemerged, smiling primly. No comment from him while we walked out of the Vatican buildings. Then, finally, yes! It could be done! I was now to speak with Ellington and find out what was the situation on his side. No date was fixed yet, not before quite a few months. But I could start the ball rolling.

However, I hesitated to contact Ellington yet. My long years of working with the RAI authorities had taught me that sometimes an enthusiastically conceived project could end thrown out the window for a number of reasons: a political change of management, new budget restrictions, anything and everything. I told the director that I would contact Ellington as soon as I received an official letter from RAI asking me to do so.

It was fortunate I did hesitate, for the letter never arrived and, a few months later, the director called me again in his office. Very embarrassed, he informed me that, due to the terrible famine that was ravaging India for some time now, the Vatican had decided to annul all forms of entertainment, obviously including Ellington's Sacred Concert. I was heartsick but relieved that my friend would never have to share my disappointment.

ACT IX—FINAL INTERVIEW

In 1969 the RAI Television producer of a very popular series called "Un volto, una storia"—literally, "One Face, One Story"—asked me if I would be interested in producing a special number for that series, dedicated to Duke Ellington.

Considering the fact that the whole series seemed dedicated to sad, tragic, unfortunate subjects with a story that was certain to be a tearjerker, often relieved by an unexpected happy ending, I told the producer that Ellington's story was anything but that of a poor black underdog who eventually acquired fame.

The man listened to me, a little disappointed at first, and then with a smile he assured me that the very fact of Ellington's fortunate life, practically from birth, would be the catching "story" of that "face." Would I please contact Ellington right away to find out his fee and a date of his choice, for the filming?

With his usual benevolence, Ellington listened to my proposal on the phone. He then asked if I would have complete and direct responsibility for the whole project; he then accepted, refusing any fee. The date he chose coincided with his coming Italian concert tour within a few weeks.

"I'll see you in Bari, my Lil; you can come and film the interview at my hotel suite after the concert, for as long as you need. I'll add just one thing. I want a contract from RAI that mentions clearly that you have the total control and approval of the operation. Will they do it?"

Of course they were willing to promise him the moon! They could have Ellington on their program and at no fee? Quick with the contract, yes, let la Terry have the last official approval, they could see no problem with me.

Thus, one fine day I was in an RAI car with the director, the cameraman, and the sound technician, on our way from Rome to Bari.

I described the fascinating personality of our famous artist, and from their questions I was amused to note that they suspected that only a very close "affectionate" relationship between us would induce such a personality to concede a TV interview deep into the night, after a concert, and at no fee. I was even more amused by the look on their faces when Ellington greeted me with his usual "total embrace."

"Uncle Eddie, I want you to know that this is a huge gift you are giving me, and I do appreciate it. Let me introduce my colleagues who are thrilled to work with you . . ."

My three TV crewmembers had come forward, and Ellington was immediately charming them with his wit and what Italian language he knew. It was decided that we would tape the interview at his hotel suite, right after the concert.

So around one o'clock in the morning the scene was set, lights appropriately fixed, a microphone hovering above us, out of sight. Relaxed and amused, Ellington answered at length the questions that the TV director and I would ask him, regarding both his personal life as well as his career. The picture that emerged was obviously unique.

He spoke of his father, who had worked as a draftsman in the Navy's printing office but also doubled as butler for high-ranking families in Washington. This last occupation had resulted in a certain genteel reflection in their own home, with proper silverware, furniture, and good manners that were taught to the children. Both parents, as well as his sister Ruth, played the piano.

His beloved mother had obviously spoiled him: "My mother held me in her hands and never let my feet touch the ground. I was completely spoiled. She educated me, taught me the importance of proper speech and good manners. She developed my taste for beauty and neatness, including my clothes, which at school made them call me 'Duke' to mock me."

The biographic interview unfolded to reveal the extraordinary benevolence that fate had bestowed upon him from birth. He had acquired an education that had been equal to that of any white youngster. He spoke of his childhood music lessons with Miss Clinkscales, although his foremost talent, painting, had earned him an entry to the Academy of Arts in Washington, D.C., his birthplace. He had earned some money painting signs and backdrops.

Continuing his piano lessons, he had begun to play, at first, in all kinds of spots and dives, with some success. He then had created a small music combo that eventually would convince him that music was his best choice. It had become his real interest, and he had decided to become a real musician; so he had acquired a real teacher, studying harmony, composition, and what he called his "music foundation"—reading the lead sheets and recognizing chords. In addition, he listened carefully to unwritten negro music as well as the old-fashioned piano rolls. He had then formed his first orchestra, "Duke's Washingtonians," and his career had gotten off to a great start.

When the TV director asked him about the fact that he was known to have more than one hundred suits and that they were all blue, Ellington gave us an amused look and answered that blue happened to be his favorite color, perhaps because his mother had always clothed him in blue. Why such a vast wardrobe? Because it was useful, an inheritance from the old days when all the musicians of his age would choose to dress very carefully. He scoffed at the improper way the younger musicians would dress on stage, trying to look eccentric at all costs. He considered his appearance had to be dignified at all times, as a form of respect for oneself and for the public.

When asked about the difficult situation in the United States regarding civil rights, and if he was taking any action, Ellington replied that he had been protesting since the 1930s, long before protest would become almost fashionable. That closed the subject.

When asked about the fact that many jazz musicians used drugs because they said they needed the strength to keep going, he replied very clearly on the subject:

"It's commonly thought that being a jazz musician is synonymous to being a drug addict, but the fact of taking drugs has nothing to do with the music; even if, among my generation, there have been some eccentrics, using drugs and alcohol and living their lives where music and drugs were essentially one. But those were other times. Today not all addicts are necessarily jazz musicians. Look at me, for instance. I tour the world with a small case full of vitamins. I use vitamins. I need vitamins because I work very hard, I give much of myself in all the things I do."

Remembering our early days in Juan-les-Pins, I teased him, asking if it was true that he drank large amounts of hot water at breakfast? He gave me an amused look and answered very seriously that he now drank lots of green tea instead.

The director asked him if he spoke any Italian, and Ellington replied breezily: "But of course! Uno, due, tre, quattro, cinque, sei, sette, otto, nove . . ."

Asked if the three Sacred Concerts he had composed were a sign that he considered himself some kind of missionary, he replied that being a missionary was not at all his vocation. Each man prays in his own language and Ellington's language was music. He could only say that he had seen God. He could close his eyes and see God. But he could not make anyone else see his God.

We spoke of his popularity among all walks of life, from a simple "shoeshine" to the Queen of England, as well as the recent "Legion d'Honneur" he had received in France. Reminded that he had celebrated his seventieth birthday at the White House, invited by President and Mrs. Nixon, he reminisced: "Ah, yes. At the table I was sitting next to the First Lady, and I asked her if she was aware that she had gone beyond all limits. Surprised, she asked me why? So I answered that there were limits, even for a president's lady, and that she was lovely beyond every legal limit. She had laughed and answered: 'Ah, don Juan, I have heard all about you!'"

The TV director was truly delighted with the portrait that was emerging, and he motioned for me to continue with my enquiry.

"One last question: At your age you have really obtained it all: honors, fortune, success. . . . What else is missing? Is there still some special thing you would wish from life?"

He considered his answer, and then nodded: "Well, yes, there are very many things . . . some shows I have written that I would like to see performed . . . two operas and one ballet. But then, perhaps the most important thing would be to present my last Sacred Concert to the Holy Father at the Vatican . . ."

Once again, I was secretly heartbroken, remembering the cancelled Vatican concert because of famine in India, and once again relieved that I had never mentioned it to him.

After a while I noticed he was looking tired, so I closed the interview with the usual words of thanks and "arrivederci soon" and told the TV crew that we could fold up and prepare to drive back to Rome.

Ellington drew me aside and asked if I could not stay with him and return to Rome the next day. As usual I hugged him and, thanking him, declined his invitation, assuring him I was very flattered and perhaps another time? But instead of answering me with one of his flirting phrases he sighed and asked, "But will there be another time, Lil? Time is a thief. The distance gets shorter . . ."

"But you are the eternal Ellington! Time will never catch up with you."

His wise, amused smile, one last "total embrace," and then he let me go.

In the days that followed I transcribed on paper the taped English dialogue and sent it to him, as usual. I then proceeded to translate the interview into Italian, streamlined it to fit the time allotted to the TV show. I chose the actor who would dub the voice of Ellington in Italian while I would speak my part. I spent two days in the dubbing studio and finally brought the definitive result to the programming director. Excellent work as usual, Lilian. They would let me know the date set for airing the interview.

Fortunately, I had good friends among the recording technicians who one day called me urgently to their studio, but on the hush. I discovered to my horror that the producers had decided that Ellington had to appear, at the beginning, as the poor, discriminated, hungry, black street urchin. The story had to be "from rags to riches," from the "slums" to the Royal command performance. I could just imagine Ellington's reaction to such an offensive invention. Perhaps that's why he had wisely requested that I have the last legal word of approval before airing the show.

I went to the executive director and told him that Ellington was not going to be misused for one of their sob stories, especially as his story was extraordinary enough to interest our public as it stood. The director was extremely annoyed and tried to insist on their version. I finally reminded him that the contract had been very clear, I had the last say before airing it, and I was saying no to this offensive invention.

"Very well then, in that case the interview will not go on the air at all" was their menace.

Knowing Ellington, I was totally at ease in telling them that I withdrew the interview and forbade any use of his image. When I tried to recuperate the original interview, I was told that "orders from the top" had requested that the film and the sound, as well as the dubbing, be totally destroyed.

Of course, I was never to produce anything else for that particular TV section.

When I called Ellington to inform him of the outcome, he must have sensed my disappointment and frustration. He told me it did not really matter, as the main reason for accepting their proposal had been for the pleasure of our getting together again.

"I got one last 'total embrace' Lil."

"Not last! There will be many more, I promise you."

ACT X—"FARE THEE WELL!"

We would never embrace again. On May 24, 1974, he was gone. I did not fly to New York for his funeral. I was an incredulous orphan; how could he leave us? I could only bear our loss by casting aside the thought of his disappearance. He would reappear in his own good time, for sure.

To this day, his memory has not abandoned us, including the daily breakfast ritual of two glasses of hot green tea, when I raise my glass to him: "So here we go, cheers!"

Yes, an incredible miracle had happened long ago when I had been drawn into the magic land of Ellingtonia, the world of an eternal magician.

But then, I do believe that to this very day each one of us, young or old, shares this feeling of belonging to his ageless music.

"So here are four kisses to thank you, Maestro, and please believe us when we strongly affirm that 'we want you to know that we do love you madly.' Always will."

Juan-les-Pins, 1966—*"Maestro Ellington, I shall never forget your kindness!"*
Courtesy of Pierre Lapijover

Juan-les-Pins, 1966—*"It depends on the wishes of La Plus Belle Lil . . ."*
Courtesy of Herbie Jones

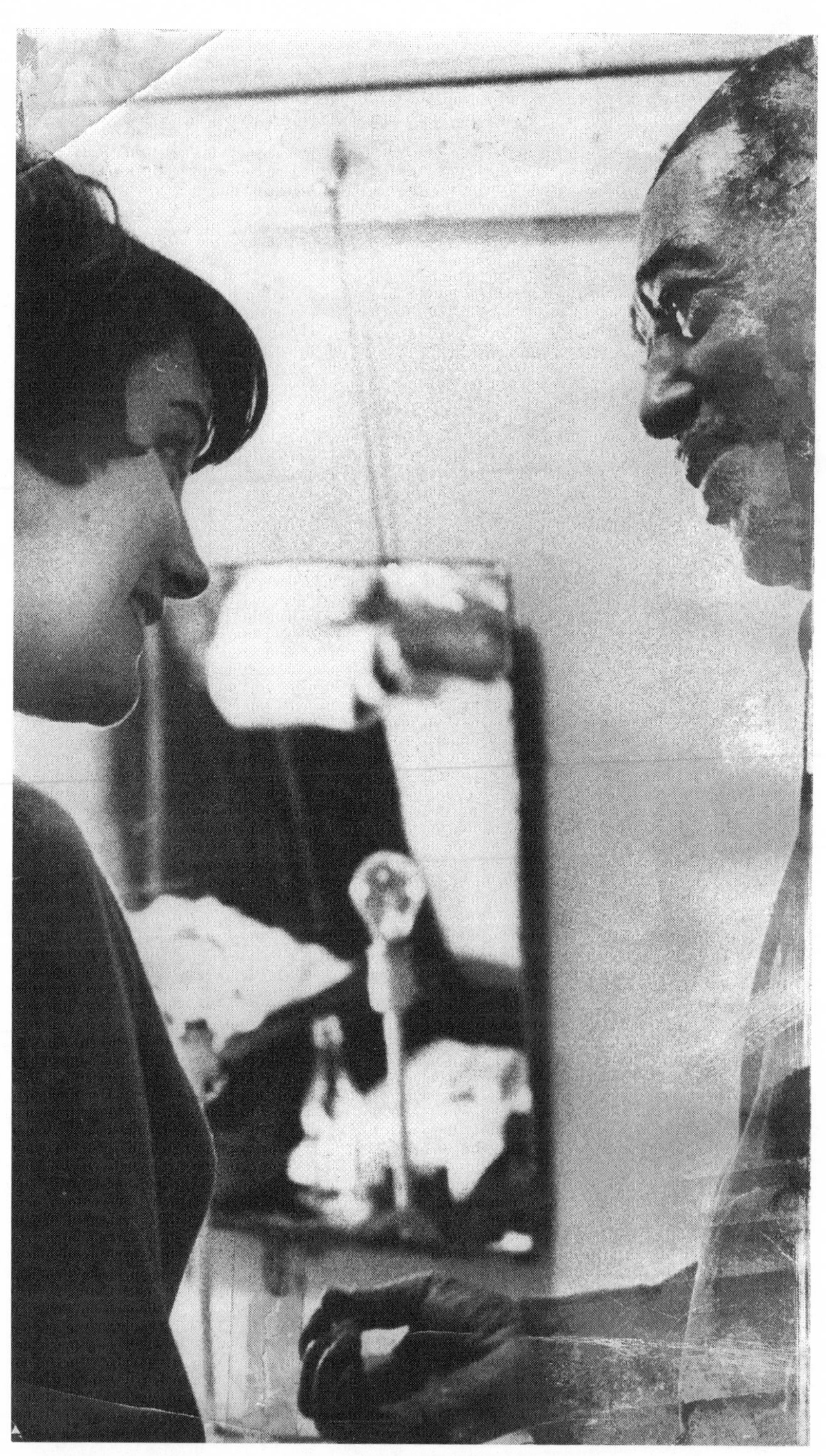

Italy, 1969—*"Fare thee well."*

Courtesy of Giuseppe Pino

ABBEY LINCOLN AND MAX ROACH

Introduction

Act I—Abbey Lincoln and Max Roach: Handsome couple, bright, intense, very interesting. From a business meeting in Milano then on to Rome, where they become welcome members of my family for the rest of their lives.

Act II—Sister of the Soul—1967 to 2010: There is total trust between us, she tells me of her life, her hopes and plans. Her success in films as well as her deep disappointments.

Act III—Separation: The divorce from Max is a terrible blow from which she will never recover, but she will dedicate herself to her art: singing, acting, writing, and painting.

Act IV—Memories: The many touching memories of her life, she shares my home and my family, while I am at home in New York under her wing.

Act V—Last Messages: Toward the end I would have her news through my son Francesco, who assisted her with her music. There were letters and phone calls, but we knew we would not meet again in person.

Act VI—The African Lion—1967 to 2007: Parallel with my relationship with Abbey, I can entertain the same sincere, open friendship with Max even after their divorce. He is often involved in my work, and I am his interpreter during his clinics in Italy.

Act VII—University of Massachusetts at Amherst: When he becomes part of the teaching system at Amherst, he gives me a detailed, amusing interview regarding the pros and cons of teaching in a university.

Act VIII—Family Ties: Through the years, Max remained an active member of my family, especially with regard to Francesco, who would give me regular news concerning both Abbey and Max.

INTRODUCTION

Abbey Lincoln and Max Roach were undoubtedly the most interesting couple of modern jazz. They were brilliant and intelligent, and we are all aware of their artistic accomplishments as well as the political and social importance they were deservedly given. For my part, I can speak of them remembering the friendship that developed between our two families, from our first "business" meeting in Milano and on through all the years that followed.

ACT I—ABBEY LINCOLN AND MAX ROACH

In the summer of 1967 Max was invited to Milano by Meazzi—Italy's leading percussion firm—to discuss his endorsement of their Hollywood Tronic Drum. When Meazzi invited me as well, the idea of meeting Max and Abbey was most stimulating, for I had been aware of the couple's involvement in the political scene of the United States from their first Long Play, "We Insist! Freedom Now Suite," and their social involvement in the Black Power movement had been of great interest to all of us.

The Meazzi director had asked me to act as his hostess with the couple, who stood, tall and very handsome, among admiring Italian musicians and journalists. Everybody was eager to hear this odd Tronic Drum boom into life at the magic hands of one of the great drummers of all time, and I could tell our artists felt slightly out of place in this typically noisy and good-natured Italian crowd.

When we were introduced formally, Abbey and I measured each other with feminine curiosity. I smiled at her, admiring her African headdress.

"You know, *that* turban will be the envy of all the fancy Milanese ladies at today's luncheon, especially as they could never hope to wear it with the same results. Actually, you and Max are a very handsome couple. Another thing, your record covers don't do you justice. You're much more interesting in real life."

Shaking hands with me with an amused smile, they accepted my compliment and Abbey asked: "Oh yes? Well thank you. And which records do you refer to?"

"Good Heavens! I'm a *mess* with titles of LPs but, of course, I do recall the 'Freedom Now Suite' and especially the one called 'Abbey is Blue.' I am always playing on my radio program your version of Kurt Weil's 'Lost in the Stars.' With that lightly rasping voice you have, it really gives the lonely feeling of those lyrics."

"Yes, it's one of my favorites."

She was amused by my outspokenness. We talked for a while about African clothes and the way they were being worn by black Americans as a political statement, and I could see that she was trying to figure me out. "Where are you from?" she asked suddenly, "You're not European . . ."

"Nope, I was born and raised in Egypt, but my father was Maltese and my mother is Italian. You might say I am Mediterranean."

She shook her head, amused, and exclaimed, "You know, what you really are . . . is a *mess*!"

"I just told you so; but then, why not?"

She asked, pointing a finger at me, "So you are *not* a Soul Sister . . . ?"

"No, my dear, but I *am* a Sister of the Soul."

"I love that!" She laughed out "A Sister of the Soul!"

And with that phrase our friendship was set. There were no more barriers between us but instead a light teasing camaraderie.

A few days later they came to Rome, where my mother and son were eager to meet them. Mother admired their looks and their elegance, declaring Abbey "Una Dea Africana," an African goddess. As for Max—mother always had a weakness for tall, strong men—she said, "You are the powerful African lion, the king of the forest!" My seven-year-old son Francesco sat next to Abbey in speechless admiration.

The next day we went to the beach at Fregene, and while Abbey and I stretched in the sun gossiping, Max took Francesco by the hand, asking for his assistance at the ice cream stand. They were gone for some time, and when they reappeared Francesco was nursing in his arms a huge motorboat, grinning from ear to ear. I scolded Max for spoiling him, but he shook his head, saying, "Francesco said something to me in Italian that I didn't quite catch. It was about black and white people, I think?"

Francesco repeated his Italian phrase so I could translate it for my two very attentive friends.

"I said that I know now the difference between black and white people . . ."

"And?" asked Abbey, cautiously.

"Well, black people have a very kind heart and treat children much better than white people do!"

She gave him her special harsh laugh, pulling him onto her lap and, rocking him, she said:

"Well, bless your little heart, Francesco!"

A year later, when Francesco was given his First Communion in Rome, he received a personal cable from New York congratulating him for this very important day of his spiritual life: "Congratulations and may God be with you all of your days, signed Abbey and Max Roach." And that's how a bond was created that grew and strengthened between our two families.

Yes, through all the remaining years I was their "sister of the soul" through the joys and pain they shared and inflicted on each other, especially with their divorce. It was obvious they never stopped loving each other, long after they had each developed a new, separate life of their own. And I was grateful to be able to enjoy their friendship equally for the rest of their lives.

ACT II—SISTER OF THE SOUL

Across the years Abbey and I had established a pattern. During her tours in Italy she would come and rest at our country home near Venice, where mother would ply her with tasty goodies while giving her wise advice on how to treat men in general. In turn, it became customary that I accept her hospitality at her New York apartment at 415 Central Park West—and later in Harlem at 940 St. Nicholas Avenue. In New York I would cook special pasta dishes for her, on condition that she should also eat vegetables, which were not her favorites.

We would always find the time to "take our shoes off" and curl up in our armchairs to talk. She would laugh, grumble, criticize but above all review her life, her mistakes and her hopes, her defeats and her victories. Gradually I could put together her history from the 1950s starting with her extraordinary evolution from a pretty, sophisticated pop singer called Gaby Wooldridge or Gaby Lee—who charmed the patrons of supper clubs in Honolulu for a few years and then moved on to conquer the Big Apple—to bloom finally into Abbey Lincoln.

Riverside records began recording her evolution toward a more jazz-oriented repertoire, and in 1957 the same Riverside studios were witness to the birth of an inevitable earthquake when Abbey Lincoln met Max Roach. By the time they were finally married in 1962, she was well on the way to becoming politicized, as shown by her deliberate Angela Davis afro, and later the African braids.

Abbey admitted that Max had opened her door of perception to the events going on around them, socially, politically, and culturally. She became aware that being an attractive jazz singer was not enough; in fact, she rejected that definition, choosing "black artist" instead. With Max she became interested in the Black Panther Party for Self Defense, joined actively most of the public protest meetings, such as the one at the United Nations regarding the murder in 1961 of Patrice Lumumba, the first Prime Minister of the new Democratic Republic of Congo.

In 1968 she phoned her excitement regarding the film she was about to act in: *For Love of Ivy* with Sidney Poitier and, some time later, her joy at the success of that film. In 1969 the film had obtained her nomination for the Golden Globe award.

That success and recognition, however, did not spare her one huge disappointment she endured. One day we had gone downtown to celebrate great news with her friends. She had been interviewed for the role of her dreams: the life of Billie Holiday! We all felt certain that the outcome would be positive, for she was evidently *the* one actress-singer who would represent Billie to perfection, not only for the particular quality of her voice and her singing style, but also as far as stark physical appearance.

It could only be Abbey Lincoln. The word went around and everybody congratulated her. But Diana Ross decided she wanted that role and obtained it, turning Billie Holiday into a "Supreme" eye-batting doll.

But Abbey was a strong spirit, and the deep disappointment somehow enhanced her will to express herself with all the means that nature had generously bestowed upon her. She was a musician and a poetess, a writer, a performer, and also a painter. Above all, she lived her life battling for her social ideals.

Our discussions, in either of our homes, were always filled with frustration at the unfairness of the world and finding comfort in the end as we managed to laugh at life, at our men, and mostly at ourselves and our illusions that we could save humankind.

ACT III—SEPARATION

In 1970 came the painful, reluctant separation from Max Roach. It touched Abbey deeply, and for some time she was unable to move away from the building where they now both lived in separate apartments, as if she were hoping for a possible reunion.

"I'm an 'eyes wide-open' fool, Lilian. But I can't believe that there's nothing left between us; after all we have lived through together, the political battles, creating our music, loving each other totally. . . . When I think of those horrible years when his mind was shot to hell and he was going down the drain; yet I stayed with him, by his side, facing together each stage of his cure. . . . And, when he was finally out of the woods, that's when I broke down and went to pieces in my turn and, would you believe it? Roach left on a long international tour. . . . He was strong enough not to need me anymore, but what about me? I needed him; I still do, damn it!"

Then in 1975 she phoned that she was going to visit my homeland, adding "sort of." Miriam Makeba was leading her into the heart of Africa to discover her roots. From that extraordinary voyage she had emerged more set than ever in her battle in favor of the underprivileged, of whatever race. In Africa she had also been given a new name: Aminata Moseka.

Sometime after the divorce Abbey moved back to California, where her family resided. Incidentally, by then my grown-up Francesco had entered USC in Los Angeles and was very dedicated to his jazz piano. Abbey, who lived in West Los Angeles, would meet him regularly, and he would work with her, transcribing her songs—melody, chords, and text—onto music paper with his neat Virgo scores. They also composed a song together, a $\frac{3}{4}$ tempo called "Children."

After she returned to New York at the end of 1982, she further developed her writing and painting skills. In 1983 Francesco, invited to spend his spring break at her home, now in Harlem, had sent me an enthusiastic description of the night when she had sung at the Harlem Apollo Theater, accompanied by pianist Cedar

Walton. Francesco had mentioned the huge black limousine driving them to the theater with equally huge black bodyguards. Through the years, they were in regular contact. She would speak to him about "Roach" when she referred to Max; and about Black Power, referring to the whites as "the Europeans" and to the blacks as "the Africans." And, of course, she spoke to him of oppression and emancipation; she was as indignant and angry as ever at the social situation, especially regarding the old "bag ladies" who trailed in the streets.

When Francesco became a husband and father, living in New Jersey at the time, Abbey was present in church for the baptism of his baby Alice. When many years later Francesco was living again in Los Angeles, he used every business travel occasion to drop in on Abbey in New York. His last visit was in 2005, when she was living again on Riverside Drive.

He wrote that her sight was failing her, that she had seemed particularly fragile and a little absentminded. She had proudly shown him her "naïf" paintings inspired by African subjects in bright jungle colors. She was always as beautiful and as angry at racism as ever, especially with regard to the milieu of music and the arts. He finally mentioned that she did not seem at all in good health, and he was worried he might not have the chance to see her again.

In fact, in 2007 she was undergoing open-heart surgery.

ACT IV—MEMORIES

We have so many memories of that wonderful woman, such as the time I had recorded a successful LP with Tommy Flanagan in 1982. One day, in Rome, I had received her call from New York to tell me that WBGO, the New Jersey radio station, kept playing the whole LP from top to bottom and daily. She had thought it would please me to know it and that she loved it. The next year she sent me her latest LP, "Talking to the Sun," scribbling on the back:

"Dearest Lilian, I love you for everything you are. Thank you for friendship. It's love. Abbey Aminata Anna Marie."

I have it right here on hand, today.

At Count Basie's funeral in April 1984, I had been Abbey's guest in Harlem. Calling Dizzy Gillespie on the phone, we had made a date for the next day, when we would meet him at the Abyssinian Church in Harlem and, after the funeral, he would come to Abbey's home for his special "pasta" lunch. When we got there, Dizzy was immediately grabbed and ushered into the church. There was such a huge crowd trying to enter that Abbey chose for us to join the many other fans and friends in a bar just across from the Abyssinian Church, to have a drink to Bill Basie's memory instead.

Finally, Dizzy, Abbey, and I were at her home and, while I went into the kitchen to prepare "farfalle, pisellini e gamberetti" (butterfly pasta, sweet peas, and baby shrimp) and Abbey set the table, Dizzy sat at the piano and played romantic ballads for us.

At lunch we spoke of various things, remembered some of our friends who had gone ahead, others who we had been glad to discover were still alive; in all, it was a very relaxed, philosophically thoughtful afternoon.

During Abbey's European tours we would often organize some concerts also in Italy. In Sorrento I had organized for a huge banner to span the main avenue from side to side with the largest words to read "Welcome Abbey Lincoln." Driving into Sorrento, there it was, flapping its greeting to her. She had gasped then exploded in her brilliant laughter. "Oh, I love it! I love it!"

When the jazz milieu of New York finally realized her worth, the Lincoln Center organized a series of concerts in her honor at the Alice Tully Hall. On the phone she was very happy, on the one hand, yet melancholy. I wrote her a note of congratulations:

"I am sure that during these coming evenings at the Alice Tully Hall you'll be thrilled and excited and will be your beautiful overwhelming self. How very appropriate that they should honor you, considering what you represent not only for jazz but also for the dignity of women anywhere in the world. Am very proud of you, my girl, and trust you will contact me as soon as you are relaxed enough to sit and write all about it."

Of course she preferred to answer by phone.

ACT V—LAST MESSAGES

My last message to her, typed in large letters to ease her failing sight, went as follows:

> Happy Birthday, Anna Marie, Gaby, Abbey or Aminata!
>
> As I told you in my phone message, the French/German TV station ARTE passed a long Special dedicated to you, recorded a few years ago. It was wonderful to watch you sing, talk, laugh that brilliant laugh of yours—and so touching to see that you can still get tears in those eyes—that I got homesick for our old times together. If we could talk (and laugh) so meaningfully years ago when we still had a lot of living and learning to do, can you imagine our future get-together?
>
> It was extremely interesting to see your paintings and just what exactly went on between you and Jean-Philippe Allard, hum? I was very moved by your rendition—in French, I say!—of the famous song by Léo Ferré, "Avec le temps." Actually, with your contract with Universal you have become practically French! I love your latest "Abbey Sings Abbey" but although I love all your songs, the one I like "very best" is "Throw It

Away" of course. As for me, as you know our CD "Emotions" comes out in September and I wish you were here for good luck! Francesco did a very good job as pianist, arranger, and producer. But then he was a pupil of yours.

From September onwards I'll be living definitely in Nice and I hope to have you here, during your French excursions, if only to eat all the veggies you love so much . . . Of course including foie gras and champagne . . . OK, now the ball is in your corner. I enclose a magazine cutting regarding your TV presentation, for your files.

Love, as ever, from your sister of the soul.

When she did answer by phone, she told me that while she sent me all her love she also considered it unlikely that we would ever meet again in person.

It was so. On August 14, 2010, our beautiful girl left us with the poignant memory of a very special and unforgettable human being. She was an extraordinary artist as a singer or poetess, actress or painter. She wore her heart and soul on her sleeve as shown by the text of her songs; and she never stopped caring for the "underdog," expressing her anger on their behalf.

Our favorite song remains "Throw It Away," and we can see her radiant smile as she sang it:

Throw it away, you can throw it away!
Live your life. Give your love, each and every day.
And keep your hand wide open, and let the sun shine through.
For you can never lose a thing, if it belongs to you."

Abbey Lincoln was much loved by all who knew her: man, woman, and child. She was unique, irreplaceable, and is forever missed.

ACT VI—THE AFRICAN LION

When Max and Abbey parted, I was relieved to see that my relationship with either of them continued unhindered by their reciprocal problems. Max remained our very good friend, and we enjoyed both his company and his music for the rest of his life.

He was obviously a charmer with his sharp sense of humor and his brilliant mind. His art—both as composer as well as performer—was definitely outstanding, growing through the years in the eyes of critics and public alike, the world over.

As mentioned, our friendship had begun in 1967 in Milano, through the Meazzi Company, who then invited me to the Chicago Music Fair in 1968, where Max was presenting their Hollywood Tronic Drum. Obviously, Max attracted a very large amount of public attention as he sat regally powerful, explaining the very complicated secrets of an electronic set of drums. The Meazzi engineer stood by his side, ready to give further insight into the workings of the instrument, in Italian, while I translated into English what I hoped was a coherent spiel.

It worked enough to impress Max, who decided, through the many years that followed, that, whenever I was free, I would be his assistant in Italy during his seminars and clinics. I would explain his lessons in Italian and act as interpreter between his questioning students and the Maestro Massimo Roach. I remember that he would close each lesson by playing for his admiring students his particular version of Chopin's "Minute Waltz" on his drum set, provoking their enthusiastic applause. In Italy I also organized some concerts and radio and television appearances for him.

On the other hand, during my visits to the United States he was ready to accompany me whenever I requested his assistance to approach particular artists for my radio program. We were often joined by Papa Jo Jones, as when we would go for a good soul-food meal at the Boondocks, or the time they drove me by car to the Newport Jazz Festival and we ended up as guests of Lucky Luciano's brother-in-law at the Cliff Walk Manor. Here is what happened.

We were driving from New York to Newport in a pale blue convertible car. We were enjoying the ride, listening to Otis Redding and singing along with him, approximately, and at the top of our voices: "Oh, I don't know what you're doing to me, baby, but you're so GOOD to me!" I was there to tape—for my Italian Radio program—a number of interviews with any jazz artist I could approach during the festival. Max had patted my shoulder reassuringly: no problem, I was to pick out any artist I fancied and just point him out.

At the Newport Motel—where the Italian Radio office in New York had reserved three rooms for Terry, Roach, and Jones—the reception clerk told me, after eyeing my two suntanned friends, that unfortunately they had only one room left, for me. Yes, three rooms had been confirmed but it just so happened that . . .

Indignant, I had walked out with Max and Papa Jo, who warned me that it might be impossible to find rooms anywhere else at that point of the festival. And right they were; not even George Wein could help us, at least not for that first night.

"Better go back to the motel, Lilian. Don't worry, we'll find a pad."

"Never! We came together, we share together. This is my first personal contact with discrimination, and we're in 1968! They'll never believe it in Italy when I tell them!"

"Italy!" exclaimed Max to Papa Jo, who answered: "Sure. Nick!"

And with those mysterious words they drove me out of town to a beautiful cliff with a breathtaking view of the ocean and an elegant hotel called the Cliff Walk Manor.

"What a lovely place! Look, the sign says the hotel is closed. Yet look at all those limousines. . . . They must be having a wedding."

Max and Jo exchanged a knowing grin, nodding, and then Max turned to me: "Well, Lilianah, looks like you're going to have another American experience. You're going to be the guest of a very important family. I guess we've run smack into one of their reunions. I'll go find out."

While waiting for Max to return, I asked Papa Jo the name of this family, but he laughed and shook his head: "Just you wait, girl."

Within minutes Max was back, waving for us to emerge from the car.

Flanked by my two artists, I entered the large hall where a very friendly man by the name of Nick Cannarozzi came to greet us.

"Say, great! Nice to meet you! So you're from Rome, ha? Come on in and meet the folks! We've just finished lunch and they're eager to meet you."

I was ushered into the center of the huge dining room where I saw a number of men and women, all dressed up, sitting at ease around an imposing horse-shoe-shaped dining table. I considered that this was a rather large crowd to belong to just one family . . .

Meanwhile Nick Cannarozzi was being a perfect host, introducing me around, and everyone was happy, glad, delighted, and pleased to meet me . . . and what was new in Rome . . . and when had I last seen the Pope? Shaking hands and answering with a smile, I raised my brows at Max and Jo, who were standing back with huge grins on their faces.

To cut a story short, the three of us were made welcome to stay as guests at the top floor of the Manor for as long as we liked. It was understood that we would use the other entrance and be discreetly invisible.

It was only the next afternoon, when we had found accommodations elsewhere, that Max told me, greatly amused, that we had been the guests of Lucky Luciano's brother-in-law, in the midst of an important Family business reunion.

My heartfelt comment was: "Well, I'll tell you one thing. If it hadn't been for Nick, we would have ended up sleeping in the car. Long live Nick Cannarozzi and Italo-American hospitality!"

During those four days in Newport I saw many old friends and made some new ones, like Joe Zawinul and Cannonball Adderley. There was also Ray Charles, who accepted willingly to give me an interview in New York some days later and from which meeting there developed a long and lasting friendship, across the continents, for more than a decade. But that's another story.

Max Roach was my mentor and my guiding spirit in Newport as he saw to it that I should meet all the famous artists I wished to include in my Italian Radio program. I interviewed Mahalia Jackson and Bill Basie, Dizzy Gillespie and underrated saxophonist Vi Redd. I taped a very pleasant interview with Tal Farlow and Barney Kessel. My greatest prize, however, was when Max introduced me to Nina Simone as his "sister of the soul" from Egypt. He obtained that she consider me with friendly curiosity, resulting in an invitation to her home in New York. An exceptional interview was recorded on that occasion.

ACT VII—UNIVERSITY OF MASSACHUSETTS AT AMHERST

When Max became a faculty member of the University of Massachusetts at Amherst, I was truly happy for this well-deserved recognition, and we celebrated when he came to Italy. I could not help wondering if, being now part of the Educational Establishment, his outlook regarding the racial situation had modified.

In one of our "conversations" for my radio program I questioned him about it.

"Massimo, today that jazz is being played all over the place, in all countries, all continents, therefore by *all* races . . . can one still say that there is a *white* way and a *black* way of playing jazz?"

He obviously loved that question!

"Well, let's examine jazz *itself*, from a musical but also a *political* vantage. Jazz is the most democratic form of any music on the face of the earth today. It deals with racial participation, racial contributions, et cetera. Jazz is the complete opposite of European classical music, in the way it is performed and created. Classical music is imperialistic in its *political* nature. There are two main people involved: the composer and the conductor. The rest of the orchestra, singers and all, are no more than robots doing the will of these two characters. That's why I say imperialistic."

"Whereas jazz is . . . ?"

"Whereas jazz is democratic in the fact that *everyone* has a voice in the makeup of the composition itself. There may be a composer . . . say Mister Ellington, or Gershwin. . . . We may use one of their pieces as a *theme*, but we have an opportunity to develop *that* theme the way *we* feel about the subject, provided we stay in the boundaries of the harmonic, rhythmic, and melodic structure of that particular piece. That we preserve the *ambiance* of the piece: exiting or peaceful, whatever. It's democratic because we are free to express ourselves *within* those boundaries. That's why the music itself is so attractive to so many musicians around the world."

"But they have to learn the rules . . ."

"*And* it's no small matter either! A lot of people think improvisation is just where you do what *you* want to do. But certain structures are set up, and you have to be able to improvise *within* these musical guidelines. And even though it's *free*, it's really *not* free. There must be harmony among the group as the *whole* performance has to get on; we are all free to participate but . . . intelligently. So our music expresses what true democracy *is* because it's the music that comes from *ordinary* people, regardless of race. It's not an elitist type of music."

"Although many people will say that jazz is an elite music, for an elite public."

"Yeah, those who see this as an elitist type of music are usually middle-class and bourgeois. But jazz came out of the creativity of people who were *not* of the elite, it came from the bowels and guts of the working-class people, of every persuasion—people who have created a culture that is viable and just as technical. It has its own laws about perfection, and about what makes the true jazz artist."

"Following precise standards?"

"We *do* have standards by which we evaluate a person."

At that point I remembered that Max had begun to play the drums at a very young age, soon becoming a recognized performer when he had joined the new bebop scene.

I asked him if he had ever studied percussion academically.

He answered, grinning, "I had quite an experience, you know, when I decided to go to the Conservatory in New York City."

"How old were you?"

"Well, I guess I was about twenty."

"And how long had you been playing?"

"I started playing when I was still in school because in New York City at the time . . . music abounded in every nook and cranny, out of the walls, twenty-four hours a day. I'd been making all these records and things . . . this was in 1944/45. So I said, "I'll take an audition to get into the Conservatory," and naturally my instrument would be drums; though I had been playing piano since I was very young, from the church."

"So you're also a pianist, like Dizzy!"

Nodding, he went on with his story:

"When I went to the professor—his name was Albright, a famous teacher—he gave me the sticks, put some music before me, and told me to read it. So I picked up the sticks . . . and before I could even strike the drum, he told me I was holding the sticks incorrectly! Now I was paying my way through this very school by working on Fifty-Second Street making records with people like Coleman Hawkins, Charlie Parker, and Dizzy Gillespie . . . playing the drums, the way *I* play the drums."

"Well, of course!"

"Now that was not an insult to me, for right then and there I changed my major to composition, which was *really* a blessing. And it taught me several things about the United States."

"Such as?"

"First of all, that although we have several cultures here, the only one *recognized* is the Germanic culture. We only speak *one* language even though we have a nation of Italians, of French, Chinese, Japanese, all kinds of people. We should know *more* about folks who live next door. Know something about Asiatic cultures, about different European cultures, but we are only taught *one* culture and this is my big fight since I'm in education now. The United States are *one-dimensional*, culturally speaking. And it's a tragedy."

He shook his head. I moved the subject forward.

"So when you changed your musical studies . . . ?"

"Well, I changed my major to composition, and I smiled because I knew that with Mister Albright's military technique for classical music . . . well, there would be no way I could use that technique down on Fifty-Second Street and perform with people like Charlie Parker and Dizzy Gillespie! They'd drive me off the stage, of course!"

We laughed, imagining the scene.

He went back to the original subject:

"Many students ask me, like you did: Is there such a thing as black and white jazz? Now in my lectures, especially in the United States, I talk about the *history* of the music and the major contributors to different styles and different periods of the music. Almost always, they are black, and there's a reason for this, Lilian, because the *seed* of this music is in the *United States of America*. Nowhere in *Africa* do you hear this kind of music, or in the history of *European* music, or *Asiatic* music. It's peculiar to the United States of America, because it's a fusion of *all* these cultures; although the U.S. itself denies these cultures. They say the only thing that's valid is the Germanic culture: English, Shakespeare, Bach, Beethoven, they call this 'high' culture."

"And what do you teach your students?"

"My students ask me: 'We've listened to your lecture and very seldom do you mention the contribution of white musicians,' and I say there's a *political* reason for that. A culture is a result of a way of life, of your family life, the things that your sensibilities are bombarded with from the time you come out of your mother's womb, until you become an adult. What I'm saying is: In the U.S.A. blacks were not allowed *by law* to participate in the white way of life, become part of the *white* part of town. And whites were not allowed to become part of the *black* part of town. We all know that Bessie Smith died when she was in an automobile accident, down there in the Deep South. The first ambulance that came was from a *white* hospital, but they could not take her *legally*; they had to go back and she had to wait for an ambulance from a *black* hospital, and that is why she died."

"Yes, such a tragedy!"

"So whites were not allowed on our side of town . . . and *we* weren't allowed to go to theirs. Consequently, *we* have produced no Beethovens or Bachs, or Gunther Schullers, and by the same token *whites* have not produced any Charlie Parkers or Billie Holidays. This is a sociological and a political problem."

"Even today?"

"Today of course that condition is lessened because people are becoming more civilized, in the United States. We learn to live in close proximity to one another. But the beauty of this music is that, even before racial segregation became illegal, boundaries had been crossed earlier. It's because Louis Armstrong and Bix Beiderbecke and all these people intermingled, *in spite* of the segregation laws."

"Thanks to jazz."

"Thanks to jazz. It started many, many years ago. Take the techniques that are essential with jazz, on a professional level; everybody had a hand in that: Europeans, Africans, everybody. From the instrumental standpoint, from a harmonic, melodic, and rhythmic standpoint. So it's really a combination of that democratic process that's *supposed* to exist in the United States of America."

"*Supposed* to exist?"

"Supposed to exist. But jazz really personifies it. I can get on a bandstand with Zoot Sims, Stan Getz, Miles Davis, and Ray Brown; and something happens, something *really* happens, because we all know the techniques that are involved in making this music a *living* piece that has high order, design, and form. It has clarity: a beginning, a development, and an end."

Listening to his reasoning, I couldn't help thinking with some amusement at how his strong personality must have affected some of the formal classical professors when he became one of them at the University of Massachusetts at Amherst. So I asked him, hoping for an interesting reaction. He reacted.

"With my cohorts, who are music professors themselves, we have faculty concerts during the semester. Sometimes they do an "improvisational piece" but with music in front of them that will say . . . to the percussion part: "throw a dime up in the air and let it drop on the snare drum and then dampen it."

"And this is improvisation?"

"This is improvisation. Or: 'Play a series of four eight-note phrases, but in this three-minute period you cannot use the same type of stick as a percussionist.' That means you play 'da-da-da-da' with a brush, 'da-da-da-da' with a mallet, and then 'da-da-da-da' with something else."

"And that's improvisation!"

"That's improvisation. Now, as far as the voice part is concerned . . ."

"Yes?!"

"You get the telephone book . . ."

"Oh, come on!"

"It's true, this is a *piece* now. And for one minute you read the names at random from any page in the book. Then from any other page, at random, for thirty seconds. While this is going on, the trumpet player may be doing something or other. This is *their* improvisation. Now jazz is not like that."

"I should say not . . ."

"In jazz the properties are all laid out and we all know the law. Like in a democracy, everybody has to be intelligent enough to know that we have to govern these properties together, *equally*, and that's what jazz is about. And the reason it came about in America is because the U.S.A. is, on *paper*, a democracy. It's a reality because a common man can become a president, like Richard Nixon . . . or Gerald Ford. There's no "upper class by *birth*" in the United States, so it has eliminated the *imperialistic* quality of the country, and our music personifies that attitude, politically. It originated in the U.S.A. and then spread out to the world where there are some people who may do a better job than the originator."

"But would you still call it jazz at that point?"

"If we're going to deal with just labels . . . I think *music* is the proper term"

"Afro-American music?"

"I don't call it Afro-American music *now*. You see, we named it Afro-American or black music as a reaction to the social system that was there *then*. We, as black people in the United States, were always denied everything. So in order to fight back we'd say 'well, this is *black* music!' you understand? Because everything else is white, it's tacitly understood. So, 'Afro-American music' or 'black music' is a reactionary statement. This music is made of a combination of cultures that exist in—and could *only* have existed—in the United States."

"Yes, but then would you say that there *is* a white way and a black way of playing jazz? That they are similar but different?"

"Well, are there a '*white* European classical music and a *black* European classical music?' I mean, we have a lot of blacks who come out of the conservatory and write wonderful music but who would know of any great black composers in the European classical music tradition? Most people would say 'I don't know of any.'"

"That's true."

"So I say to you: Lilian, when you look at the history, at the development of our music, it's almost totally black. Now, usually this insults a lot of white people, and right away they cry 'racism!' But we'll just look at the history of the trumpet, for example. We'll say: King Oliver, Louis Armstrong, Roy Eldridge, Hot Lips Page, Dizzy Gillespie, Miles Davis, Freddie Hubbard. Now why didn't I say Bix Beiderbecke, Chet Baker, Harry James, Red Rodney . . . why didn't I say that?"

"Why didn't you?"

"Well, it's obvious. Red Rodney was influenced by Dizzy Gillespie; Chet Baker was influenced by Miles Davis. I'm talking about the *original* people, OK? So now when I listen to *black* composers who compose in the European classical tradition, I hear a little Stravinsky, a little Debussy. . . . So I would not say they now are as great as any European composer; there's no way in the world I could say that. The question I am trying to answer to you . . . I have had so many debates, even here in Italy, and I have been accused of being a racist when it comes down to culture . . ."

I have to laugh.

"No, don't laugh; I'm very serious about this. I maintain that whites have not had an opportunity to *really* become involved in jazz on as serious levels as blacks. Because if *we* want to participate in music seriously, we have to become engaged in jazz music, whereas Europeans can become engaged in European classical music and 'incidentally' become involved in jazz music as well. As fine a musician and as creative a musician as Mister Ellington is—and as much music as he has written—he is still classified as a 'jazz' musician. And I might also tell you that Duke Ellington never referred to his music as jazz."

"I know! He would ask, 'What is jazz?'"

"Mister Louis Armstrong never did either; he called it: 'This is New Orleans style.' A lot of these names don't mean that much anyway, they come and go. So when you say 'jazz,' it's a cover up for everything. Who is jazz? What is jazz? The King of Jazz is Paul Whiteman!"

I burst out laughing, nodding. Max continues:

"That's the truth. Historically, the King of Jazz is Paul Whiteman. The King of Swing is . . ." (*we name him together*) 'Benny Goodman!'"

"But why is it so?" I ask him.

"Well, publicity! Somebody says that. When you listen to someone like Eubie Blake expound on the music, and the forms of it . . . you learn that *jazz* came as a later word. Another thing, they had soul music, rhythm and blues music and all of a sudden they changed it to rock and roll. Now when they have the big contest about who sold the most records . . . well, in the rock category there are no black people. Black people are relegated to what they call soul and rhythm and blues. So right at *this* point in time things are really a bit confused."

The tape had come to an end. We agreed we had a lot of very satisfying material on record, so we let it go at that, and I drove him home, where mother had prepared a very special Italian meal for him.

ACT VIII—FAMILY TIES

His relationship with my family continued through the years. Max was always ready to welcome Francesco whenever his concerts coincided with my son's whereabouts. In 1982 I would receive enthusiastic reports about Max playing at a club on Washington Avenue in Venice Beach. On that occasion Max had invited Francesco to his beach apartment on Manhattan Beach. My son had noted dutifully that Max, very casually dressed at his beach home, had then appeared on the club stage impeccably dressed in an Armani suit! He also described the complex, sophisticated arrangements, such as "Round Midnight," played with a highly interesting fast swing.

The last time they were together—some years later when Max had been integrated at the University at Amherst—he had invited my son to his home in Greenwich, Connecticut. There, Francesco had met his daughter Maxine, who was playing cello in a string quartet, and his son Raoul, a very busy producer. Max discussed his last project, "M Boom," and gave Francesco one of the first CDs coming out.

There was just one melancholy observation from my sentimental son: while at every meeting Abbey would sooner or later mention "Roach," as she called Max, since their divorce Max had never once mentioned her name.

One vision that will never fade is that of the magic concert held in the breathtaking Arena of Verona. There were only three names on the large poster, and they were three exceptional artists: Dizzy Gillespie and his United Nations Orchestra; Miles Davis and his most recent experiment; Max Roach with his "M Boom," including Maxine Roach and her string quartet.

The last time Max Roach and I were together was in September 1987 in Bassano del Grappa, where Dizzy Gillespie had adopted my Popular School of Music, giving it his name and with a regular annual appearance of encouragement among our enthusiastic students. The occasion of that last meeting, officially named "Dizzy's Day," was most important to all of us. The City of Bassano had decided to give Dizzy an honorary citizenship, and at the same time I was to produce our official celebration of Dizzy's seventieth birthday with a huge concert at the Velodrome with about eighty international jazz musicians and more than five thousand fans gathered together to celebrate our artist.

From the United States I had immediately invited Max and Milt Jackson, plus Randy Brecker and Johnny Griffin, who lived in France. There were musicians from Spain, Switzerland, Yugoslavia, Denmark . . . they came for Dizzy, and the music flowed from 6 P.M. to 3 A.M.

Being in charge of the whole operation, I was unable to spend all the time I wished with my closest friends, but the obvious mutual pleasure of being all together was rewarding enough. My last visual memory of Max Roach is that of a handsome man sitting powerfully at his drums, giving the heartbeat to the music and to thousands of enthusiastic fans.

Max left us on August 16, 2007. Three years later, almost to the day, on August 14, 2010, our beautiful Abbey said goodbye. Somehow, we have never been able to really think of them as two separate individuals, even after the many years that followed their divorce.

They gave my family their affection and their trust, and I was fortunate indeed to be considered their "sister of the soul."

Milano, 1967—*"No, I'm not a soul sister, but I am a sister of the soul."* Photographer unknown

Milano, 1967—His personal Italian/English interpreter through the years.

TELEGRAMMA

= FRANCESCO CROSARA ANTONELLI

15 ROMA

= CONGRATULATIONS AND MAY GOD BE WITH YOU ALL OF YOUR DAYS +

. ABBEY AND MAX ROACH +

0425 A

Telegram from New York to Rome, 1968, addressed to Francesco, age eight, on the day of his First Communion.

Abbey and Francesco in Rome, 1981.

Max Roach on Dizzy's Day,
Bassano del Grappa, 1987.

HORACE SILVER

Act I—The 1968 Chicago Music Show: Max Roach presents an Italian electronic drum; Horace Silver's drummer Billy Cobham is fascinated by the drum, but will Horace accept it?

The Plugged Nickel Jazz Club: We meet and become good friends; he will come to the Music Show the next day to listen to this drum.

Act II—Chicago 1968: Horace accepts the drum for Billy, then takes me to the South Side radio station, where I meet Muhammad Ali. He then takes me to dinner on certain conditions: before ordering any meat, I must first eat the vegetarian dishes Horace will order for us.

Act III—New York 1968: Horace takes me to his favorite Italian restaurant.

Our Phoenician Roots? We discuss the ancient history of the Mediterranean.

Act IV—We tape an interview-conversation regarding his successful career. We part.

Act V—Italy 1987: We are together again after nineteen years! In Bassano del Grappa we tape a last "conversation" on all aspects essential to his life.

Act VI—Italy 1987: He discusses his music, his business, his Religious Quest.

Act VII—A Final Magic Concert

ACT I—THE 1968 CHICAGO MUSIC SHOW AND THE PLUGGED NICKEL JAZZ CLUB

Remembering Horace Silver, the first thing that comes to mind is Chicago in June 1968, when I had been invited—in the role of interpreter by Meazzi, Italy's leading percussion firm—to the Chicago Music Show, where Max Roach was endorsing and promoting their Hollywood Tronic Drum.

One day a pleasant young man had entered the drum room while Max was absent. His name was Billy Cobham, drummer with the Horace Silver quintet performing in town at the Plugged Nickel. He had heard of this Italian drum, so could he . . . ? By all means, Horace Silver's drummer was most welcome to sit and experiment! He sat and he was off, drumming with all the might that Billy Cobham showed his fans throughout the years.

Signor Meazzi and Max returned to a room full of people excited by the performance of this young percussionist, and, upon learning that the Horace Silver quintet was to play at the Newport Festival the following month, Billy was asked if he would like to play their drums at that Festival.

"Wow, yes!" was the answer, "but first I'd have to ask Horace, because this drum is something else! I would need to learn more about it. But I'd love to play it."

Max was immediately agreeable that Billy should come in and rehearse with him, any time. There remained only the problem of convincing "the boss" to accept to play with this unknown Italian rhythmic entity backing him, but Billy smiled at me:

"I know what . . . you come to the Plugged Nickel tonight, and I'm sure Horace will listen to you."

Why not? And that was the beginning of my special relationship with a delightful human being by the name of Horace Silver.

The Plugged Nickel was THE Chicago jazz club that year and obviously packed with Silver fans. Billy led me backstage to meet Horace, who had been advised of my visit.

"Here she is! This is Lilian Terry, a jazz singer friend of Max Roach. She lives in Rome but she's from Egypt. She has a very interesting . . . suggestion."

A humorous expression in his eyes, a half-moon smile, evidently amused by Billy's agitation, Horace greeted me with curiosity as we shook hands. Just then his trumpeter, young Randy Brecker, spied me and came over exclaiming:

"Mama! How *are* you? What are you doing in Chicago? You look great!" He then turned to Horace and Billy, explaining: "Lilian practically adopted me the time I was stranded in Vienna and we drove down all the way to Rome in Cicci Foresti's car. She is my Italian mother!"

At this point Horace was really curious and amused, so he turned to Billy: "So, what's this suggestion?"

Eagerly, Billy gave him detailed information about this great Italian drum set that Max Roach was presenting at the Chicago Music Show. He had tested it, and the Meazzi owner was willing to let him use it when they would play at the Newport Festival—if Horace were agreeable, of course! Horace turned to me.

"I see. And you represent this Italian firm? It's Lilian, isn't it?"

"It is. But I don't represent the firm; I'm here tonight just as a friend, as well as a fan of yours, of course . . ."

This time he grinned openly as I exaggerated my "fan" attitude.

"Yes, of course. Tell you what, Lilian; tomorrow afternoon I'll come to the show with Billy to examine this 'extraordinary' instrument. Then I'll take you to dinner and you'll tell me all about Egypt. OK?"

The next afternoon at the show Max greeted Horace while Billy sat at the drum set and showed off with enthusiasm. Horace, taken aback by the strange, modified sounds of the instrument, asked if it could also play in the normal non-electronic way. By all means, it could be turned on and off by a simple button. Well then . . . long silence while Billy sat in motionless pleading . . . then the half-moon smile signified that Horace would humor his young drummer, but on two conditions: that Meazzi should deliver the drum set directly on the Newport Festival stage and that Billy should play the normal way during the performance of the quintet. At a given moment, he would have the stage all to himself to show off his "electronic mastery" to the surprised festival public.

So everyone was satisfied, the delivery details were given, and finally Horace turned to me: time for dinner. However, once outside the Hilton, he mentioned that he would first like to take me to meet some interesting friends of his at a radio station on the South Side.

ACT II—CHICAGO 1968

Ever curious, I was immediately interested when I noticed that the crowd in the studio was all black. I recognized some excellent singers and actors and was again amused by the magic worked by the mention that I came from "Cairo, Egypt," which earned me an armchair and friendly conversation.

Suddenly, there was movement by the door, and someone said, "He's here! He's coming in!" and I saw a tall, powerful, and attractive young man enter the room among welcoming calls and hugs from the ladies. He greeted each one warmly, and when he reached my side, I saw him hesitate until Egypt and Rome were mentioned. He held my hand in both his own and sat beside me, telling me he had been in Rome in 1960. Yes, of course! I remembered the occasion, the Olympics! I then added that in Italy we admired him not only as boxing champion but for his strength of character in his stand against the Vietnam War and all the unpleasantness that had followed. He listened, smiling, but was soon whisked away to another side of the room, where other fans waited to meet him. I watched this young giant, both in shape and fame, as he moved about with that friendly smile on his young face. Yes, I was pleased that my hand had been held by Muhammad Ali's own, and I thanked Horace Silver when he finally took me to the restaurant.

Once on the street he asked: Any particular place I favored? Ah, well, in Chicago any of the famous steakhouses would be perfect! Horace agreed and proposed his favorite place, but on condition that *he* should choose the menu. And that's when I discovered the teasing sense of humor of our pianist. It turned out that he was a firm vegetarian at the time. He took me to the famous Chop House, where I could see interesting meat plates passing by, but as soon as we sat down he lectured me against the dangers of eating meat. At the doubting expression on my face he proposed that if—after the menu he chose for me—I still felt the need for a Chicago steak . . . well, I would have one.

Horace then ordered various tasty vegetable and corn dishes. When he saw I could eat no more, he gave me his Cheshire cat smile and offered the Meat Menu. I declared him the winner, and as a consolation prize he promised that, once back in New York, after the Newport Festival, he would take me to his favorite Italian restaurant, where I would eat whatever my heart desired.

I accepted, hoping I would change his mind and be taken to the Boondocks instead. But that was not considering Horace Silver's charming firmness, and, once back in New York, the Italian restaurant it was.

ACT III—NEW YORK 1968

Seated at the table I informed Horace that, in Italy, his name would be translated into "Orazio Argento." He was amused and repeated it slowly, nodding. Through lunch we talked, and while he told me about his family's Portuguese origins in the Cape Verde islands, I told him about mine in the Maltese islands.

"Ah, then you *are* an Arab!" he declared, grinning.

"Not really. The Maltese are essentially Phoenicians."

He was curious, so I continued my story.

"The ancient Phoenicians were great shipbuilders, sailors, explorers, and traders who built cities all along the Mediterranean coastline, from Sicily to Greece, then around North Africa and across to Spain."

"When was this?"

"About one thousand years B.C. They built special boats that allowed them to sail and discover large parts of the world. They crossed the Strait of Gibraltar and navigated up the Atlantic to the British Isles and down along the African coast. In fact, you too could be of Phoenician Atlantic origin."

"Then what happened to them?"

"They merged with the local populations, building cities like Phoenicia, Byblos, Canaan, in places now called Lebanon, Syria, Palestine, and so on. And they developed the first modern alphabet that was then adopted and became Greek, Latin, also Arabic, Hebrew, and Indian. They wrote from right to left, as do the Arabs today."

"So we go back to the fact that you *are* an Arab." He teased me.

"Undoubtedly a Phoenician Mediterranean islander, as you are an Atlantic one."

"Well now . . . I'll have to ask my father about this, maybe the Phoenicians *did* come over long before the Portuguese?"

"Why not? My dear Orazio Argento, we could be related to each other from one thousand years ago."

After lunch we went to his apartment to tape an interview for my Italian radio program. While I struggled with my tape recorder I asked him to play the piano for me, though he confessed that his instrument was "a little off key." It was, very much so, but he played even as we joked about it.

Finally, we taped a very friendly, lighthearted, conversation.

ACT IV—HIS CAREER

"First question, Orazio: How old are you?"

"Do I have to tell?"

"Yes!" We both laughed.

"I'm thirty-nine."

"When did you start playing?"

"When I was about twelve years old"

"Did you start with the piano?"

"Yes."

"Ever played any other instrument?"

"I played the tenor and the baritone saxophones during my high school days and for a few years after."

"But you also played the piano?"

"Oh, I played the piano all the time, yes. But with the school band and orchestras, I always played the saxophone."

"Did you decide from the very beginning that you wanted to be a musician?"

"Yes. I always loved music. I knew from a very small child that I wanted to be a musician."

"And is there a *tradition* of musicians in your family?"

"Well, I have an uncle who used to play trombone for the vaudeville shows in the pit band, reading parts and whatnot . . . and my oldest brother used to play drums in his youth, and I have a couple of nephews that . . . one plays drums and bass; the other plays alto saxophone."

"And they play jazz?"

"Well, more of a rock kind of jazz."

"Ah, this is one point I wanted to ask you. Your music *is* jazz but . . . like in "Psychedelic Sally" it has a definite rock feeling to it, wouldn't you say so?"

"Umhuh." He nodded. "Yes."

"So will rock be merging with some part of jazz?"

"Well, we've always done that with our music because . . . going back to 'Sister Sadie' and 'Filthy McNasty,' they were sort of borderline numbers with a bit of the rock flavor and the jazz flavor too."

"But isn't jazz music essentially to be *listened* to?"

"Of course. Jazz is a listening music, but dance music too. Some jazz music you sit down and listen to; and if it's not too far out you can also get up and dance, and enjoy it that way."

"Talking of too far out: that first tune you played at Newport, the . . ."

"'The Kindred Spirits'"

"What would you call it? What kind of jazz?"

"I don't know!" We both laughed. "That was a new tune recorded in our album . . ."

"Yes, but it's not 'just a new tune,' it has a special thing about it, a special flavor . . ."

"Well, it has an eerie kind of quality about the melodic line. I dedicated it to my brothers. Because, you know, brothers are kindred spirits. The melodic line of the composition has sort of . . . a distant eerie feeling and yet a closeness. We are far apart yet we are close together. And that's the way that melody line is written too."

"Tell me . . . you're not married are you?"

"No!" He laughs.

"Yet you have a very strong family feeling. You composed 'Kindred Spirits' for your brothers and 'Song for My Father' obviously for your father . . ."

"Well, I *love* my family, you know?" Another burst of laughter. "I love my father, my brothers, my mother . . . I dedicated the 'Serenade to a Soul Sister' to her. It's my way of telling them that I love them."

"It's beautiful, actually. That's why it's funny that you haven't formed a family of your own."

"Well, I have plenty of time for that. I have no idea whether I will marry and, if I do, how many children I'll have. I let things take their course. Que sera, sera."

He shrugs, grinning.

"Yes, but wouldn't you like a son to whom you would teach what you know?"

"Oh, yes! I love children. I have five godchildren, they're all girls. . . . I get a great deal of enjoyment out of visiting them and bringing them presents on holidays and whatnot . . ."

"And do they call you Uncle Horace?"

"Yes!"

"Now tell me, Uncle Horace, if a little boy asked you for advice because he wanted to become a pianist . . . what would you tell him?"

"I'd tell him to study hard, to practice *every* day, and to be very serious about what he is doing."

"At what age should someone start?"

"The earlier the better, if they are *really* sincere about it."

"I see. You've composed many songs; which are the ones that are most played by *other* musicians?"

"Eh, let's see . . . 'Doodlin'' has been recorded quite a bit—both vocally and instrumentally. 'The Preacher' is another one. 'Senior Blues,' 'Sister Sadie,' 'Filthy McNasty,' and 'Song for My Father' are very popular, have been recorded quite a few times . . ."

"'Nica's Dream' is yours too. That's been played a lot."

"Yes, yes."

"And your latest recording was 'Serenade to a Soul Sister'?"

"Yes, and it looks like one of the tunes from that album might become as popular as some of those tunes I mentioned. 'Psychedelic Sally' seems to be well received . . ."

"Of course! I think it will be well received, not only in the jazz world . . . but among the kids too."

"Well, I hope so, because I've found that those tunes that we record in the rock vein appeal to the youngsters who, listening to *that* tune, come in contact with the other tunes on the LP. And before you know it they like those tunes too, and after a time they become jazz fans."

"Exactly! I try to do the same with my radio program, so your type of record is most welcome—and please do more! Are you preparing anything new? Have you written any film scores? Or any shows?"

"No, I hope to do both of those things sometime in the future. But we travel all the time, all over this country and sometimes abroad . . . it's hard to find the time to sit down and write."

"Especially if you have a piano that is off-key like the one you have here!"

Laughing, he shook his finger at me.

"Now, now. We must be kind . . ."

"Tell me, how often do you change your sidemen?"

"That's a hard question to answer, you know. Things just take their course. Like you buy a pair of shoes and when they wear out, they wear out."

"What is the longest period that you have had the same people playing with you?"

"Five-and-a-half years."

"Who were the musicians?"

"Blue Mitchell, Junior Cooke, Gene Taylor, and Roy Brooks then replaced by Louis Hayes on drums."

"However, you're very happy with the group you have now."

"Very much so, yes! I have Randy Brecker on trumpet, Benny Maupin on saxophone, John Williams on bass, and Billy Cobham on drums; a very fine group of musicians."

"Another question: Is there any *new* young *pianist* that you think will emerge in the future?"

"Hah, that's hard to say . . . McCoy Tyner now is a very fine pianist, and I think he is beginning to obtain more recognition today than he had in the past."

"When he was playing with Coltrane?"

"Yes."

"Although many people listened to those records and became *very* aware of the piano work going on."

"Well, it's a very delicate matter, you know, because regardless of the quality, caliber, and musicianship in a musician, sometimes they just don't have a certain thing that appeals to the general public."

"Who are *your* favorite musicians? I mean if you had to compose your *ideal* orchestra. . . . Let's start on drums?"

"Well, I'd have to name several people on drums. I like Art Blakey, Max Roach, Roy Haynes, Elvin Jones. I like Kenny Clarke. Tony Williams is a fine drummer."

"On bass?"

"I like Ray Brown, Percy Heath, Ron Carter, Bob Cranshaw . . . there are many fine bass players. On piano I like Thelonius Monk, John Lewis, McCoy Tyner, Bill Evans. . . . Er . . . trumpet: Miles Davis, Freddie Hubbard, Kenny Dorham . . . trombone: J. J. Johnson. I also like Curtis Fuller. On alto saxophone I like Cannonball very much, Lou Donaldson, Jackie McLean. On baritone I like Cecil Payne, Pepper Adams, Harry Carney. Who else did we leave out . . . ?"

"Well, how about the flute?"

"I like Roland Kirk on the flute. Herbie Mann, Frank Wess. Yussef Lateef is very fine on the flute. We didn't mention the tenor saxophone!" He was caught in the game. "I like Sonny Rollins, Lester Young, Coleman Hawkins, Coltrane . . . I could go on, you know . . ."

"Yes, I know. Tell me now, singers. Do you like singers as a rule?"

"Yes, as long as I don't have to play for them . . ."

Bursts of laughter from both of us, as he knew I was also a jazz singer.

"I don't care for playing behind singers. There are pianists who are exceptionally good at it. I never was. But I love to *listen* to singers. What I like about a singer or an instrumentalist is originality, inner depth, and feeling, of course. Soul, you know? I really go for creativity, on an instrument or voices themselves."

"How about Antonio Carlos Jobim?"

"Well, I don't think he is much of a singer. He's a great composer . . ."

The Jobim fan in me was indignant—how dare he put down my idol!

"Have you *heard* him sing?"

"Yes, I heard him sing . . ."

"And you don't think he's much of a singer?!"

"No, I don't think *he* would say he's much of a singer. I know him. I hung out with him in Brasil."

"Is he as beautiful a person as his music?"

"He's a very fine person, and he's a great composer."

I was appeased as he went on: "But as a singer he is . . . adequate, you know? He sings better than I do, I'll put it that way!" We laughed as he went on: ". . . but I wouldn't classify him as a *singer*."

"Speaking of Jobim, what do you think of bossa nova as a form of music?"

"'Song for My Father' is a bossa nova, while 'Cape Verdean Blue'" is Brazilian too, in a sense. That's strict samba."

"You're working on your next long-play, aren't you? Because you've already prepared 'The Belly Dancer' I believe?"

"Yes . . . that's the one *you* like, right?"

"Yes, then you promised to create 'The Lazy Arab.'"

"Well . . ." He grinned at me. "We'll see about that . . ."

"OK. Now, you were in Italy in 1959, at the San Remo Jazz Festival. Was that your last time in Italy?"

"Yes. I've been in Europe several times since then. But not in Italy."

"So I think it's high time you came back, don't you?"

"I think so too! Oh yeah!"

"OK. Then we'll just say 'Arrivederci.'"

"Arrivederci."

It was time to say goodbye. He saw me out to the street and hailed a cab. Just before I climbed into it, we embraced.

"Orazio Argento. You are a special human being, and I am very glad to have met you. You have my address; give me your news when you can."

"I'm not much of a letter writer but I'll send you all my records. I promise. And keep being as lovely as you are."

A light kiss and we let each other go.

Our friendship lasted through the years, underlined by the receipt of each new recording. Our conversations were filled with equivalent parts of laughter and very serious talks. He had an extremely thoughtful, meditating soul, and he often spoke of his religious beliefs and his search for spiritual answers.

At this point allow me a brief consideration regarding the religious quest of some jazz musicians I have known well. Dizzy Gillespie of course was dedicated to the Bahá'í philosophy and furnished me with various interesting publications on the subject, as did my friend Chick Corea with papers on the subject of Dianetics. Sonny Rollins surprised me with an annual subscription to the Rosicrucian magazine, and Ray Charles was fascinated by the Vatican and its history. Duke Ellington gave us those extraordinary Sacred Concerts, of course.

ACT V—ITALY 1987

Our last meeting took place in April 1987, when I was happy to invite Horace to play with his quintet at the annual concert season I produced in Bassano del Grappa, Italy.

It was a very warm reunion with the usual laughter. When I invited him to lunch, I chose an excellent restaurant renowned for its meat specialties, to tease him. To my astonishment, he ordered and gobbled down with gusto all sorts of meat hors d'oeuvres. At my raised eyebrows, he gave me his half-moon smile, saying, "Ah, forgot to tell you . . . I've changed my mind about meat. It's good for you."

"Hah! So you still owe me a *real* meal at the Chicago Chop House!"

"Any time!" Hand on his heart.

Instead, we settled for another recorded conversation for my Italian radio program.

"Orazio. In the fifties and sixties you were one of the leading personalities, with Sonny Rollins and all that Hard Bop movement. You have no doubt influenced many other musicians, and not only pianists. So we may safely say that now, in the eighties, you are *definitely* part of jazz history. I know that for a person like you, almost shy and reserved . . . this might be embarrassing, but how do *you* feel about your place in jazz today? Can you tell me how the years have affected your music? Where do you place yourself *today* in the jazz picture?"

"Well, that's a pretty big question to answer, but I'll make a stab at it. It's evident to anybody who knows anything about jazz, that Horace Silver is part of the jazz history but, you know, I am still a relatively young man, and whatever I've contributed so far is just the beginning, I feel, with much more to come."

"Yes. You were always in the avant-garde anyway, and yet you had deep roots in *soul* music—meant as black religious music—so you were with one foot in your roots and one foot going out beyond the Afro-American experience."

"Well, I try to encompass a bit of it all. Going back from the beginning up to the present; then trying to see as far ahead as I can see, and adding that to what I'm doing. I believe in mingling all these various influences together."

"And which *are* these influences, the ones you listen to most?"

"Well, the black gospel music has been a great influence on *my* music. And the blues is actually a derivative anyway; it comes *out* of black gospel music. So the *blues* has very much of an influence on me. And, as you well know, Latin music has an influence on me, particularly the rhythmic part of Latin music. It has always intrigued me. The Afro-Cuban rhythm, the Spanish and the Mexican, all of that type of rhythmic concept is very exciting to me."

"You were one of the founders of the Jazz Messengers, together with Art Blakey, right?"

"Yeah, I guess you could say that. The Jazz Messengers just happened to evolve. I don't know if anybody in particular put them together. Art and I were mainly responsible but also all the other guys . . . Hank Mobley, Kenny Dorham, and Doug Watkins, all had a hand in it. It resulted out of a couple of record sessions for Blue Note years ago. They were just the Horace Silver Quintet. We did 'The Preacher' and 'Doodlin'' and all those tunes. We kind of liked the way we sounded together and enjoyed playing together, so we decided to *stick* together, if possible."

"How did the name Jazz Messengers come up?"

"That stems from a name Art used with a big band in New York he called "The Messengers," in the mid or late fifties. All the guys in the band were members of the Muslim faith. I happened to hear them play one Sunday afternoon when Kenny Dorham took me by; he was in the band. I enjoyed that band, and the name stuck with me. When we started to put our little group together . . . I thought of the Modern Jazz Quartet, I admired not only their music but also their business sense, the fact that they could stick together as a cooperative type of a group, you know . . . so I said to the guys why not try to put together a group like them, a cooperative thing? The name of The Messengers came to me, and we decided to put the word Jazz in front of it and call it The Jazz Messengers."

"And the first group was the quintet you just mentioned?"

"Yeah."

"How long was that group together?"

"Well, I was with the Messengers only about a year; but they stayed together longer than that."

"So *you* founded the cooperative but *you* were the first to quit?"

"Yeah, I was the first to leave, and then, little by little, the other guys left after that."

"However, there is one thing that you and Art have in common; it's this special knack of recognizing new musicians that are emerging. . . . You listen to a newcomer and you can tell that *that* young cat has something going for him. Now what do you look for in a youngster who auditions for you?"

"Well, you never know if that particular musician will wind up being a very well-known, famous musician; but you can tell that the talent is there. You can help him, but it's up to him to develop it."

"What is it you *look* for?"

"You look for the talent and hear in his playing possibilities of improvement. He's just starting, but he plays well, and something makes you think he's in a growing process; but of course it all depends on the musician himself . . . how well he progresses."

"Have you ever been disappointed?"

"I've had some guys with that potential in them, yet after a year or so with the band I didn't feel that they were growing. That made me change to someone else."

"What other musicians, apart from Randy Brecker and Billy Cobham, have you brought out?"

"Well, I'm very proud of Tom Harrell, great trumpeter. He has gone on to make quite a name for himself. I heard him with Woody Herman's band and admired his playing, and when Randy left, I hired Tom. Bob Berg joined me at the same time with Tom Harrell, and that was one hell of a team, commensurate with . . . say, Blue Mitchell and Junior Cooke."

"What prompted you to move from New York to Los Angeles, considering they are two such different cities with respect to the life a musician leads? Some say New York has more going on for the *growth* of a musician. While Los Angeles is apt to *relax too much* a musician . . ."

"That's very true. There was, and there still is, much more going on jazz-wise in New York City than there is in Los Angeles. And I miss New York a bit for that activity, but I feel that New York is mandatory for the *young* jazz musician who is climbing the ladder and is growing . . . not that I'm not still growing . . . but once one reaches a certain degree of maturity, musically, and a certain degree of success . . . I feel they can live anywhere, you know?"

"And why did you choose Los Angeles?"

"Because I like the heat. San Francisco is a beautiful city and I love it, but it's a little too chilly up there for me. It's very warm all the year-round, in Los Angeles, and it's scenic, it's beautiful. I have a lovely home and a nice view of the ocean from my backyard, and a nice view of the mountains from the front yard."

"Humm . . . where do you live?"

"I live out in Malibu, and I enjoy it, you know? It's very peaceful, very relaxing, and I do a lot of writing there because my mind is at ease and it's a good vibration, inspiring me to write. But you're right, as far as music activity, New York is the place, for a young man. I've been through all of that, but I prefer a more gracious style of living right now, at *my age*, you know?" We laughed.

"I see. . . . Now, you say that in L.A. you do a lot of writing, but do you still go regularly on tour, or just from time to time?"

"I've been going out, just during the summer, for about four months, and staying home for the rest of the year. I stay home because now I am also a businessman. I own a record company."

"You do? Congratulations Orazio!"

"I have Silveto Productions and we have *two* labels: the Silveto label and the subsidiary label called Emerald Records."

"What kind of music do you produce . . . ?"

"It's always going to be jazz because I'm a jazz musician . . ."

"I mean, not like Quincy Jones, who is also producing Michael Jackson . . . ?"

"No, not that type of producer . . . I mean, I am now a producer of all my *own* recordings, but I'm going to start recording *other* people on my label too."

"How did it all come about?"

"Actually . . . I started it because in the latter part of my time with Blue Note Records I became very much interested in the power of music for healing and uplifting . . . I mean in the *spiritual* aspect of music, you know? While before everything was instrumental; I now started writing music with lyrics that had a spiritual connotation."

"With Blue Note?"

"I did that on Blue Note, but I didn't go all the way with it because I felt that . . . maybe they wanted a strictly instrumental approach, so I did a little of each. When my Blue Note contract expired, I felt that I wanted to go *all* the way with this spiritual concept, and I knew that with *any* company I would have problems because they wouldn't understand it and I'd have a fight with them, you know?"

"That must have been quite a decision to make!" He nodded.

"So I decided I would put my money where my mouth was and go into my savings and invest my *own* money in a company and start my *own* record business. I wanted to express the spiritual thing through my music, and that's why I started the Silveto label. We've got four Horace Silver releases."

"Who sings? *You* do?"

We laughed remembering a previous occasion discussing singers.

"No! A couple of albums have a vocal duet, man and wife team, while Andy Bey sings in my latest album . . ."

"So will he sing some of your songs at the concert tonight?"

"Yes, he'll sing some of the old ones and some new."

He resumed his story.

"Then I decided to start a subsidiary label called Emerald Records—an *instrumental* label because I didn't want to lose those people who were not in tune with the singing. I have one record out called "Horace Silver Live 1964," made from a tape recorded in a club. We had Joe Henderson on tenor and Carmel Jones on trumpet, Teddy Smith on bass, Roger Humphries on drums, and myself."

"Quite a collection there!"

"Yeah, it is. It's selling pretty well, too. And I'm coming out in September with my *first* Emerald album featuring *another* bandleader. I haven't told anyone the name of the guy yet, but it's somebody famous, and I'm excited about it."

"That's very good. I'm very happy for you."

ACT VI—ITALY 1987

"Now, another matter, Orazio. . . . You mention this music for healing. I agree that music *is* a power, and we should know how to use it and be worthy of the opportunity given us through music; so I am very interested in what you said. So, is your music being *used* for healing, actually?"

He considered his answer. "Well, I feel it is; in the general-public sense. You see, along with our Silveto Record Company and our feelings about music for healing, we also have a prayer group in which we pray for healing sick people."

"Who do you mean by prayer group?"

"Anybody can sign up and join our prayer group and take a portion of their 'prayer time' each day and ask the good Lord for help for whoever is on our healing list. People who are sick either call us or write and ask to be put on our list to be prayed for. We have two chiropractic doctors who are part of our prayer group and *they* use our records."

"You have produced more than one?"

"Yes. Our very first record was called "Guides to Growing Up"; the music is straight jazz but with lyrics, and the recitation on the album is by Bill Cosby, and it's directed to small kids. A lot of schoolteachers told me they've used this record in the early grades and it's been very useful. So that makes me very happy."

"I can see why. But what is the music like?"

"The music . . . I call it *self-help holistic metaphysical* music. First of all, it's music for entertainment, but it's also music for enlightenment and healing. It goes to the general public, but if they listen carefully to it, they can do some meditation and get some spiritual insight."

"People who are mentally disturbed can be very affected by music. Either over-excited or soothed. Ever looked into *that* part of music for healing?"

"Oh yes, definitely. I mean we are only scratching the surface so far, but I'm very aware of what you're talking about, and we'll be getting into that too. Basically, now we are putting in music the type of lyrics that will help people to think positive and uplift their emotions into a positive train of thought. The music does its part, but it's the philosophy and the psychology in the lyrics that help to heal the mind and in turn . . . the body."

"Tell me, this 'healing,' which seems to be a philosophy but also a sort of religion—how did you come by it?"

I thought about Kant and his view on metaphysics.

"Well, somewhere in the sixties I started to read about the civilization of Atlantis. I read that they used music for healing, very effectively, and that kind of excited me. I've always felt that there's some concept behind those notes that goes far deeper than what mankind knows about, so far, and I am still searching to get those answers."

"In what religion were you brought up? You have a very personal concept that might not be linked to the *main* religions?"

"Well, I have respect for every religion, for there is some truth in every religious concept, *some* way that will help *some* person at a certain point of his life. I was born and christened a Catholic, and it was good for me when I was a child. When I got into my twenties there were questions that I would ask myself *about* myself in relation to God and religion that Catholicism could not answer for me. After that, I kind of dabbled around a bit."

"And now?"

"What I follow now is a study of metaphysics that encompasses all the other religions and goes beyond. I've read many books on the life of that great psychic and healer Edgar Cayce . . ."

"Ah, yes! With Gina Germinara . . ."

"Yes, I've read many of his books and he's a fascinating man. . . . He was a channel of healing to so many people . . ."

"He was indeed fascinating."

"Then I read a lot about this Self-Realization Fellowship founded by Yogananda from India; I've dabbled in their philosophy and I'm in tune with them. I don't belong to any particular group, but the Church of Religious Science, founded by Ernest Holmes, is very much akin to metaphysics. And so are the Unity Churches. Their philosophy is very much in tune with metaphysics, as are the spiritualist churches. Are you familiar with *spiritualist* churches?"

"Do they have anything to do with the Brazilian 'religion' called Kardecismo, inspired by a Frenchman called Allan Kardec? He's the father of Spiritism. Are you familiar with him . . . ?"

"No. I'm not familiar with that particular person but the ministers of spiritualist churches are psychics and mediums."

"Allan Kardec was the penname of Hyppolite Rivail. In the nineteenth century he was an educator, had degrees in science and medicine and studied psychic phenomena such as clairvoyance and telepathy. In Brazil they linked the teachings of his books to beliefs from African religions. But let's go on with *your* beliefs. Do you believe in reincarnation?"

"Very definitely."

"And how do you feel about your evolution in *this* life?"

"Well, I feel good about it. I have evolved to get to the point where I am now, with my music as well as spiritually. Of course, who is to say if I have to be reincarnated again? I will not know until I pass out of the body. But I feel happy where I am now, because I firmly believe that what I'm doing is very valid and important."

"I could envy your faith!"

We smiled at each other and he patted my hand.

"I mention in one of my records: 'We all have a part to play in God's plan for mankind.' Everybody has a part in it, and once you start to pursue it, you get a sense of fulfillment. You think life has a greater purpose now than it ever had before because *this* part of the plan He's put in your charge is important. And you *feel* that life has taken on a different meaning."

"Doesn't it affect your *private* life? I mean, either you find a companion who believes totally, fully, in what you do, or your family will feel put in second place."

"Well, I look first and foremost to the *world* family. Actually, I *have* a family, I'm a divorced man, and I have a son who is fifteen years old."

"He lives with you?"

"No, with his mother. I live alone, but I'm very much aware of my family, of my son, my relatives, and I love them very much. But I look at humanity first, to serve them. Now, as far as finding a companion, it's extremely difficult to find one who would be able to live with me, under the same roof, doing what I'm doing and believing the way I believe, you know?"

"That's for certain!" We laughed.

"I'm not opposed to remarrying again, if I should find such a woman. But this work is very important, and I would rather live alone and be happy as I am now than be straddled with a woman who doesn't understand and is fighting me."

He grinned then repeated:

"I would only remarry if I found somebody as dedicated to this work as I am, and *that's* improbable!"

We both nodded, smiling.

"OK, Orazio, one last question. You don't come very often to Europe. People here wonder, 'Whatever happened to Horace Silver?' Don't you feel you should give more time to your *performing* career?"

"Well, yes and no. I must pursue my work as a businessman, and it takes a lot of time. I cannot be on the road *and* run a record business."

"Yes, but what about your career as a performer?"

"Well, as a performer I try to make myself available once a year for three or four months, whatever, on the road. Besides, I'm at a point in my career where I'm expanding and shifting gears, and I'm writing more music now than I've ever written before. I'm extremely prolific at this point."

"Are you recording all of it?"

"No. I have a backlog of material that has to be put out. But I need the time to take my music into other areas—on stage with symphonies and motion pictures, *and* there are books that I want to write. A lot of projects are at the back of my head."

"Tell us one of them?"

"I was very fortunate to have been commissioned by ASCAP to write some special music for Duke Ellington, a couple of years ago, and it was performed by a philharmonic orchestra, and it was a very big thrill for me to play with them."

"I can imagine! Did you tape it?"

"No, but I recorded this music on my latest album on Silveto Records with the Los Angeles String Orchestra, and that whetted my appetite because I would like to do more things with a symphony orchestra. I don't want to do *just* that, but occasionally; and not only in the United States but around the world, with various symphonies. But I need the time to write the music for this type of thing. It's a big endeavor."

"How wonderful for you! I heard that Tom McIntosh gave you a hand?"

"Yeah, he helped me get my start with it."

"He's a wonderful man. . . . Now here is another question. Do you teach?"

"Yeah, at El Camino College; I have a course once a year, called 'The Art of Small Combo Jazz: Playing, Composing, and Arranging.'"

"You mentioned writing. Do you have a book out?"

"I'm in the process of writing a book right now, actually, but I haven't finished it yet. If I keep getting out on the road, I'll never finish it!"

"Are you implying it's also *my* fault, for inviting you to play here?"

We both laughed as he shook his head.

"OK, Orazio. Well, I hope to be able to welcome you back to Italy and perhaps also organize a seminar. I mean on the 'music' part, not the 'healing' part, as yet. However, I'm very happy to have had this occasion to bring Horace Silver back again to Italy. I know that the public tonight is looking forward to the concert. We have people coming from various towns all over Italy. May I say, then, 'Arrivederci Orazio,' not only as an entertainer, but as a teacher . . . and especially as a good friend?"

"Thank you, Lilian. It's been a pleasure to see you, after all these years. You're looking lovely and your spirit is still very beautiful."

"Why, thank you!"

ACT VII—A FINAL MAGIC CONCERT

I wish to close this story going back to that last concert in Bassano. Something quite extraordinary happened. The theater was totally full of people, even from faraway Sicily, as this was Horace Silver's first and only appearance in Italy after long years of absence. The quintet had begun the second number when there was a sudden, drastic blackout sinking the whole town and surrounding villages into total darkness. Followed a great distress: no juice for the loudspeakers or the instruments! The public was beginning to react when the stagehands appeared with hurricane lamps.

Horace rose from the piano and went to the edge of the stage and asked for silence. Then he told them briefly that if they would all sit *very* quietly, his quintet would play for them. In the amazed hush he went back to sit at the piano and began to play in the semi-darkness. It was an exceptional, totally acoustic concert that remained a conversation piece for all the people who had been fortunate enough to witness it.

We did not meet again in the years that followed, and he said goodbye to the world on June 18, 2014. With his warm friendship, his teasing sense of humor, and that half-moon smile, he will always be very present in our memories.

RAYMOND CHARLES ROBINSON

Interviews—Conversations 1968–1979

Act I—New York, July 1968—Newport Jazz Festival: Getting acquainted through a pleasant conversation, recorded while he acts as my technician. He mentions the "Sickle Cell Anemia" medical research. We speak of blindness, Black Power, and drugs.

Act II—New York 1969: Brief recorded meeting declaring his regret not to be coming to Rome yet.

Act III—Rome 1969: He comes to Rome after all. He brings his most recent compilation, and we tape a relaxed presentation.

Act IV—New York 1970: We tape his choice of his most famous songs with anecdotes.

Act V—Rome Again, 1978: We tape a conversation on the different aspects between black and white musicians. Does he consider himself a jazz musician?

Act VI—Rome 1978: We realize our relationship is already ten years old!

Act VII—Rome during the 1970s: We tape his personal consideration of the negative and positive aspects of his entire life.

Act VIII—Rome 1979: He talks openly about the political situation in the United States at that time, also related to religion. We say goodbye.

ACT I—NEW YORK, JULY 1968

At the Newport Jazz Festival in July 1968, Joe Adams, business assistant and manager to Ray Charles, had set up an appointment for me to meet the artist in New York as I wished to interview him for my jazz program on the Italian National Radio network. I admit I was not specifically a fan of Ray Charles. I was a Sinatra "bobbysoxer" from age twelve and, where other male artists were concerned, my preference went from the "unforgettable" velvet of Nat King Cole to the volcanic "Sittin' on the Dock of the Bay" Otis Redding—alas, gone too soon—as well as a very sentimental spot for Satchmo's "Wonderful World." However, I did appreciate Ray's very personal voice and his choice of diverse styles that gave him a large range of followers, including my radio listeners.

The Newport Festival ended, and some days later I was in Ray's hotel suite in New York, sitting beside him on the sofa and hugging my new portable tape recorder. Ray was kindness itself and proposed that we start with an afternoon snack he favored. Reaching for the phone by the sofa, he ordered pineapple ice cream for two, plus a serving of hot French fries. That odd combination of ice cream and hot fries amused me enough to relax me, and we chatted while waiting for room service. He seemed curious about me, about Italy, about Rome and the Vatican. It must be added that, through the many years of friendship that followed, the history of the Vatican was a recurrent subject.

When came the time to start taping our talks on my recorder, Ray grabbed it with curiosity and, examining it with his fingertips, told me to go ahead with the questions while he would take care of the technical side.

So we began taping what was more of a conversation than an official interview. By the time we stopped recording we discovered that more than an hour had flown by most enjoyably.

I recall that at one point we stopped recording as Ray answered the ringing phone, apologizing. He was very much the boss with whomever he was talking, and the lilting, almost hesitant voice he had used with me was now strong and sharp. For a second I was tempted to turn the recording button on, but it seemed unfair. In any case, he was soon on the sofa next to me, and we resumed our conversation. Here is the gist of it.

He was born on September 23, 1930, in Albany, Georgia, but the family had moved to Greenville, Florida, when he was but a few months old. His passion for music had begun at age two or three, thanks to the next-door neighbor, who was a boogie-woogie pianist and who encouraged Ray at age four or five by teaching him simple chords. At the Saint Augustine Institute for the Blind in Florida he was further assisted in his music lessons. His first public appearance was at age thirteen.

At my question regarding a choice between being a singer or a pianist, he laughed and declared that, if forced to choose between the two, he would give them both up and do some other kind of job altogether.

When I asked what essential advice he would give to young blind students, he considered the question then answered firmly. He declared that the drawbacks of blindness were minute. His deaf and blind friends at the Institute had all emerged according to whatever desire or passion they had entertained. Today, one man was a jeweler, another girl was a seamstress, and so on.

However, he declared most strongly the importance of the parents who were not to shelter their blind child but to develop his attitude positively, to encourage him to lead a normal life and not nurture his self-pity but help him to fight for whatever he wished to become: "Parents need to instill in the child the fact that he may have lost his sight, but not his mind."

Ray also insisted that if schooling could teach the "technique" of playing, still the fundamentals had to begin at home.

However, I do recall the surprising information that emerged, during that first long interview, when I asked him his other interests in life, apart from music.

"Oh, well now, good question, hmm, where to start?"

So I asked if he was active on behalf of the youth in the black communities, and he replied that they organized benefits in various colleges in exchange for scholarships to help all the kids—of whatever color or creed—who were not as fortunate as others, yet just as deserving.

He then mentioned that he was the National Chairman of the Sickle Cell Foundation and was active in organizing donations in order to provide the transfusions that were a constant need. Just as important was the action of familiarizing the medical world that did not seem to be too aware of sickle cell anemia. He went on to explain that it was a lesser-known but often deadly form of genetic hemoglobin anemia that seemed to be present mostly in Americans of black descent, as well as in the populations of the Mediterranean and black Africa.

When we started talking about politics and his involvement, if any, in the Black Movement, he replied that all he wanted for black Americans was a right to dignity, an opportunity to make a living and therefore to be entitled to a good education, the same as anybody else. He was definitely not in any kind of separatist movement. He considered it unworkable and unrealistic and explained why:

"You cannot live in a society that is controlled only one way—like this one in America is—yet you can't live apart from it, it's impossible."

Therefore, he was against violence, which he considered sadly hopeless and ridiculous, for it would be as if one side gathered stones and bricks to throw against the other side that handled machine guns and bombs. The only way would be through the courts, through legislation, and through people getting together and talking to one another. He gave me an example:

"There are many people in this country that are not *aware* of each other; certain areas where the white people are not aware what the black man is *like* and vice versa. So there should be more dialogue and more meetings, gatherings where people could get together and talk, and get to enjoy each other. I saw the other day where some parents in a community sent their children over to another community so they could have a chance to play and work and do things together with these other kids, which had never been done before. They were going to do this for about a month and then reverse the process and have the kids come over to the other side. This way people will have a chance . . . because there are a lot of tales about this person being this way, that way. . . . There's no such thing, people are just people. If people communicate a little more, work together more; go to school together so they get to know each other better . . . this is the way to do it, because if the black man in this country starts a war, it's impossible for him to win a violent type of thing."

"And yet, that's what it looks like . . ."

He shook his head, depressed, and explained: "If you look at South Africa, they've got a majority there that is black and they can't win with the minority, because the minority has got the power. So how in the world can *we*, as a minority, win when the *majority* has got the power? It's idiotic!"

"But it could be done gradually, by obtaining the power?"

"In this country what power is . . . it's to be able to get into key positions. We have now a couple of black men who are mayors—one of a very big city like Cleveland, Ohio, and one in Gary, Indiana. We have a senator and a few congressmen. This is the way to do it, getting people into office, into politics, doing it politically. You can't do it with violence because the odds are against you."

At this point I questioned him on another delicate matter: the use of drugs and the excuse that they enhance your personality and help you perform much better. Knowing his past legal difficulties on the subject, I hoped he would not mind answering my question. His answer was clear and direct:

"Let me put it this way and say this. If you can think of drugs as you think of alcohol, drugs react as a stimulant the same as alcohol to the point that they don't make you *do* anything any better, but make you *think* that you do, which is absolutely ridiculous. The same as people who drink, you know? It doesn't make a person drive a car better; or become a better pianist or a better singer when he drinks. He may *think* he is, but actually, anything that you can do behind drinking or drugs, you ought to do it much better without them."

Knowing how popular he was with my young radio listeners, I asked him various questions regarding his personal life. Ray spoke about his own recording company as well as his publishing company, declaring he was not centered only on his own career but was interested in doing some talent scouting regarding singers, musicians, composers, and so on . . .

I mentioned the admiration my radio listeners had for him, and he smiled, thanking them. He then promised spontaneously to make himself available, on his next visit to Rome, to meet them personally. I mentioned the reaction such a meeting would provoke!

He reassured me: "I'll be happy to do so."

When the interview was over, we both mentioned how very pleasant and relaxed it had been. I told him he was a kind and thoughtful person and quite different from the general impression one had of him as an unapproachable "star."

He gave me his private phone number, asking me not to hesitate to call him whenever I was in the United States again, and he memorized my own phone number in Rome.

ACT II—NEW YORK 1969

Upon returning to Italy I informed my listeners that we had a friend in Ray Charles who might be coming to Rome and might have the time to meet them over the radio network. I received dozens of letters, in Italian and in English; they were addressed directly to Ray, asking me to forward them, which I did. I recall one phone call from Ray, in the early morning, thanking me for the letters that had just been read to him.

That very first contact in New York proved successful because, when a few months later I was back in New York on a "working" holiday, I obtained an immediate appointment with Ray at his usual hotel. He was on the point of flying off to Los Angeles, so we taped a very brief interview for my young listeners, explaining the fact that he would not be coming to Italy as early as had been planned.

"So you will not be coming to Rome after all?"

"No . . . no, and I'm very, very sorry we won't be, 'cause I had planned it with so much enthusiasm. I have never been there before and through the letters I received, through you, about the enthusiasm of the kids . . . however, as I understand, maybe with a little bit of luck we can get to Rome next year, I hope. And be able to stay for a couple of days and make up for it."

"Do you know around what time it will be?"

"Our promoter . . . I don't know if he's going to have it in the spring or the summer; they're still trying to get the information together about the halls and so forth. This is what I understand."

"So can we say that it's just postponed?"

"Yes, it *is* just postponed. And believe me; you have no idea how sad I am about it."

"OK. Then let's just say 'arrivederci'?"

"Yes. All right."

My consolation was the fact that he seemed to regret it as much as I did.

I was also flattered by the fact that, following that second meeting, from time to time he would phone me "in the wee small hours of the morning" as the song goes—often just to say hullo—and he obviously had a very personal notion of time. A phone call at dawn could only be from him, so I would answer: "Ciao, Raimondo Carlo . . ."

"Hey, were you asleep?"

"Well, it's 3 am over here . . ."

"Gee, I'm sorry, I'll call you some other time."

"Was there anything . . . ?"

"No, no, just wanted to say 'hi'—you go back to sleep now, g'night!"

ACT III—ROME 1969

In 1969 he phoned to ask me to meet him upon his arrival in Rome. It was a very friendly reunion and, because he'd brought me his latest compilation, I suggested we tape an informal conversation regarding the songs on that record, which I would then present on my radio program with his own voice announcing them.

When my portable tape recorder refused to function, Ray reached out and settled it on his knees. He fiddled with it for a few minutes, corrected the problem, and told me we could start talking while he would be my recording technician, again.

Very patiently he answered all my questions regarding each song on the LP, which gathered a number of well-known songs that had been successful as single 45s and were now offered together as a compilation. I chose the most famous ones for him to describe to my radio listeners.

"Here comes a song that is synonymous with Ray Charles. 'Unchain My Heart.'"

"Right! It was by a fellow who had never written a song in his life, but he brought it to me and I liked it. We recorded it, and it turned out to be very good. In other words, people think that entertainers only pick songs from established writers, but if the song is good, I'll take it from anybody."

"And now, of course, comes the one and only 'Georgia on My Mind'!"

"Well, yeh, that of course . . . when you say 'the' 'Georgia on My Mind,' obviously it's self-explanatory. We recorded songs that had names of states, like 'Alabamy Bound,' 'California Here I Come'; we decided that here was a song called 'Georgia' that was so pretty, you know? And I think when Hoagy Carmichael wrote it, he had in mind the state of Georgia, so we used it in that respect."

"And it came out rather well!"

"Yeh, it certainly did!" he laughed.

"Tell me, which song has been the biggest success, I mean from a sales point of view?"

"Well, it depends on how you mean it—over the years or in just a short period of time. For instance, 'I Can't Stop Loving You' has sold more records in a short period of time than any record I've ever had. On the other hand, 'What Did I Say?' has sold far more records because it has been around much longer and people are still buying it almost like it was new."

"Now here's an 'oldie' that has become a classic, really, and I must say I do like *very* much the way you sing it. It's 'Ol' Man River.'"

"Thank you very much; it's one of the songs that really touched me, until I actually really cried in the session! I felt very embarrassed after the thing was over but it is a very touchy song, and from the heart."

"Ah, and now here is one that has a very funny title: 'Let's Go Get Stoned,' rather peculiar, isn't it?"

He laughed, nodding his head.

"Well, you know, strangely enough that song created a lot of controversy . . . although the song was self-explanatory because we said 'a bottle of gin' you know. . . . But the reason it was controversial is because, in America, when you say 'stoned' that means you want to smoke a little pot or something. So many of the radio stations banned it because of that reason . . ."

"Banned it?"

"Oh yeah, they wouldn't play it, you know? Obviously, we didn't mean that, but just by the word 'stoned' . . . and of course the fact that the kids listen to my records . . . so the stations thought, 'Well, it's a bad thing to be telling kids to go out and get loaded!'"

"But it's ridiculous!"

"Well, I think that because of the controversy, strangely enough, it really made the record sell more than it probably *would* have sold!"

"Well, we'll want to hear *that* record!"

Thus, the list chosen for my radio program was completed.

His time in Rome being brief, we were unable to organize a visit to the Vatican; however, he was happy to order "real Italian ice cream" at his hotel and asked me to share it with him as we relaxed and talked on into the evening.

At this point I must explain the relationship that developed through the many years. Since our first meeting in New York in 1968, followed by regular annual encounters around Europe and the United States, we had become very close friends who trusted each other and enjoyed each other's company. In Italy it could be referred to as "an affectionate friendship," meaning not a real love affair but a close, loving, relationship. We had agreed that it should be protected from prying eyes and ears. I had suggested to him: "We shall be each other's secret!" and he had repeated this phrase, highly amused, patting my knee and nodding.

I am happy to say that we succeeded for more than ten years, meeting in New York or traveling together around Europe, whenever I was free to join him. We would travel together using a different air flight and hotel than the one used by his staff and musicians. I never appeared backstage when he was performing, and our privacy was respected through the years.

ACT IV—NEW YORK 1970

One late afternoon in New York, Ray announced that he had a surprise for me. He was going to take me out to dinner to his favorite restaurant, just the two of us, and he would act as lead and guide. Sensing my surprised hesitation, he had smiled and taken my arm, leading me firmly out of the suite, onto the elevator, then out through the main hall into the streets. Obviously amused by my surprise, he led us down the avenue, walking along two blocks while regularly stopping at the crossings. Then he said: "Now we turn right . . . and the entrance should be about here. . . ." And so it was.

By the friendly welcome he received and the table obviously reserved for us, I realized he was really a habitué of the place.

When I asked what was his secret and how could he move about the streets of New York by himself and with such ease, he smiled and patted my hand:

"Sweetheart, I have my special system, but don't you worry, I'll always take good care of you. You're in good hands with me."

Actually, through the years, I would be constantly surprised at the ease with which he moved around his various hotel suites, whether in Rome, Brussels, Paris, or New York. One time I asked him if he was really totally sightless, as I had never seen him reach out around him while he walked with confident speed.

He had smiled and drawn me to the window, wrinkling his eyes as if he were really peering at me and, cupping my face, he stated: "Sweetheart, I can tell you one thing, I can see you are a lovely young woman. I see it just by listening to the way you talk to me, and the things you say, and also because . . . because Joe Adams told me so, from that first meeting years ago, in New York! In fact he's very jealous; he was very interested in you himself . . ."

Ray concluded, throwing back his head with his amused laugh.

As I have mentioned earlier, every time we were together Ray enjoyed using my portable tape recorder as if it were his personal toy. He would check its good functioning, and then he would invite me to go ahead with the questions, which were often suggested by my young listeners. This time they were curious about the way he would choose his repertoire, both when recording as well as when he performed on stage. He considered the question and then replied:

"Well, some of the songs I write, and some I take from *other* people who write. As far as what we do on stage, I try to select songs that are favorites, shall we say? Then add some new things, and some older songs they haven't heard for some time. I've been playing for a long time, you know, since 1948! So I play the tunes they've come to hear. A musician owes his best to the public, and you do that by playing the songs that they know you for."

"In Italy, if you ask anyone, two of your songs come out immediately. One, of course, is 'Georgia,' and the other is 'Yesterday.'"

"Well, we always do 'Georgia' in every concert, and we do 'Yesterday'—I think that came out last November—and of course there are songs like 'Hallelujah I Love Her So' and 'What'd I Say' that people have loved over the years. So you've *got* to play them, and it's one of the reasons why I've been around so long, because I sincerely feel this way about it."

"That might be one of the reasons, but the main reason is your talent."

"You know, I'll tell you. I've known people who do have talent but they have the wrong attitude. Very talented musicians who come out on stage to do what *they* want to do and the devil with their public! Use your talent in a way that the public will appreciate; this is what an entertainer should do."

So that was one of the secrets of his lasting fame.

Another subject had me wondering: "Tell me, who are the singers who have influenced you?"

"Well, now! That's interesting . . ." he frowned in concentration. "Oh well, Nat Cole was a great influence in the years gone by. Then some of the old blues singers I used to love, T-Bone Walker and Lightnin' Hopkins. They were the backbone of the blues, like Bessie Smith. . . . Of course, nowadays Aretha Franklin is really Boss in my opinion. I like Sinatra; I like Ella Fitzgerald . . . and of course you know I like jazz too."

"Talking of jazz, you are in a unique position. You are one of the biggest names in the pop world, yet you are also playing in the jazz field, as well as some rhythm 'n blues that some critics consider like 'the poor cousin' of jazz."

"Right, and that's sad because . . . I consider myself as a fairly good musician and I can play it either way. If there's a jazz concert . . . then I'll play jazz, you know?"

"But when you play jazz, do you also sing?"

"Actually, like I said . . . I am there to please the public, and if they want me to sing, then I'll sing. Because I *like* to sing, so why shouldn't I?" he laughed.

"Right! Let me see . . . oh, I'm sure there are hundreds of questions I'll wish I had asked you . . ."

He patted my hand. "That's all right, my dear. If there is anything else that you think . . . that you decide you want to ask about me, all you have to do is write it down and when I see you in Rome, then we can talk about it."

"OK! I'll do that."

ACT V—ROME AGAIN, 1978

The next time he returned to Rome I was producing a new subject for my Radio program, "Jazz: Black and White," and, as he took possession of "our" tape recorder, he was ready for my questions.

"Ray, nowadays that jazz is played all over the world, in all continents by musicians of all races, can one still say that there is a difference between black jazz musicians and white jazz musicians and their way of expressing this music?"

"Oh . . . that's a very . . . hum, that's so good a question you know? I think, though, that you can find excellent jazz musicians in both races, black *and* white. However, you might find jazz musicians have more *feeling* in the *black* community, and the *blues* feeling shows up in the black musicians' *sound*. But that's because they've been doing it *longer*. But I think that white musicians are catching up fast."

"Is there any white musician that you can think of, who plays in a 'black' way?"

"Let's see . . . well, I think Stan Getz is pretty good, you know? I must say. And . . . do you know the fellow from Denmark, from Copenhagen, bass player . . . Niels . . . ?"

"Niels-Henning Ørsted Pedersen?"

"Right, I think he's really mean, you know? Oh yes, there are some guys who are really excellent players. There's no question about it. But then most of these guys have lived around black musicians so long until they have learned the ins and outs of the *feeling* of jazz, I think. I don't want to make it a racial thing; I just think it *is* kind of true."

"OK. I have another question that regards you and jazz. Some years ago I had an interview with Quincy Jones, and he told me that practically all he ever learned about jazz, at the very beginning of his career, he learned from you. And many other jazz musicians consider you *definitely* a jazz musician. However, I only remember one 100 percent jazz record of yours, the one called 'Genius Plus Soul Equals Jazz' with the Ellington musicians, I think. You also said your first influence was Nat King Cole, so why don't you play *more* jazz music?"

"Well, you know . . . first of all you are correct; I have not made a lot of pure jazz albums . . . I did the 'Genius Plus Soul' record and then another one with Milt Jackson called 'Soul Brothers.' But the thing is . . . that I am not a *pure* anything. I'm not a pure jazz artist or a pure blues singer. I'm one who loves *all* kinds of music; I'm what they call 'utility' you know? I'm probably not too good at anything but adequate at most things. So I don't want to be put into *one* category. For anybody to say 'Ray Charles is a blues singer' implies I cannot sing anything but the blues. So, if you must give a description of me, it would be nice to say that Ray Charles is a very good *entertainer* because I like to venture into different avenues of music, other than just one thing."

"Very well, but as a jazz lover I can't help regretting that you don't do *more* jazz."

"I think that to play good jazz requires a *very* good knowledge of music. . . . Let me put it another way. You hear these so-called rock groups nowadays: this hard rock, acid rock. . . . That kind of music I can play when I sleep; it does not require any *true talent* to play it. But to play good jazz you *must* have talent, you understand?"

"Yes, but you do have talent!" I protested, but he went on with his thoughts on the matter.

"So therefore, I think the reason I don't play as much jazz as I would like to, is because the people who listen to Ray Charles, the bulk of the public, love to hear me sing. At least that's what they have indicated to me, and therefore I try to sing things that the everyday person can identify with. Jazz is a higher level of music;

the same as classical music. So I start off dealing with everyday people who like everyday songs, and every now and then I'll play some jazz just to let the people who understand music know that I can do it, if I want to . . ."

"And is that the way you plan your records?"

"Yes, I made an album not too long ago where I try to give a flavor of how I am inside. Now, if you listen to 'Oh, What a Beautiful Morning' or 'How Long Has This Been Going On?' you will know right away that I understand jazz quite well. But the reason I don't go out all the way in any one thing is because I hate labels, you see?"

"Well then, let's put it this way. Can we hope that one day, in the future . . . ?"

"I'll do another record just straight jazz?"

"Please do!"

"I'm planning on doing something like that because many people ask me, 'Why don't you play the saxophone anymore?' like I did in the 'Soul Brothers' record with Milt Jackson. So I'm planning an album where I'll play some jazz piano, some alto . . . the only thing is, I don't want anybody to think that I'm trying to be a show-off!"

"Of course not; and have you any idea who the other musicians will be?"

"Well, I know who I would *like* to have. I want to have Clark Terry, I'm hoping to get either Buddy Rich or Louie Bellson on drums, and Milt Jackson, and Dizzy Gillespie . . . I mention these names 'cause these are the people that I know. People who, when we can get it together . . ."

"Oh yes, please!"

"I did want to use Johnny Griffin, but he's in Europe. I want to get Leroy Cooper, who was with my band, then J. J. Johnson . . . I want to get these people at different times, to come in to play just one or two songs; not necessarily the whole album. Because it's pretty hard to get everybody together at a certain time, for everybody is doing different things."

"OK. Then I'll be looking forward to that! It sounds like a great project."

"Thank you, darlin'."

ACT VI—ROME 1978: *RAY*

At this point, I would like to make a statement. When I was shown the film *Ray*, I was impressed with the excellent physical portrayal by Jamie Foxx—the mannerisms, the walk, the voice with the southern drawl, that special grin on his face when he performed. On stage we saw his particular swaying walk to the piano, and his way of bending from side to side as he sang—yes, they were all faithfully there. I am also certain that all the main facts of his life had been dutifully checked with Ray himself.

But then, what had happened to the human being I had known so well? Where was his wry sense of humor when he was often making fun of himself? Above all, there was no sign of his introspection, of his quest for understanding what made human nature act as it did. The film seemed to end just as he was maturing into an outgoing, generous man.

There were just a few printed phrases added on the screen at the end of the film, very briefly depicting Ray in the years that followed. They were phrases to be read quickly, if at all remembered. Where was his personal involvement with Thalassemia? Or his action to convince his young fans of the evils of drug addiction, which he had experienced at such high cost?

Through the years of our relationship, I remember sharing long talks well into the night. There was so much more to Ray Charles than what was shown in the film, and I hope these interviews will give a further idea of the kind of man Ray Charles was.

In our sixth interview he no longer talked about his music but discussed the situation of black people in the United States. I began:

"In our first interview . . . heavens, that was ten years ago!"

We both laughed as he nodded.

"You're right! Long time, eh? Right!"

"In that first interview we were talking about integration, about the situation with the summer riots and all; and what was really needed. You said something about South Africa as opposed to the United States. How—although much more numerous in South Africa—the black people were discriminated against heavily over there. You had added, 'So how could the black community, a minority in the States, hope to fare better?' Now, in these ten years has the situation improved? And what's ahead?"

"Well, I would be very much a liar if I were to say that things haven't improved because obviously they have. However, I think that some of the underlying problems that we had still exist, but they are better."

"Well, that's good, no?"

"But they are still there. If you can think of a scale from one to ten—and that when we had that first interview maybe things were at one, at the bottom of the scale—maybe we are up to four now. You understand what I mean?"

"Um hmm," I nodded him on.

"So there *has* been improvement, but the sad thing is that people in power—whether they are in the majority or the minority—they hate to give it up. Proof is that there is so much turmoil in South Africa, although the power belongs to a *minority* there; can you imagine in the States where it's a majority? No one wants to give up his little goodies, you know? So they try to protect them. But the reason I say there *is* an improvement is because . . . there was a time when the black man had trouble trying to vote in America, now every black man or woman can vote all over the United States, whether it's in the southern or the northern part, east or west."

"That *is* a great improvement."

"Yet during *that* same period of time there was argument and very much trouble about integration in the *schools*. . . . Well, today we still argue about the *same* thing, the same *thing*! OK? There was arguing about black people having trouble to get jobs. It's still the same today; you got some cities where black people are 40 percent out of work. That's very heavy. If in the overall situation in the United States the unemployment rate is 5 percent with whites, it's certainly 12 percent with blacks; it's all out of proportion. I mean, there has been progress, but we still have some of the same underlying problems that we did have in the sixties."

"What about the right to education?"

He sighed, nodding: "On the other hand, you do have more black people who are going to universities, so there *has* been improvement, but we are still climbing the ladder . . ."

"Tell me about Jesse . . ."

"Jackson? Jesse is a fine man. I think he has a great voltage about him, a great force. He doesn't carry the power that Martin Luther King carried; however, Jesse is a highly respected leader, and he is doing some wonderful things. . . . The difference between Jesse and Martin Luther King is that when King was coming along, there were so many things happening . . . where in Jessie's case he's sort of hampered because, since then, a lot of black people, who were really in the worst conditions then, have gotten sort of middle-class living now, and so you don't have nearly as much . . . what's the word . . ."

"Following . . . ?"

"Yes . . . because you've got more black people who are doing a lot better now. . . . So today you do have a little *apathy* from the black people that was not the case in the sixties."

"But he is working a lot with young people . . ."

"That's right, Jesse has a great following and I love the man. He has great ideas and he's going about it the right way, which is to deal with the youth because, let's face it, the youth is *tomorrow*. He's trying to get the youngsters to understand that the name of the game is to get off dope, get in school, and put something in your head and learn how to *be* something; and that really is the key. But Jesse has a problem because there is not nearly as much *dissention* now as there was in the sixties, because people *are* doing a little better, and therefore he is not getting as much support as I feel he should get."

"We saw a program about him on Italian TV, with his speeches and everything . . . and it was really very interesting. He knows how to catch the attention of the people . . ."

"Oh yes, Jesse Jackson is a very *astute* man. He's quite brilliant and he does know how to say what he *wants* to say, you know? He knows exactly where he wants to go, but many times you can motivate people only when they have troubles themselves, when they can *feel* it, when it's a pain to *them*. But when you get people who are *kind* of satisfied, it's hard to get them to realize, 'Hey, *you* may be satisfied, but what about *us*?' So he's not having as easy a time of it, but he has the right thoughts because he's dealing with the young people and he *is* trying to teach them that what they need to do . . . instead of letting themselves become addicts and stuff, that they need to get something in their heads that can last them all their lives. Therefore, I have a lot of respect for Jesse, and anything that I can do to help him I certainly will try to do because I think Jesse right now is probably the strongest black leader as such."

And right at that point the tape of our little recorder informed us "game over," no more space. But the most significant parts of our conversation were safely recorded.

ACT VII—ROME DURING THE 1970S

During those many years there had been other radio interviews, alas vanished. The subjects had seldom been about music but more often about odd matters of interest to Ray, such as the various forms of power: not only the power of politics and economics but also the power of any given group, any religion, creed, or sect that could direct its faithful toward good or evil. He had been interested in the Vatican's universal influence through its religious, social, political, and financial events. The promise that one day I would "show him" Saint Peter's Cathedral and the Sistine Chapel had been made practically from our first meeting in New York in 1968, and at every Roman farewell we would say: ". . . but next year we will *really* find the time to visit the Vatican, it's a promise!"

While listening to all the extraordinary conversations with Ray Charles, I cannot help but remember his patient kindness in accepting and answering all kinds of questions relating to his private life and his private feelings, such as the time when he had returned to Rome and we were in his suite. As usual, we were both sitting on the sofa with my tape recorder firmly in his hands, positioned on his knees. We could start.

"If I'm not mistaken it is now thirty years that you have been in the music business . . ."

"That's right."

"Looking back at these thirty years, can you tell me offhand the first positive things that these thirty years have given you and, if any, the negative things?"

"Well, I think it's better to start with the negative first because I want to end up on a good note, you know? It's my being a 'Libra' or something."

"Very well, negative first."

"I think the negative part that happened in the thirty years was in the beginning, because in the beginning of my career I, along with many other black people, ran into a lot of problems just because I was the color I was, you know? It was very tough because we couldn't go in restaurants, many times we couldn't go in certain restrooms or bathrooms or lavatories. Sometimes if you had a decent car and you looked OK, you were harassed by the police. These were *some* of the negative things that happened to me, but, on the other hand, let me show you how that led me to something. These were things that taught me tolerance, you see?"

"Taught *you* to be tolerant? What a strange expression to use."

"What I mean by that is . . . because I had to learn how to deal with some of the worse conditions. I had to learn how to deal with poverty first; I had to learn how to deal with having *nothing*. Now I'm not recommending that people try to live as bad as they can live! Please don't misunderstand me, but I am saying that this way of life did teach me a lot of things. How to deal with people under adverse conditions, and, as a result, when I was able to upgrade my life, it taught me how to appreciate what was bestowed upon me, so therefore I am grateful that I know both sides of life."

"Can you specify?"

"I know how to live with *something* but I also know how to live with *nothing*, and I think that's very important because that gives you . . . that lets you feel for people who *are* suffering because you know what *it is* to be cold, you know what *it is* to be hungry, what *it is* to be ragged, you know what *it is* when people come talk down to you and do things to injure your integrity. So I think that my thirty years of music taught me a lot of how to treat people like I would like for them to treat me. In other words, I don't care *what* you have in this world or how much you *don't* have; the point is that every human being has *feelings*. A match will burn anybody, you know? I'll tell you a cute story; it won't take more than a second . . ."

"Sure, please go ahead."

"Someone came up to me one day and said, 'Mr. Charles, I've been wanting to meet you for so long. I am nobody, but I really wanted to say hullo to you.' It touched me, so I told him: 'Look, whatever you do in your life don't *ever* describe yourself as *nobody*.' You see, he thought I was so high on a pedestal and he was so low beneath me. So I learned that in the end we all have to eat, we all have to drink, and one day we all are gonna have to die, you see? Therefore, in all of my thirty years of music, I have learned to *respect* people. And that's the positive lesson."

ACT VIII—ROME 1979

The last interview we taped was scheduled in the usual form of a relaxed conversation. His favorite subjects evolved toward his country, his fellow people, and their black leaders. During these informal talks he expressed his feelings, his disappointments, his regrets, his hopes. He mentioned Jessie Jackson and Malcolm X. He worried about the presence of the powerful White Citizens Council, the Nazi Party, and the Ku Klux Klan—all still active, especially in the South—although he noted that today there seemed to be some sort of reciprocal acceptance, especially among the young people—provided they were not brought up with the old hatred.

"Ray, you say that Jesse Jackson has a harder time than Martin Luther King because the black people today have obtained some sort of . . ."

"Yeah, they're a little more comfortable than they were . . ."

"So they are not really anxious to follow him in any crusade . . ."

"Let's say they are not in any big hurry. They are not stepping up their pace. That's just my view of it, however, but I think that Jesse is on the right track, because what he is trying to do is to develop the young people and point them in the right direction. You see, I don't think Jesse is really going to get the strong support he needs until something happens . . . I mean something to go wrong."

"Isn't that a pessimistic thought?"

"It's a bad thing to say, but it's the truth, you know? Sometimes it takes an incident; like in the sixties where this woman got on the bus and they wouldn't let her sit . . . so it triggered something, or like the Detroit riots when some soldiers had shot a black person and it started something. Chances are that Jesse won't get the kind of support he should have, unless something dramatic does happen . . ."

"To make the people get angry again . . ."

"That's exactly it!"

"But if he could get through to the young people and discuss with them, then maybe he would get their support through *reasoning*?"

"Yes but that's a hard thing, babe, because let's face it, most times when you have revolutions it's usually because somebody is very mad about something. Something has happened to get the people's temper up, to make their blood rise. But as long as people are a *little* comfortable, and life is a *little* easygoing, it's hard to drum up support. I hate to have to put it this way because it doesn't sound too good—but I still think it's the truth. Take the Indian in America; he is not going to come up with anything, until something happens one day. They're going to have to go out and scalp somebody, or break into something . . ."

"You mean that violence is a necessary step?"

"I mean in the history of the black people's progress . . . *before* they had the push of the riots; they went to the legislatures, to the congressmen, and they did all the *begging* and everybody was saying, 'What are you crying for? You're *laughing* and you're *dancing* and you seem *happy* so what the hell you want?' So nobody paid them any attention, you see? It was not until somebody got *mad*. . . . Now I don't want to start *anything* but as long as people are fairly well off then *nobody* wants to rock the boat, you see?"

"So what will happen next?"

"Maybe something will come along one day and there will be a mistake, where somebody will do something to somebody else, and it will trigger some anger. It's a shame to have to put it that way, but I think *that* happens to be the only way that it *really* can be done."

"Tell me, do you think there will be another Malcolm X?"

"Well, that's a very difficult thing to say, but I certainly wouldn't rule it out by any stretch of the imagination. Oh, no, no. Because even in America *today* you do have, as strange as you may think of it—although I'm sure that you have read something about it—you do have the Nazi party, in America, *today*."

"You mean an *American* Nazi party?"

He nodded and continued:

"So when you have the Nazi Party or the White Citizen's Council or something like that, you're always going to have some kind of opposite, which you *should* have. So you got people who are extremes on both sides. I'm not implying that Malcolm X was an extremist but I am saying that you certainly do need people with the same amount of force, like Rap Brown was, you know? You need these people to come along who don't mind bombing and doing all kinds of things. . . . For the same reason that they are dealing with the opposite side—like the Ku Klux Klan who didn't give a damn about mutilating a little twelve-year-old child—you've got to have the opposite side of that."

"It's a form of war then?"

"That's right! Exactly!"

"Actually, you think that one part of the white people of America and one part of the black people are still at war?"

"Well, I don't think that it is as pertinent as it was in the sixties, I think everybody has kind of cooled down a little bit. For instance, one thing that happened in the States, and that kind of changed things around, is that the *white* people in the South found out that *black* people spend money too . . . you understand? And as a result of that, a lot of *white* people found out that *black* people were not as bad as they were taught to believe. They began to think that 'hey, they're just people like we are!'"

"So as a result to this?"

"So as a result I think that people have become a lot more educated, and thank God for the *youth*. A lot of young kids that are coming up now don't have the kind of hatred in them that a lot of the earlier kids had . . . which they were taught by their parents. . . . I think the kids are saying, 'Now wait a minute, *he*'s never done anything to *me*, so why should *I*. . . . What the hell do *I* care?"

"Ah, you do have hope then . . . ?"

He shook his head in doubt.

"But there is *still* some undercurrent things happening just because you *still* have the Ku Klux Klan, you *still* have the Nazi Party, you *still* have the White Citizen's Council, and so as a result naturally you're going to have opposite forces, although they might be very *minute* right now. Because as I said, the black people now for the most part . . . nobody's really going around doing the awful things to them that used to be occurring. If you're *now* in the South and you walk into a hotel you don't have a bunch of white people saying, 'What's this nigger doing in here?' and all that sort of thing. Most of that's gone now, for the most part."

"So there is less racism today?"

"Certainly there is *still* some racism on *both* sides but usually, for the most part, this racism is generally among the *older* people who sooner or later are going to die!" He grins. "And when *that* happens that will probably do a lot to hip it out!"

We laughed, and I turned to the next question:

"I have one last question. We are talking of black and white people. In the past ten years one of the slogans . . . or actually the strength of the Black Movement was 'Black is beautiful,' and it was actually a thing about 'the black people stick together.'" Have there been more marriages between black and white people? I mean it's very easy to be friends in school, but in private adult life, have they really integrated?"

"Do I think there has been an increase in that sort of thing? I have to tell you, I have not done any research myself. Jesse Jackson would know far more about it than I do. . . . But I'll tell you something; I think that the *white* man in America was wrong when he thought that, as soon as integration came into view, all of a sudden every *black* man was going to go off and marry a white woman."

"Or vice-versa?"

"I don't think that was the case then, and that's not the case today. I'm not positive about this, but one of the main horror thoughts in earlier segregation was: 'Well, if we let these black people do this or do that, first thing you know they're going to want to marry your daughter or marry your niece.'"

"Ah, the bad, black man!" I kidded him. He smiled, nodding.

"Yes . . . but you know, one of the things that has been proven out is that the *black* people as a rule had no more desire to jump off and marry into the *white* race than . . . I mean, it's just like saying to a woman 'I give you the right to have an abortion,' but that does not mean that every woman in the world is going to jump up and say 'Oh, wow! Let me go and have an abortion!' It's kind of stupid, you see? So now they are finding out that 'hey, we had a fear and it was unfounded,' and that has kind of cooled down a lot of people. In a way, what they were saying was "Hey, if I *want* to marry a Catholic or a Jew, then I should have the *right* to do it." Not everybody is going to jump up and do it *because* it's available. It's just nice to know that you have enough control of your life that whatever you want to do with it, you can. That's all."

"But have there been many mixed marriages . . . ?"

"I don't think so, sweetheart; let me put it this way. I'm not saying there haven't been some, but I don't think there has been any great rush for *white* men to run to black women or *black* men to run to white women. I think what has happened is that the people who wanted to do it, did it, and that was that. It was kept quiet, and nobody thinks anything of it. But you know, it's a funny thing, as I said about a minute ago, we talk of discrimination as far as color is concerned but you have that in religion too . . ."

I had to agree. "Yes, in religion too . . . you are right."

"I've heard some stories . . . pardon my saying this . . . but some tall tales about Catholicism where they said 'Hey man, if they're not Catholic, you can't marry them . . . you cannot bring them into church, so look out now!'" he grinned, teasing, knowing I was a Catholic.

We were interrupted right then, as it was time for Ray to leave right away for the airport. He said we should pick it up at our next meeting the following year. It was a promise, for sure!

But, like the visit to the Vatican, it was a promise fate would not allow us to keep.

A new sentimental event had developed in my own private life, gradually modifying my personal freedom, and, inevitably, I had to make a choice. This induced me to ask Ray, with sincere regret and unaltered affection, to accept that we say goodbye.

We never contacted each other again; we decided it was better this way, a clean cut.

However, Ray Charles remains to this day a very special part of my memories: with his sense of humor, his open-eyed wisdom, his generosity, his firm beliefs, his shy tenderness and acceptance of whatever life had in store for him.

I hope that through these "conversations" recorded over ten years of close friendship, you will have discovered and followed the mental evolution of the man. Listening to his voice over the years, one would notice how the first interview began with a definite Southern drawl, not quite at ease, hence with a light form of stuttering and hesitation. Gradually he had relaxed and, through the years, would take his time to answer with a clearer enunciation and, most interesting, leaving behind him his much-publicized musical career, he wished and enjoyed to discuss and express his feelings on politics, social matters, and even religion. Was all this evident in the film *Ray*?

Who was Ray Charles? A blind, black boy with no assets, no strength but his own purpose and his will to change his destiny. From a young handicapped man he had created the miracle of leaving behind Raymond Robinson to become Ray Charles, the famous singer of the famous song "Georgia." Worldwide fame, money, power, recognition: yes, in the end he had it all. Yet in his soul there hid a young boy who would sing "Ol' Man River" with tears in his eyes.

BILL EVANS

Weaver of Dreams

Act I—Encounter in Bologna: I finally meet Bill Evans, hoping to convince him to give me an interview. Fortunately, he is amused by me and invites me to spend the next day with him.

Act II—Invitation: We spend the day mostly strolling, talking, and recording. He plays "Emily" for me at the concert.

Act III—Farewell: A few years later I listen to his performance at the Village Vanguard in New York. He smiles at me, then bends down to play "Emily." His passing away is a huge loss.

ACT I—ENCOUNTER IN BOLOGNA

Among the many historical jazz pianists I have appreciated, I must confess to a definite preference. The incurable romantic in me was doomed upon listening to that elegant touch, that harmonic invention, the unique melodic lines that belonged to Bill Evans alone. I am obviously aware that it is a preference shared by many other listeners, including some well-known pianists who admit their enormous debt to our artist.

When I was informed that Bill Evans would be playing in Bologna, in the mid-1970s, I was also warned that he was a very private person who did not give interviews easily. My radio program at the time was called *Portrait of the Artist* and offered a list of very important jazz musicians, so how could I not at least *try* to capture my very favorite artist?

On the day before the performance I was invited to meet Bill Evans at a reception given in his honor, but was also told that any interview would have to be obtained on my own strength. So, leaving my faithful tape recorder in my hotel room, I had donned an appropriate cocktail dress and crossed my fingers. When I finally shook hands with him, I must have said something amusing because he gave me a sharp look behind his professorial eyeglasses and a reluctant smile opened on his sober face.

Ah, I had his attention, so I expressed my total admiration for his compositions, his pianistic style, and even dared express my approval of his unique, balanced choice and use of the trio form. I expressed my regret for the tragic loss of Scott La Faro and my relief upon listening to his excellent new bassist Eddie Gomez. He must have realized how well I knew his work, for with another sharp look he asked me, "What was your name again?"

That evening we found common ground, and I explained about my radio series on great jazz artists; could I possibly ask him a few questions, whenever it suited him . . . ?

There was a pause, and then he asked if I was free to spend the next day with him until the afternoon sound-check. Speechless, I could barely nod. He gave me the name of his hotel and said he would expect me at eleven, for breakfast.

ACT II—INVITATION

Our relationship began at a breakfast table where Bill ate an enormous plate of scrambled eggs with Italian ham while I sipped a cappuccino. He was in excellent spirits, revealing a surprising sense of humor. As we chatted, I realized that his reputation for being unapproachable, withdrawn to the edge of rudeness, was rather a form of shy privacy. Our conversation began lightly, almost politely, till I made some comment that elicited his nodding smile. His amused reply opened the door, and finally he let me into his private world.

One of the first things I noticed was the fact that he seemed in good health, which confirmed the news of his recovery from the heroin addiction that had been destroying him—even if it now meant relying on methadone.

As I asked him what would be his advice to young students of jazz music, he stressed the importance of a study of classic music, whatever instrument one chose to play. Unless you happened to be Errol Garner or Art Tatum, he added, smiling. In other words, the musician was never to stop learning, discovering, experimenting.

He then asked if I played an instrument, and I replied, sighing: "I did study the piano till I was seventeen years old."

"Then what happened?"

"I went to a concert with my piano teacher, at the Uffizi Courtyard in Florence. It featured the great Alfred Cortot playing Chopin, and we were seated practically in his lap. All through the concert I felt as if my heart and soul and mind were there, spread on the piano keys, at the mercy of those hands. When I went home, I shut my old piano and gave away my music books: Chopin, Debussy, Satie . . . all of them. And that was the end of my piano studies."

"But you stayed with the music anyway?"

"Yes, in my home music was a fixed background: opera, classics, ballet, and jazz. I would sing my head off since childhood and, before I knew it, I was considered a jazz singer! However, my piano studies have helped me appreciate the performance of others. And that's where you come in; for when I listen to *you* play, I find the same reaction inside my heart and mind as that night in Florence. The tenderness, the wistfulness you express in your way of playing ballads, like 'The Londonderry Air,' brings tears to my eyes every single time. Why, it's almost physical, a strange form of sensuality, though not erotic. Do I sound weird to you?"

I hesitated . . . had I overstepped? He was smiling, amused, and shaking his head, so I took advantage of his benevolence.

"Please tell me honestly if you mind my asking you some questions for my radio program? We can stop whenever you wish."

"Go ahead."

So began our interview-conversation:

"Bill, how would you explain—to someone unversed—just what jazz music is about?"

"Jazz is a spontaneous proceeding to make music within an organized area of sound and not, as many think, a particular *style* of music. So for me, also Bach, when he improvised, would be playing jazz. It's a spontaneous, mental, musical proceeding. It's like living within a certain tradition, a certain surrounding, therefore the language can change with time but the proceeding remains the same."

"What do you think of free jazz and avant-garde jazz?"

"To my mind, each one is free to do as he pleases: he can kill, he can steal, and he can vomit inside a microphone if he wishes. But I will not waste my time listening to the frustrations and self-indulgence of *any* individual. If some people enjoy listening to someone indulging himself, then that's *their* business. I should add that I am not much into that world, nor familiar with many of its disciples, so perhaps today someone new has arrived who has finally managed to put it all together in a way that makes sense; but from what I've gathered of the basics of that music, it seems rather an excuse to avoid a lot of hard work. I think that, when I'm a listener, I expect the artist to offer the *best* of his art, his best feelings. The rest, the suffering, that's his business, his privacy, not mine. I have my own private portion of personal troubles and problems, and they are enough!" He smiled to relieve the harshness of his judgement.

"Who are the musicians who have influenced you at the very beginning of your career?"

"I would say, first of all, the classic musicians, all of them. As for my first jazz influence, it came from the big bands, when I was a kid, you know. Tommy Dorsey, Coleman Hawkins, Earl Hines."

"Ah, just like me; the Second World War years!"

"Right; but what *really* hooked me to jazz was when I began playing with small groups, like with Miles Davis."

"In fact, I believe your real rise into the general public light began with that fantastic 'Kind of Blue' group with Miles, wouldn't you say?"

"Absolutely; playing with Miles opened the doors to a *personal* career, for many people began *listening* to me, when they would not have done so otherwise. However, you see, it's not something that happened overnight. In my first recordings I was twenty years old, and at times I feel as if I don't play as well today. Furthermore, some qualified critics will tell you that today I am fundamentally the same Evans as when I was eighteen. Maybe today I am more sophisticated, but no change took place overnight."

"Now another important question: If some young person came to you declaring he wished to dedicate himself to jazz music, what would be your advice?"

"Well, it would depend on the quality of his decision. Unless it is because he has simply an absolute need to play exactly *this* music, I would not count much on his future happiness, and I would tell him to leave it alone. Yet if he went ahead to study anyway . . . then he would be absolutely right!"

"So you have no regrets? Is there anything from the past that you would change today and do over again?"

"Do over? Well, you see, I feel that it was never really in my hands. I mean my destiny. What happened had to happen, and I have absolutely no regrets."

"Exactly for how long have you been playing? And which have been the best and the worst moments?"

"Let's see . . . I am forty-seven years old and have been playing jazz music for over thirty-five years. The best moments are when I play the piano in total solitude, without the public; for I confess that I am not a 'concert' pianist. When alone, I can communicate completely with my music. The worst moments—ah yes, when you have to play on a broken-down piano!"

A fleeting smile crossed his face, as if remembering. I pressed on:

". . . And has it happened often?"

Still smiling, he nodded: "Unfortunately, yes; there have been times when the piano was *so* bad that I had to forget playing *melodic* pieces and concentrate only on rhythmic tunes to mix up things!"

"What type of music do you prefer to play?"

"I would say the personal, intimate kind. Oh, I know that they consider that I play this way because I don't like upbeat tunes, because I am unable to play them! But I assure you I can play just any type of music, from a polka to bar mitzvah music, to Dixieland and to society music. It's not a matter of ability but of *choice* for me. After all, it *is* the music that *I* am playing. By the way, I just remembered, going back to free jazz . . . I have to admit that I did record a long play with George Russell that had great success, and I probably even enjoyed recording it, but I did not wish to repeat the experience, so evidently it's not the 'genre' that satisfies me."

"How do you choose your repertoire?"

"You might say it's one of my characteristics, maybe. I need a point of reference, organization and a clear picture—a solid background that holds everything together. Maybe that could be considered my weakness, but that's how it works for me and I'm satisfied, I'll tell you." He smiled again.

"Which are the tunes *you* have composed . . . that you prefer?"

"Well, I'll say that they are all my children . . . perhaps 'Young and Foolish' or 'Peace Piece' or even 'Spartacus' from my album *Conversations*."

"Do you go through periods when you are particularly attracted to a single tune, at the risk of playing it to the ground?"

"I do it all the time. Right now it's 'Emily'—do you know it?"

"Ah, that's a *lovely* ballad, and you're so good with the slow $\frac{3}{4}$ tempo. Will you play it tonight at the concert?"

"I might."

"Please do! Here's another question. How many albums have you recorded?"

"In my entire career? Ten years ago I counted them up and there were about sixty of them. After that, I stopped counting them."

"Which is your most *successful* composition?"

"'Waltz for Debbie.'"

"Of course! It's another delightful 'almost-waltz,' with the Bill Evans smiling melancholy. And I'm sure you like bossa nova?"

"Very much, especially the first records by Gilberto and Jobim, the Brazilian records, with tunes like 'Chega de saudade,' 'Desafinado,' all very beautiful."

The waiter brought us our cappuccinos, as I turned a mental page: "I have another question. What is the actual situation of jazz today, in general?"

He sipped thoughtfully before answering: "From what I hear around me, it's all moving very slowly and, of course, it's much more difficult for a young musician of talent to emerge today. But at the root, the situation hasn't changed all that much. I have not a single doubt regarding the spreading of this music. There is too much meaning, a history too important, it has such magnetic strength . . . look at me, I began my classic studies when I didn't know the word 'jazz' even existed; and I did the whole program, you know? Conservatory, et cetera . . . well, I never really took the decision to enter into jazz music, I simply went in."

"Yes, I know what you mean! So going back to jazz today; many musicians complain there's not enough room for them, enough venues open to jazz."

"Of course; there are many obstacles on their path. The business, the commerce of music, and, naturally, rock music that is *big* business and has therefore reduced the presence of jazz on the radio, TV, in the clubs . . . and in some recording companies it's even off the budget. There's a lot to be done for the survival of jazz, and only dedicated people who *really* care for this music do it. But even without records, or radio, or TV and what else, jazz is definitely part of our modern life and will continue to exist anyway."

Such positive belief was reassuring. It was the right moment to close our conversation: "And you, Bill, will continue to play for us, creating an enchanted land of elegant sounds and tender, wistful, melancholy dreams."

"What you just told me is very beautiful, and I thank you. And I seriously hope to return to Europe. Think of it: Italy is the only country that I don't know well and perhaps the only one that I sincerely wish I could visit, perhaps live here for a while . . ."

"Now *that* would be an incredible dream come true for your fans in Italy. Besides, who knows what fate has in store for us? So let's just say 'Arrivederci a Roma'?"

He nodded with a little smile, and the interview ended there.

We strolled through the streets of Bologna, on our leisurely way to the theater, chatting and enjoying the afternoon sun on the golden stones of the town. He was curious about Roman history, about ancient Egypt, and about Italian cuisine. We arrived at the theater together with Eddie Gomez, in time for the sound check.

A brief hug, and as we parted I called out: "Please remember 'Emily' tonight? For me?"

He nodded, and later that night he did play it; and I told myself it was his gift to his most passionate admirer.

ACT III—FAREWELL

A few years later I was in New York visiting with a friend in Greenwich Village. She told me that the Village Vanguard had announced a performance by Bill Evans for that same night. We queued patiently and luckily found a corner to squeeze in, behind the pianist.

I listened to him, noting that he had grown much thinner, had let his hair grow long, and was also sporting a beard. He looked older than his age, and with his large glasses he resembled a scholarly prophet. Yes, he had changed with time, and I wondered about his health, but his music moved one deeply as ever.

At the applause of his enthusiastic public he turned, nodding his thanks. His gaze fell on me and I smiled, knowing he could never remember one day in Bologna some time ago. He seemed to smile back and then turned to bend down low, over his swollen hands resting on the piano keys, about to play again, while I felt like a teenager before her idol.

No, he could not have remembered . . . and yet he was beginning to play a tender, dreamy $\frac{3}{4}$ tempo ballad called "Emily" . . .

That night at the Village Vanguard was my last encounter with Bill Evans: the magic weaver of dreams. May I suggest you listen to his solo performance of "The Londonderry Air" while you close your eyes and surrender to his soothing melancholy?

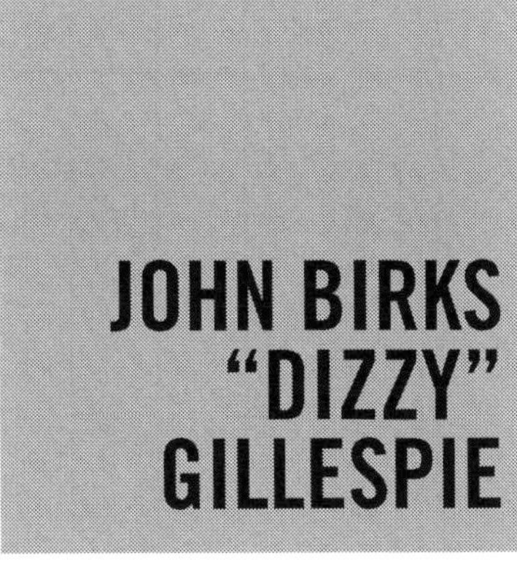

JOHN BIRKS "DIZZY" GILLESPIE

The Joyous Soul of Jazz

Introduction

Act I—To Begin: A portrait underlining basic, if lesser-known, aspects of our artist.

Act II—A True Roman: First meeting on a TV set in Rome, where his irreverent humor almost costs me my job.

Newport: A second meeting revealing an unexpected religious aspect.

Act III—Getting Together: Turning point in our friendship during a TV special: "Gillespie in Rome."

Act IV—A Radio Interview: Discussing the birth of Bebop, Charlie Parker, Miles Davis, and Dizzy's plans for the future.

Act V—"To Be or Not to Bop": The throes of translating his autobiography from Afro-American "jive" English into a modern Italian language.

Act VI—The Magic Mimic: The Jazz Festival of Pistoia, Italy. A huge storm soaks all equipment; Dizzy decides to play acoustically, informing—with theatrical gestures—thousands of amazed fans in the huge wet piazza.

Act VII—Gillespo, Italian Style: An amusing interview on his relationship with Italy: the fans, the friends, the food.

Act VIII—Cubano! His relationship with Cuba—before and after the advent of Castro—and his victory with the State Department regarding his freedom to travel there.

Act IX—Another Radio Interview: Dizzy speaks of Lorraine and family, the Bahá'í religion, and his future Cultural Center in Laurinburg.

Act X—A Symphonic Gillespie: Confesses a secret wish to perform with a real European symphonic orchestra. Two years of discussions with the RAI Radio and TV directors, and the contract is signed.

Act XI—Like von Karajan: The hectic rehearsals, the typically hair-raising press conference, and other problems.

"Annow . . . laydees an' gennelmen . . ." The actual concerts, the satisfaction of charming a "long-haired" audience, and the usual unexpected, irrepressible humor.

The French Riviera. A worthy conclusion of the symphonic adventure.

Act XII—"Once again now, Eemilio!" In Campione d'Italia (Switzerland), Dizzy is given an important international award in recognition of a Life Career in Music.

The Award Festivities: Dizzy decides to come with me to the inauguration of my Jazz School in Bassano del Grappa.

Act XIII—"On the road": During the long ride to Bassano we discuss his hearing aid, Egyptian love songs, various aspects of the Koran and the Bahá'í religion.

Act XIV—A School Is Born: His first meeting with the town of Bassano del Grappa, his "home-from-home" for the last nine years of his life, and the inauguration of the school.

Citizen of "Bazzano": his favorite view from the bridge and annual visits to discover the town.

Act XV—The Children: His involvement with diabetic children in Italy.

Act XVI—"Oo shoo-be-doo-be": Recording a CD together in Milano.

Act XVII—Odds and Ends: Brief anecdotes.

Act XVIII—Woody 'n You: A surprise encounter in Washington, D.C.

Act XIX—Monsieur Dizi' Jillepsi': Various meetings in Nice and Antibes.

Signor Giovanni Gillespo: Magic concert in Verona.

Act XX—"Dizzy's Day," September 1987: A huge "concert party" celebrates his seventieth birthday at the Velodrome in Bassano del Grappa, with eighty musicians and more than five thousand fans. He is named Honorary Citizen of Bassano, and our music school inaugurates officially a special section for the blind.

CODA—On January 6, 1993, Dizzy says goodbye.

INTRODUCTION

This story is not about Dizzy Gillespie seen as the world-famous artist, the musical innovator, the composer and arranger who led the way to new, daring, harmonic and rhythmic inventions. Nor need we refer to the amazing instrumental performer.

We shall not dissert on his historic importance, nor will it be a biography, there being an excellent *To Be or Not to Bop* translated into many languages. Dealing mainly with his adventures in Europe, you could consider this an addition to that biography, which does not mention his longstanding relationship with Italy.

It could also be useful to the "lay" reader interested in the general world of music thus discovering a stimulating, unusual personality, a hero of the Afro-American culture for which the United States is admired and appreciated the world over.

You might consider this book a "bedside" companion, aimed at giving you a different insight on the private, humorous, and thoughtful human being that was John Birks Gillespie as we knew him.

ACT I—TO BEGIN

Having an exuberant, multifaceted personality, Dizzy Gillespie has no doubt amused, amazed, annoyed, angered, and perhaps scandalized people with his irreverent "so what?" and "why not?" attitude. In an interview he had explained that, living as a black boy in the Deep South, therefore in a dangerous world, he had trained himself to face any harmful problems from early childhood. In fact, for many years he had carried a pocket knife to defend himself from the attacks of drunken rednecks on a "Saturday night nigger spree." He still had a vivid recollection of the horrible death of his friend Bill, who had been tied down to the railway tracks and run over by a train.

"Good heavens, Dizzy! That must have shocked you for life! Was that what made you so aggressive?"

"Heck no! I spent all my childhood getting into mischief. I was small and skinny but real fast and real mad. In the end, even the big boys would stop heckling me and steer away."

"And at home?"

"Well, I was the youngest, so my brothers and especially my sister were really pushy with me." His big laugh: "In fact, one day Eugenia really pushed me . . . out the window! Said I was too wild! "

Another facet of his irrepressible personality were his outspoken political ideas, albeit formulated with humor. Some might recall that in 1963 he had given election politics a shake when, tongue in cheek, he had presented his candidacy for president of the United States, running against Barry Goldwater. What had begun as a joke, with Ralph and Jean Gleason prompting the whole affair, was soon taken up all over California, where students wore "Dizzy Gillespie for President" buttons. From California the action spread out, reaching the media throughout the United States. It was obviously treated as a joke, and yet this "why not?" stunt may have contributed to open eyes—and eventually doors—with regard to future black statesmen.

A delicate matter had been his heavy drinking problem, which had developed in the 1960s and would eventually lead him to an emergency hospitalization. Once again, his wife, Lorraine, had taken him in hand, nursing him toward definitive recovery. However, concerning drugs and other addictions that were rampant, especially in the jazz milieu, he was firm and adamant on the mortal harm that could ensue.

It should be added that through those many years when Charlie Parker and Dizzy Gillespie were creating a musical revolution that would change the sound of jazz forever, his strong bond with Charlie made Dizzy watch over him to the day Bird died. He not only disapproved of and fought Bird's addictions—which would lead him to a tragic end in 1955 at age thirty-four—but he stood by him with enduring devotion.

He also took in hand, with a committee of other artists, the harrowing decisions and actions needed to extract Bird's body from the Bellevue morgue, to be sent to his mother, and to be buried decently in Kansas City. Dizzy said that Norman Granz paid practically all the bills.

Through the years, especially during the difficult problems Dizzy had to face because of Parker's hectic behavior, the press would try to obtain from him some negative comment regarding Bird, but Dizzy would smile, sphinxlike, and enunciate clearly: "My association with Charlie Parker is far above anything else I have ever done musically. He gives me tremendous inspiration, always and at all times."

After Parker's passing away he declared: "It is said that our Creator chooses great artists. There is no other explanation for the fact that an artist like Charlie Parker had so much talent other than he was divinely inspired."

And he would conclude: "Charlie Parker was the other side of my heartbeat."

Dizzy Gillespie was a mixture of wiliness and ancient wisdom mingled with a juvenile naiveté. His flamboyant personality is probably foremost in the memory of the general public. To this effect, one excuse he would offer to explain his tendency, sometimes, toward an explosive behavior, was the fact that, having been born on October 21, 1917, he was a child of the Russian Revolution, which had "exploded" then.

However, leaving all these well-known stories behind us, for you can find some of them as part of his official biography, with this chapter I wish to pay homage to the very special human being he matured into, during his later years. Consider it a collection of memories lived over a period of two decades. Perhaps, while reading, you will catch a shadow of his laughter, his joy of living, his sharp humor, and his husky-nasal voice, and feel as if he has never really left us.

ACT II—A TRUE ROMAN

In the mid-1960s in Italy I was dedicated to the diffusion of that "elite" music called jazz by presenting a weekly jazz radio program and working on national TV not only as a singer but also producing, presenting, and interviewing famous international jazz artists.

That afternoon I was to meet "the great Gillespie," whose quintet was to perform in a TV special. In those years he was not the mellow, wise, and relaxed human being who would bloom later; he was peppery, wisecracking, electric, and devil-may-care. He had the reputation of being a most unexpected personality who might create problems with the straight-laced TV producers of those years.

We were very formally introduced, and he gave me the big eye. I began explaining how the program would unfold, but he kept leering one minute and frowning in mock concentration the next. Aware that he was not really listening, I stopped talking altogether.

He nodded, grinning.

"OK-OK. What did you say your name was?"

"Lilian. Lilian Terry"

"That's not Italian . . ."

"No. I'm British, born and raised in Egypt. However, my mother is Italian."

"Bet she makes great minestrone, huh? I love minestrone!"*

I smiled and gathered up my courage to ask if he could possibly play one of his earlier tunes that held a special meaning for me, like a good-luck chant.

"It's the one that goes 'Oo shoo-be-doo-be, oo, oo.'"

He shook his head—sorry, no. They had taken it off the book and now were playing newer tunes. At my disappointment he smiled: "But one day I'll play it for you . . ."

He wiggled his eyebrows in a mock leer and whispered loudly: "If you promise we'll sing it together . . ."**

We still had a few minutes before the show was to go on the air, live. Now, any friend of Dizzy's will tell you how risky his live appearance on any show could be,

---

* Many years later he would be sitting with my mother in the kitchen of our country house in the Venetian hills, eating with relish—at four in the afternoon—from a large serving bowl of freshly made minestrone while simultaneously gobbling down the contents of a basket of fresh figs. Mother would be laughing while explaining to him what the mixture of hot minestrone and fresh figs could do to his insides.

"No problem, mama!" he would exclaim, slapping his tummy. "These are made of rubber!"

** Twenty years later we would be singing the song together in Milano, while recording an album called "Lilian Terry Has a Very Special Guest: DIZZY GILLESPIE," subtitled "Oo, shoo-be-doo-be, Oo, Oo."

but, in my innocence, I asked him if we could work out some Qs and As so as to have a smooth interview.

"Oh yeah? Don't you like surprises? They're the spice of life!"

"I love surprises, but unfortunately they don't." I pointed to our stage supervisor. "You see that gentleman in the grey suit? His job is to check that everything is according to RAI standards, including the dialogue, and they are *very* formal."

Dizzy smiled, one finger to his chin and head bent coyly to one side:

"Oh, yeah? And just what would shake them up?"

My instinct rang a bell, so I answered breezily: "No problem. I'll begin by explaining your leading role in the birth of bebop, so the public is made aware of your importance in the history of jazz. There will follow a brief interview where you'll answer me in English and I'll translate into Italian."

"Ah-ha! So you'll clean up any bad language . . ."

"Of course not!" I replied in a mock stern tone. "Because I'm certain you're going to be the perfect gentleman!"

He gave me an odd look: "Hey! For a second I thought I had Lorraine there! My wife. You sounded just like her."

"I take that as a compliment. Ah, there we are, they're calling us onstage."

Lights, OK. Cameras, ready. We roll at zero. Ten, nine, eight. . . . Rolling!

Standing next to him, in front of his musicians, I told the public how very lucky we were to have the great Gillespie play for us for the next twenty-five minutes. A brief, relaxed interview followed in English and Italian. Yes, he was indeed happy to be back in Rome. Matter of fact, he always looked forward to coming to Italy at least once a year. Such culture, all those art treasures . . . not to mention the delicious food! The cappuccino! Ah, yes, he had many friends in Rome, where he felt very much at home. In fact, he was learning new Italian words every day. Like the Roman slang compliments that the guys shouted at the girls on the street; very, very interesting . . .

My instinct again . . . so I beamed at the camera: ". . . but enough small talk now. It's time to enjoy the wonderful music of the Dizzy Gillespie Quintet."

Turning to him, I motioned: "Maestro? It's all yours! Prego . . ."

He watched me walk away, fiddling with the horn and grinning, then roared out with gusto his favorite, very brief if rather heavy, Roman compliment: "Aaaah Bonah!"

Such "compliment" could be translated approximately into "Rather appetizing!"

There was a sudden combined reaction. Simultaneously, I froze in my steps, the cameraman barked a laugh quickly smothered, while the inspector almost fell off his highchair. Satisfied, Dizzy flickered the pistons of his horn, counted off, and they exploded into "Birk's Works."

I was not sacked that day, but it was some time before they would let me produce another TV special concerning any jazz artist.

At Newport

Two years later, in 1968, I was on my way to the Newport Jazz Festival to interview as many important jazz artists as I could approach, in order to produce a special radio series for RAI, the Italian National Network. Fortunately, I was driving up from New York with Max Roach and Papa Jo Jones in Max's blue convertible. He led me through the four days, from artist to artist, like a kindly guiding spirit.

Among the artists to be interviewed, Dizzy's name was underlined with a large question mark as I cringed at the thought of what might come out of his laughing loudmouth, but Max had said not to worry—come along and we might catch him in a thoughtful mood.

With my faithful tape recorder in hand I stood outside Dizzy's dressing room waiting, as agreed, for Max to call me in. It was unusually silent inside. Had I missed the appointment? Crossing my fingers, I knocked and peeked discreetly around the door.

Dizzy was there all right, with Max and other musicians standing or squatting around him and listening intently as he read in a very intimate voice from a book he held open in his lap. Max motioned for me to come in. This was a most unusual scene and a strange lecture from a man renowned for his aggressive good humor and unconventional behavior. It sounded like the teachings of the Gospel, the Koran, and the Old Testament sifted together. Very interesting, and for a fleeting instant I considered recording it, but, from the sober look on Dizzy's face as he read, I realized this was a very private moment, so I walked out on tiptoe, signaling to Max "later," which he acknowledged with a nod.

Years later Dizzy explained that he had been reading from a book on the Bahá'í faith.

So there I was again in Dizzy's dressing room, introduced by Max as a good friend from Italy; a singer who wished to interview him for the Italian radio.

Dizzy, once again the hyper entertainer, immediately started reciting dramatically:

"Ah Roma! Cappuccino, tortellini, carbonara, calamari. . . . Say, how is Nunzio? You know my friend Nunzio?"

"Nunzio Rotondo? Yes, we've recorded an LP together with Romano Mussolini."

"Ah yeah! Romano and that beautiful wife of his! Did you know she's Sophia Loren's sister? Lucky guy! And Loffredo, how is he? Say hullo to his mother for me. Tell her next time I come to Rome we'll take her to meet the Pope. You know she lives in Rome and has never met the Pope?!"

"Well, neither have 90 percent of the Romans . . ."

While talking, he kept eyeing me suspiciously, trying to trace me to some memory at the back of his mind; I just smiled at him.

The radio interview unfolded very pleasantly with the Gillespie verve, and he was obviously enjoying himself, trying to speak Italian in a message to all his

Italian fans. A knock and a voice, announcing he was on next, brought the meeting to a close.

We parted with hugs and patting on the back. See you in Rome this autumn. Absolutely! Ciao! As I walked away from the dressing room, satisfied with the interview, he stuck his head out the door to call out: "Hey, wait a minute . . . ! That walk . . . I remember you now . . . !"

His big laugh, then his yell: "Aaaah Bonah!"

ACT III—GETTING TOGETHER

By the mid-1970s, through various occasions to interview our artist, Dizzy and I would gradually discover points in common—similar reactions to particular happenings and those items that slip out in a conversation to enlighten you on the "other" side of the man: the simple human being, as opposed to "the entertaining star."

A regular meeting would take place at the Jardin des Arènes at Cimiez during the historical and irreplaceable annual Grande Parade du Jazz in Nice, France. It was produced and organized by George Wein and Simone Ginibre, and every year I recorded various interviews for my Italian radio program.

My son Francesco, in his teens, was a budding piano student at the Rome Conservatory and totally mesmerized by Dizzy's brilliance. Throughout the festival days he would follow the Gillespie quartet from one stage to the next, noting diligently their tunes, absorbing each solo like blotting paper. On the long drive back to Rome he would give his blow-by-blow description of what eighteen-year-old Rodney Jones had played on his guitar; Mickey Rocker's fantastic drumming; the solid bass backing by Ben Brown; and how guest saxophonist Eddie Daniels would fit smoothly into Dizzy's phrasing. Not to mention the incredible repertoire with nuances of flamenco, as well as his famous Afro-Cuban of course . . . and a touch of funky . . . and even some rock! And what an entertainer! Concluding with: "He is sheer genius, he *IS* jazz!"

The turning point came when RAI accepted my proposal to produce a TV "Special Performance" with Dizzy Gillespie, who was to spend his day off, between concerts, in Rome. We had our theme: Gillespie in Rome. And what could be more Roman than the Coliseum?

The whole program was taped by the TV crew as it unfolded from his arrival at Fiumicino airport to his direct transfer to the Coliseum where, among a curious crowd, Dizzy went into his antics: a large cowboy hat perched on his head, humorous comments on the history of the place, all religiously recorded by the TV cameramen, as well as a crowd of Japanese tourists trailing behind with clicking and whirring cameras.

I was slightly alarmed at the thought of spending a whole day with this force of nature, when a small group of music students arrived and one of them presented Dizzy with a large color drawing representing him dressed in a

Thousand-and-One-Nights costume, playing his periscopic trumpet from which emerged the Genie of Jazz. Dizzy was instantly interested and touched, and, giving all his attention to the young people, he listened patiently to their questions, which he would answer while the young artist translated both ways.

It was finally lunchtime, and Dizzy was informed that a jazz club had opened its kitchen to fix a special luncheon for him. The top Italian jazz critics had been invited along.

"You see, if they meet you when you are relaxed and nursing a contented stomach, they might discover a different Gillespie, not only the artist/clown you usually show onstage but the 'other' Giovanni Gillespo . . ."

He had been eyeing me in his shrewd way, miming a fake offense.

"The artist/clown? The other . . . what was it . . . Giovanni Gillespo? OK, I'll be Giovanni, but you'll be my interpreter and you'll translate *exactly* what I say, OK?"

And from that day on, throughout the many years, I was to act as his interpreter—and often regret it—translating not only his normal answers but also some of the most outrageous explanations he would give to that worn out question: "How did you get to play a twisted horn?" Most of his fellow musicians and friends have heard the different answers he would give, according to the pleasantness of the interviewer, but there were times when he would say such incredibly embarrassing things, expecting me to translate them faithfully, till I would give him the "Lorraine" glare and he would burst out laughing.

On that day at the Roman Jazz Club, he plunged into his special chicken dish with great gusto. The Italian critics, chatting and eating along, were enjoying this unusual press conference where he was truly relaxed and mellow. He was willing to listen to everybody and answer every question: personal, musical, religious, or political, and at one point our eyes met and he gave me a most benign smile, something of the wise Buddha. He nodded his approval of the "day in Rome" I had organized for him and, to punctuate his satisfaction, he offered us—journalists, fans, and complete TV crew with rolling cameras—a very discreet series of burps.

During another special moment that afternoon, Dizzy sat at the club piano with the young music students from the Coliseum crowding around him, most attentive and inquisitive. He would explain—illustrating his words on the piano—some of his solos on his famous records. The young artist who had translated for Dizzy at the Coliseum was right there with his questions, showing how deeply he had studied Gillespie so that later, stepping out of the club for a digestive stroll, Dizzy had pointed him out, expressing his surprise at the boy's knowledge of Dizzy's music.

I had called the young man over: "Francesco . . . Dizzy is surprised at how well you know his repertoire . . ."

My son had grinned and replied: "Well, so I should, with all the festivals where I've been lucky enough to follow you around . . . thanks to mother . . . ," pointing at me.

Caught off guard, Dizzy's eyes had widened, and he had started the long "aaah . . . ?" which turned into his famous rolling laugh; he grabbed each one of us by an arm as we strolled along.

From that Roman day onward there was a subtle change in Dizzy's attitude. The superficial benevolence he usually bestowed on everybody matured into a different behavior toward me. The "flirting" attitude gave way to a relaxed familiarity. It was as if we had always known each other, feeling at ease like old friends. When we commented on this "at ease" feeling he shared with my family—for also my mother had entered into the picture with her excellent "minestrone per Dizzy"—his amused explanation had been that we had probably all lived together in a previous life. He had opened his arms asking: "Why not?"

We had an open invitation to join him whenever he would appear in Italy, or at the annual Grande Parade in Nice, and during the long years that followed we established a firm relationship with "Giovanni Gillespo"; Dizzy had adopted the name immediately and through the years he would phone—sometimes at dawn—and roar his good humor: "Prontow? Buon-gee-ornow, this is Gee-iovanni, comee sta-eeh?!" and be delighted at my complaint for the ungodly hour. We would then gossip until he would say: "OK-OK, that's enough now. Go back to your beauty sleep . . . you sure need it! Hah! Hah!"

And he would ring off.

ACT IV—A RADIO INTERVIEW

In 1979 my "Portrait of the Artist" radio series presented—through interviews and special recordings—the most famous jazz personalities available. Evidently, Dizzy was included.

We began taping the interview after a satisfactory lunch and a brief "Jew's harp serenade" with our artist in a benign, reminiscent mood, as he sipped the cappuccino he favored.

"Tell me, Dizzy, just what is your secret?"

Raised eyebrows over the coffee cup and a surprised smile. I explained: "If I remember well, your very first bebop combo was organized in 1944, with Oscar Pettiford, to play at the Onyx Club on Fifty-Second Street, right? And who were the other members of the group?"

"Oh yeah. We had Don Byas on sax to begin with, then he was replaced by Budd Johnson. George Wallington on piano . . . but he was later replaced by Clyde Hart, and Max [Roach] on drums. But the *real* first combo was formed earlier, in December '43 with Lester Young, Oscar Pettiford, Monk, and I."

"However, the secret I want to discover is the following: If we listen today to your Verve recordings made in the forties and fifties, like 'Groovin' High' or 'Manteca,' they are as fresh as if you had just recorded them. I mean, you belong to today's music even when you offer practically the same sound and repertoire you played back then. In other words, you can't be pinpointed to any particular era . . ."

"Well . . . the truth is that the 'new' style we created in the forties was itself directly developed from the ingredients and the atmosphere of the late thirties; and from that moment the evolution of our music, having those solid roots, simply developed right into the music that's played today."

"Yes, but there's also the matter of your own very personal style . . ."

"As for my style . . . well, when you establish a certain style, you sort of stick to it, regardless of what you do. You try to resolve all the different possibilities, which are limitless in any given way. The style of the music I play is simply *my* way of playing. Whatever I'm playing, my phrasing will always be that way. If you are always cognizant of fundamentals, you hardly ever go wrong because you've got one foot in the past and one in the future. You're fundamentally the way that things have gone before."

"Yet there's something particular about you. Many other excellent musicians who have remained true to their personality have experienced long 'off' moments with their public. You have never suffered from it."

"I think another reason is that I'm also an entertainer, and I had good experience! I worked under some great entertainers such as Cab Calloway, Lucky Millinder, and Earl Hines, who is a real master showman! I watched them, and tried to find out why the public liked *them* rather than somebody else."

"And what did you learn?"

"I discovered it's that personal touch, and the people know that I'm sincere, they detect it even if they don't know the language I'm speaking in. They can hear it in my voice and my demeanor, so that's another thing. There are lots of things you learn as you go along, you know? I am completely at the mercy of an audience. I know that it's my duty to reach *them*, not for them to reach *me*. An audience has no obligation; it stopped when they put their money in the box office. From that point on it's the obligation of the artist."

"You mentioned Earl Hines. Some years ago he came to Rome to play at a jazz club called 'Meo Patacca' in Trastevere. During the radio interview, we got talking about his fantastic big band in 1942, with you, Bird, Sarah Vaughan, and all those other great artists. As we say: 'la crème de la crème.' He reminisced and spoke especially about you and Bird, how you would study together to develop your own special patterns that nobody else could figure out at that time. You were inventing together unusual things that you would then insert in the changes of the tunes, when playing in public."

"Yeah. . . . We had like . . . a meeting of the minds, we were constantly inspiring each other. You could say I was more advanced harmonically but Bird was very advanced rhythmically. He was a great influence for all of us."

"Going back to your way of reaching your audience: one fact on which all your fans will agree, no matter where you appear, is that while you do clown around on stage—don't frown, you know it is true . . .—yet the moment you count off and put your horn to your lips . . ."

"I know." He grinned, ". . . I play my ass off."

"Err . . . yes. . . . Now here's another question. Have you ever been curious, tried any of the new hybrid things that are being played nowadays?"

"Listen, I was doing that stuff they call rock-jazz or fusion music—whatever they call it now—way back. I mean, they're doing things *now* which we did in 1946, the same exact riff that we did then, so it's nothing new to me, nothing I hear from that angle that I haven't heard before, in some context. You could say I play that 'new music' too, because we've been doing it for a looong time!"

"Yes, but what you play has logic to it, while some of the things we hear today have very little to do with jazz as we know it. If we go all the way to free jazz: apart from Ornette, Paul Bley, and of course Mingus and his "free form" music, and a handful of others—what do you make of it? For instance, some of the electronic things that Miles Davis has been experimenting with recently . . . ?"

"Well, I can't comment on what Miles Davis does because I wouldn't dare to take it upon myself to comment on an artist such as Miles."

"That's exactly what is puzzling us. Because an artist of his stature, who has created a special world of music "à la Miles," has no need to turn his back on it and look at the rock world for something . . . which he may not have found yet, or has he?"

Dizzy shook his head with a large grin: "Well, he's found a lot of money, I'll tell you that! Ha, ha, hah! So maybe that's what he was looking for? But seriously, you know? I've been trying to figure it out myself, and when I ask Miles, he kind of fences me off, saying, 'You know what it is, 'cause you taught me.' And all that kind of stuff."

"But in your own opinion?"

"I figure that, perhaps, it's because at one time Miles had the perfect vehicle for his personality and his creativity, you know? He had Wynton Kelly, Jimmy Cobb, and Paul Chambers, but I don't think he's found *that* anymore, since then. Of course, at one time he had Red Garland and Philly Joe Jones; and that was something where he got off . . ."

"I know, and we can't forget the Kind of Blue period with Bill Evans! That's the Miles Davis I miss *very* much. Or those eerie heartbreaking sounds he gave us with Gil Evans?"

"Ah yes. But, you see, maybe right now, when he found that he can't find another Paul Chambers, or a Wynton Kelly—and they were just perfect for what he wanted then—well, maybe now he doesn't want to play any of that music without those guys . . . and he's got to wait until he gets to heaven to do so! You know, there must be some reason for him not wanting to play the way he used to."

"I guess it's his right, even if I do wish he would surprise us romantics just once. Ah, well . . . I have another question for you. What's happening to jazz in the United States nowadays?"

"Oh, there's a big . . . but *big* upsurge in jazz now. I see a lot of young people in the public, and that's *very* good. And the new cats, they play real nice. You know, most of the time, in the past ten years, you used to look around and say, 'Hey, I'm middle-aged, cause all my fans are middle-aged people,' but now all the young kids are coming out, to play and to listen."

"You're right. In fact, most of the young people in Italy are definitely your fans. And they are discovering Charlie Parker, Sonny Rollins, and John Coltrane, and also the fact that the music called bebop, which you guys invented in the forties, is a very basic moment in the history of jazz music, leading to what is being played today. But would you tell us more about yourself and Parker . . . ?"

Once again, he was drawn back into his memories:

"Well . . . Yardbird and I just blended together from the moment he came to New York in 1942. They used to say we were like twins; our contribution just blended naturally. We were a great influence on each other's musical development, and in the way we played our notes, which were so close together. His enunciation of notes, the way he went from one to the other . . . that's what set the standard for phrasing our music."

"In an interview, Miles said you and Bird played the same chords, played the lines together just like each other so he couldn't tell the difference. And Benny Carter explained that when you and Parker were playing those 'other' tunes within the original chords of the melody, the two of you were a natural irresistible association. He declared you simply turned the whole jazz picture around."

"Well, like I said, Bird came to New York, to The Street, in 1942 and he sat in with us. That night I was hooked just by the way he assembled his notes together, and we sort of recognized ourselves in each other as colleagues and decided to play and exercise together every chance we got. By 1945 nobody played closer than we did; just listen to 'Groovin' High,' 'Shaw 'Nuff,' and 'Hot House.' When Bird came in my life, he brought a totally new dimension on how to attack a tune and how to swing it. Our difference was that he had this 'sanctified' rhythm inside him. His accents had a definite bluesy feeling, while I got my accents from percussions. I guess we inspired each other with our differences."

He grinned, remembering, and added: "But the real difference in our development was that I had to work constantly and hard, while Yardbird just grew into it naturally!"

"Just now you were saying that Bird played with a 'sanctified' rhythm?"

He grinned again and explained: "In Cheraw the blacks were divided into many levels of Christian churches. Starting from the top we had the Second Presbyterian Church, then the Methodist, the Catholic, the Peedee Baptist, and the A.M.E. Zion. The last and lowest was the Sanctified church where the whole congregation shouted. I would sneak in there, though I was raised a Methodist, and that's where I learned the meaning of rhythm and harmonies and how it could transport people spiritually."

"Was that a 'spontaneous combustion' sort of thing?"

"Oh yes! There were four brothers in that church: one played the snare drum, another one the cymbal, another the bass drum, and the last one the tambourine. They had at least four different rhythms going on at the same time, and then the congregation would add the foot stomping and hand clapping, and jumping up and down on the resounding wooden floor. And the singing! It was just mind blowing. That's what I mean by 'sanctified' music."

"What an experience that must have been! But what is happening *now*, jazz-wise?"

"You know, I honestly believe, actually I *know* that our music is conducive to what they are playing now. Our music and their rhythms. . . . In fact, I'm gonna make an album for the kids, to show them that our music is perfect for their kind of rhythm, because our music is really multi-rhythmic."

"There's that record you made in 1977, with the 'Shim Sham Shimmy' and those other tunes that have the Gillespie imprint but are of easier reach, for those people who are not particularly jazz oriented."

"Yeah . . . !" he smiled, reminiscing: "'The shim sham shimmy on St. Louis Blues,' that was fun!"

"Tell me, has this idea of a new record for kids just come to you?"

"No, actually I have already made one, not with my compositions but with Lalo Schifrin's. It's called 'A Free Ride.' Now I'm gonna try with *my* music, and it's really groovy."

"We'll look forward to it. Well, I needn't ask you when you're coming back to Italy, as you are practically an Italian by now, especially with your 'marranzano' Jew's harp. So have you any special message for your Italian friends? Apart from 'Ah bona!' possibly . . ."

His wide grin: "Yeah! Ciao! Arrivederci Roma! Wait for me! I'll be back!"

ACT V—"TO BE OR NOT TO BOP"

I was acting as his interpreter at a press conference when Dizzy suddenly turned to me: "Do you also *write* translations . . . like . . . could you translate my book into Italian?"

"Yes, but do you have an Italian publisher?"

"Well, Doubleday tells me this Mondadori guy is interested . . ."

"It's not a 'guy' but the largest publishing firm in Italy. They're probably interested because Arrigo Polillo works with them."

"Polillo!? We're friends from way back! So you think you could translate the book?"

"Well, I was interpreter-translator with FAO of the UN in Rome for seven years. And Ellington requested my translation for some articles for an Italian editor. But at Mondadori they surely have their own translators."

"But would you like to do it for me?"

"Obviously. It would be interesting and amusing, I'm sure. . . . But you should let me have a copy of the book so I could tell you if I am up to it."

"Here, write down your address and I'll have them send you a copy, and I'll tell them I want *you* on the job. I'll tell Polillo!"

Doubtfully, I complied. I was wrong to doubt, for in April 1980 our friend and jazz critic Arrigo Polillo had obtained Mondadori's decision to publish the book—even if Mondadori was not particularly interested in jazz—and the translating job for me, adding with a little laugh that he might not be doing me a favor, as I was given a firm request that of the 502 pages of the original story, plus about fifty more as selected discography, filmography, honors and awards, and index, there should remain—after a heartless slimming diet—only about three hundred pages, all items included. Otherwise, the cost of the actual printing would not be covered by the number of copies they were expecting to sell.

I wrote to Dizzy on April 22, 1980:

> Dear Giovanni, I have this minute been informed by Mondadori that they have acquired the rights to publish *To Be or Not to Bop* in Italy, and I am to translate it. They are also asking me to render the book attractive to the non-jazz Italian reader as well. So here we start with two main problems we must solve, together.
>
> First of all there is the enormous number of pages that Mondadori requests me to chop off here and there, as the book is too voluminous. We'll have to examine that together. Next, I must point out that although you speak at length of the many European countries where you played, naming various musicians, critics or whatever, you do not mention Italy or Italians at all. It would be very diplomatic if you were to add some Italian anecdotes. I am sure that interesting or funny or drastic things must have happened to you also in Italy. So please put down these paragraphs for me, as it would make the book more attractive for our Italian readers. Let me know how you wish to go about it. Meanwhile, I shall get on with the translation.

Now, a professional translator will understand my plight, as I had not only to translate from a black American jazz idiom into an Italian language "hip" enough to reflect Dizzy's personality; but I also had to choose where and how much to "slim it down" by a good 250 pages. Rolling up my mental sleeves, I opened the book with a dubious heart.

I was soon in total despair, and I called Dizzy and told him so. He asked me to give him a few days to talk to his co-author Al Fraser and they would come up with some advice.

Some time later I did receive a very pleasant and encouraging letter from Al Fraser, who wrote, among other things: "Dizzy and I have discussed the matter of foreign language editions, and because of his friendship with you, I am confident that you will complete an excellent translation." He then gave me a few points of advice and encouraged me: "Feel relatively free to make small cuts where the book seems too repetitious or digresses too far from the narrative's thrust. Everything must be done to preserve the book's value as modern jazz history and points of disagreement between Dizzy and other narrators should be preserved at all costs. Every effort should be made to retain the spoken rather than the written quality of the narratives in order to convey the idioms and the rhythmic and poetic qualities of the jazz musician's speech." More suggestions and advice and then a closing phrase: "I'm counting on your translation to help make *To Be or Not to Bop* the book Italian readers will dig with all their hearts and souls."

Feeling relieved, I thanked him and Dizzy. However, I suggested that they also speak to the American editor, so Dizzy in turn spoke with Sandy Richardson of Doubleday in New York, with whom I subsequently spoke on the phone as well, and finally I was told to go ahead.

When I mentioned my worries Dizzy simply laughed, saying blithely, "Listen Lil, I trust you. So you just use your judgement."

"It means I'll have to chop off here and there."

"OK-OK!"

"I mean abundantly, lots."

"OK-OK!"

"Well, fortunately you do have the habit of reiterating words more than once."

"Oh, I do?"

"You do."

"OK-OK, just follow your instinct, and do your best. Ciao Bonah!"

And he rang off. That was all the assistance he gave me.

It took me two excruciating years to translate the book into "soft" Italian slang, while chopping off a repetitious paragraph here and there. When the first draft went to the editors in Milano, they sent it back with compliments for my effort but asking for further slimming and to please make it a little more "good Italian," as their readers were used to a different style of language . . .

Some time later I wrote to Dizzy:

> The Italian editor invited me to lunch the other day, coming all the way from Milano to ask me to take the book in hand a second time and give it a further slimming diet, as it proved too bulky and expensive the way it is now. He explained once again that, should it cost more than what

> they expected to earn in sales, they wouldn't be able to publish it at all. I hope this does not cause a harmful delay in the publishing date. What with repeated printers' strikes, strong attempts at "taking over" from another publisher, and various judicial haggles and all. . . . But, like we say in Egypt, it's 'Maktoob': Fate will have its course. So here we go again, Giovanni Cappuccino!"

I turned out a last, slimmer, "good Italian language" version, and Mondadori promptly paid me.

Epilogue

However, our troubles were not over, as, by then, Mondadori had become involved in a long financial/legal/political/judicial battle, and in time it changed owners. In the end the new owners decided to cross off about 40 percent of the manuscripts about to be published. Jazz not being essential to their cultural image—they had most of the famous Italian and foreign authors—I was informed that the book would not be published at all. Heartbroken for Dizzy, I asked if I could offer the book to another Italian editor, considering it was translated and ready for publication. The answer was a firm NO, they had already informed Doubleday and in fact they had sent the bulk of my manuscript to the shredder. If some other editor wished to start the whole business of approaching Doubleday . . . fine, but they would have no access to the translation I had produced.

I asked Polillo at Mondadori to inform Dizzy personally and officially, before calling him myself. We were both very disappointed, and I was particularly upset for him. However, in the end Dizzy, God bless his nature, was the one to console me.

ACT VI—THE MAGIC MIMIC

It was 1981 and he was appearing as "guest star" at the Pistoia Jazz Festival. Just as they were setting up the bandstand for his group, all at once, the skies had burst open like a gigantic water balloon. They had never seen anything like it. Huge drops fell like liquid hail-stones, drenching not only the large piazza, mounted into an amphitheater—with the public running for shelter in all directions—but also and especially the very large bandstand, drenching the sound and light equipment, and anything that could have been used for the concert.

The young organizers were dashing all over the place trying bravely to mop up a constant pouring, checking over and again the useless state of the stage, while their faces expressed their distress and helplessness to deal with the catastrophe.

Finally, they came to where Dizzy was sitting backstage, in a makeshift dressing room. They explained how, to their despair, the stage had been declared definitely out of use by the Fire Department. Dizzy, relaxed and benign, puffing on his Cuban cigar, looked out onto the stage, up at the skies, around at the public in hiding under the scaffolding, and then asked: "What if we don't use any electricity at all, will the Firemen give their OK?"

The two men looked at each other then at Dizzy as if he had gone mad.

"But . . . Maestro! It's a huge Piazza, how could we hold a concert without any amplification?"

Dizzy gave his amused wise smile and pronounced: "I have done so much . . . with so little . . . for so long . . . that now, I can do anything . . . with nothing at all!"

Uncomprehending, they stared at me for a translation. They listened, speechless. I added that if Dizzy was willing to try anyway, then perhaps they should hurry and issue the information before the public gave up and left the place. They nodded, galvanized, and went out to shout the news, asking the public up front to pass back the information:

"Dizzy Gillespie is going to play for us as soon as the rain stops!"

His musicians and his manager, Bobby Redcross, expressed their doubts and worries, but Dizzy just laughed, reassuring them.

It took half an hour for the rain to gradually turn into a light, sporadic drizzle.

Unannounced, Dizzy stepped out with his musicians and, while the mopping and cleaning went on frantically behind him, he walked to the very edge of the high-perched stage and stood there, looking at the public and fiddling with his trumpet pistons. Eventually, more and more people noticed him standing there, till there was a roar of applause and they all rushed back to their wet seats, in excited disorder. Dizzy kept fingering his trumpet, looking around at the entire facility, and then made up his mind.

He bent down toward the large group of young fans standing, drenched, by the bandstand at his feet and motioned for them to hop right onto the stand, which they did immediately with enthusiasm. This produced a huge roar of protest from the public way back to the farthest rows, but Dizzy knew what he wanted.

He blew a long, high note then put his finger to his lips and went "Shhhhhhhhh. . . . ."

Then he shouted out: "Hey back there . . . you hear me? Listen to me, you guys. Just listen to me!"

There were various cries of "*Silenzio! Ascoltiamolo!*" till the whole crowd was miraculously silent and expectant.

There followed a most efficient scene of mimicry. He pointed to the skies, looking up and bending sideways in biblical fear, and then put his hands in his hair, shaking his head in despair. He pointed to the various electronic instruments, lights and all, and then motioned to cut his throat, staggering. At this point the crowd was giggling but waiting earnestly for the rest of the improvisation. What would be the finale? He pointed to his temple. Idea! He pointed around at all the public, inviting the people to come down from the farthest seats and as close as possible.

By then a good size of the front crowd had settled right upon the bandstand at his invitation, till the Fire Department and the police had stopped any more ascents for safety reasons.

With practically all of his public as close as possible, and mimicking his words with his hands, in a most Italian style, he said loud and clear:

"OK-OK. Now if you guys, all of you—*TUTTI*—keep perfectly silent, SHHHH . . . we'll play for you and I promise you'll hear every note. So all you guys: SHHHH . . . We: *MUSICA!* OK? OK? OK?"

By then the whole audience was yelling OK.

Meanwhile the musicians had set up their instruments alongside him in a single line, close to the edge of the stand. There were young men and women all around them, delighted with this forced change of seating. At that moment the drizzle stopped falling altogether.

Dizzy looked up and, smiling, shouted his thanks to the heavens in his rough Cheraw-born voice: "*GRRAZZIEH!*"

Thus, on that magic summer night a huge, drenched, crowd practically held its breath and enjoyed a miraculous, totally acoustic concert as Dizzy counted off and they all went to spend "A Night in Tunisia."

ACT VII—GILLESPO, ITALIAN STYLE

During the ongoing editorial struggle for the ownership of Mondadori, the final translation of *To Be or Not to Bop* had been approved, but there was still that lack of Italian anecdotes for the Italian version of his autobiography. Therefore, I had been requested to please grab the author during one of his tours and obtain the needed material from him. It would be inserted in the book as a special chapter, a bonus, for his Italian readers.

Joining him in his Roman hotel room I offered him a steaming cappuccino on condition that we tape a long chat about the Italian Gillespie. OK-OK.

"Giovanni Gillespo, you don't love Italy."

". . . Are you kidding? I feel at home in Italy, got lots of friends here. Lorraine loves Italy too."

"Yet in your biography there is not one single line regarding your Italian memories. Think how your Italian friends will feel when they read the Italian version . . ."

"Hey, but . . . are you sure? There's no mention of Italy in the book?"

I shook my head and he went on.

"But I remember my very first time in Italy like it was yesterday! It was even before I came with Jazz at the Philharmonic. I remember arriving at the airport and there was this band waiting for me, with Nunzio Rotondo and Carlo Loffredo . . ."

"What year was this?"

"Oh, I'd say in 1951. That's when I became friends with Nunzio and Carlo. Did Nunzio ever learn to speak English after all?"

"I don't think so."

"You know, it was really very funny the way we communicated. Neither one spoke the other's language so, while we were sitting together, Nunzio would suddenly jump up and rush to the nearest phone to call a girlfriend, who spoke English . . . no, I'm not kidding you. Anyway, he would tell her something in Italian on the phone, then pass me the receiver and this girl would say in English, 'Nunzio wants to tell you that . . .' (*Dizzy started laughing*), so I would answer her in English and pass the receiver back to Nunzio; I swear I'm not joking, that's exactly how it was. And, you know? This went on for years and years, always the same girl and always on the phone."

"But why didn't you just bring her along with the two of you?"

"I don't know!? For years it went on this way. Nunzio would say something in Italian, shake his head . . . and off to the phone!"

". . . with the two of you standing there, facing each other and not speaking directly? Madness!"

"Yes, yes! That's how it was! It was so funny . . . how we laughed! And then I remember the time we took Carlo Loffredo's mother to see the Pope. Think of it, to live in Rome and never have seen him! It was the Pope before Pope John, what was his name? He was a tall, thin guy."

"Well, Pope Pius XII was tall and thin with a very ascetic face . . ."

"Yeah, that's the Pope we went to see . . . and she had never seen him before. We had lots of laughs that day, and then we all went to their home. Ah, Rome . . ."

"What other Italian cities do you know? Ever been to Venice?"

"Yeah, sure. That's the city with all that water . . ."

"Well, you might describe it so . . ."

Poor Venice, reduced to a "city with all that water."

"Ah, and then Torino, Bergamo. . . . Wait, here's another funny story. I was coming from Paris to go to Bergamo and I was on this train by myself. I didn't know I was supposed to change trains in Milano so I just stood at the train window, looking around, and there was this guy with a beret that said 'Interpreter.' He asks me in English, 'Do you need a hand?'"

"No, no, thanks, I'm OK."

"And where are you off to?"

"To Bergamo."

"What?! Bergamo? Jump off the train immediately if you have to go to Bergamo!"

And he helped me get off and change trains. You can guess how we laughed! I've often wondered where the hell I'd have ended up if I'd stayed on that train."

"But with what band were you playing?"

"I think it was an Italian band because at the time I was on my own. Maybe with Romano Mussolini . . . must have been in the late fifties."

"Very well. Now, if you think of Italy what is the first thing that comes to your mind?"

"Sophia Loren! Hah, hah!"

"Have you any unpleasant memories happening in Italy?"

"No, I really can't think of anything unpleasant relating to Italy. I recall when I came with my own band, and Lorraine was with me. We played in that theater in Milano . . . could be the Teatro Nuovo? Anyway, I remember I had lots of fun with the Italians when I'd find out they didn't speak English. I would tell them lots of strange words, totally invented, and they would laugh. Once when I was with the stagehands I asked one of them, 'Hey, do you speak English?' and he said, 'No capish. . . .' The second one shook his head, the same with the third guy. So, looking bewildered at them, while they were laughing, I started exclaiming 'What? You mean none of you guys speaks a word of English?' and we went on like this, joking with my fake indignation, till Lorraine came to the door of my dressing room and told me, with that unmistakable voice of the wife who tells you off . . . she just said, 'Dizzy?!' And then you bet the stagehands understood English! They laughed like crazy! Just the tone of her voice was enough to straighten me up!"

"You said Lorraine enjoyed Italy?"

"She likes Italy very much. We were staying at the Hotel Duomo, nice place . . ."

"Tell me about the Italian public; have you always been happy with it?"

"Well, you know, Italians are a very particular people. Just think of the concert the other night when the rain ruined everything. I invited them to join me on the stage and it all went well, what more do you want? I don't know, I feel really at home among Italian people. It's as if I knew each one of them; there's a spontaneous link that's created between us."

"So you had no particular problems in Italy?"

"No . . . ah, but yes! Wait, you've gotta hear this. I was part of Jazz at the Philharmonic, and we were playing this theater in Rome. Stan Getz was playing, and I was to close the show. Stan gets a big hand of applause and, as the time is almost over, Norman Granz motions to Stan 'OK, that's it. Dizzy, get ready, you're on next . . .' and he walks out on stage to announce me with a long spiel in English. The public—maybe because they didn't like him—starts throwing coins at him. My god, did Norman get mad! 'That's it!' he said. 'Nothing more!' But I hadn't played yet, and the public was ready to tear down the theater, so I said to him, 'Hey Norman, I haven't played at all!' 'Damn! Well, go ahead and play just one number and then, no more!' So I went out, played my tune, got a lot of applause, and then withdrew backstage. Well, do you know that, to make a long story short, they had to call in the police to protect us? We stayed in that theater for over three hours, with a mad public waiting for us outside!"

"Yes but, as you said, it was because of Norman's special way of coming onstage with his raised eyebrows, talking endlessly in English when the public wanted to hear the musicians, not him!"

"Yeah . . . ah, Rome . . . I remember one night, maybe the same of that concert, when we went on the Via Veneto to Bricktop's. It was very nice. Via Veneto was really beautiful then . . ."

"Did you take part in the Italian 'Dolce Vita' of those times?"

"The what?"

"The 'Dolce Vita,' you know . . . the famous film by Federico Fellini, with private parties, sexy girls . . ."

"Hell no. All I saw of Italy was a row of hotels and theaters. Ah, yes, and I saw the Pope!"

"Do you notice any difference between today's public and the old one?"

"Well, yes. They are all very young today. And at that time, in the fifties, the Italian public was more oriented toward traditional jazz rather than avant-garde. I mean not like in Sweden, or Denmark, where bebop was really at home even then. Italy was definitely more for traditional jazz."

"But today you see many young people who do love bebop very much."

"You're right, and I'm very glad. After all, it's like the music is going round and round; sooner or later you've got to get back to bop. Yes . . . the Italian public is really very warm—look at the other night, how disappointed they were when the sound equipment had gone for good, because of the storm. I got them to climb onstage and they were very cool. Actually, it was Bobby Redcross and the other guys who were nervous and scared. It didn't matter if once in a while some guy would get up to stretch his legs or smoke a joint . . ."

"Ah, by the way; that evening they offered you something . . . when you bent down toward the public on the edge of the stage, right?"

"Right! A big pipe full of hash! I was wondering what it was and that guy just offered it to me. I smelled it and gave it back . . . hell, it was hash!"

"I thought so. Unfortunately, in Italy we have a big problem with the heavy drugs. Many kids lose their lives."

"It's what happens in the States, you know? Over there if some guy has an urgent need of a dose, and if he's very sick, he could even harm his own mother just to get it."

"And what's the solution?"

"Perhaps if they could obtain it without harming anyone else . . . maybe helped by the State itself . . . who would then take them in hand to help them get cleaned up. Well, if after that you really want to kill yourself, then that's your own business. But I'll tell you something. There's too much money involved in the drug business. And every time there's too many dollars involved, you can be sure of one thing. They'll look for every possible way to fight it, except the right one."

"You're right. But let's talk of something lighter—some other memory, some other name?"

"Romano Mussolini. I was very impressed when we first met, especially because he was the son of Benito, obviously. And do you know he invited me to his wedding, with the sister of Sophia Loren? I believe she was a singer too. Are they still married?"

"With Maria? Unfortunately not. I like Maria very much; she's a very sweet young woman and did sing rather well. But I'm not sure she really tried for a career."

"Ah, I have another memory, when I think about Italy . . . the food!"

"I'd never have guessed . . ."

"I tell you, I discovered that in Italy they love to watch you eat and enjoy your food, and that's beautiful. There's that restaurant in Bologna . . . can't think of the name now but, I'm telling you, the food is really fabulous there. Now, you know that we usually eat whenever it's possible. It can be two in the morning or four in the afternoon, depending on the gig. So we were in Bologna to play a concert and then off again, and it was six in the afternoon. So I rush out of the hotel, get to the famous place . . . and it's not open yet. Closed to the public! Very disappointed, but, seeing some people moving inside, I start knocking and calling till they come to the door. I explain that I can't wait for the evening but if I cannot eat at their place I cannot say I have tasted a real meal in Bologna, worthy of its name. Anyway, the owner comes to the door, unlocks it, and invites me in. He leads me to the kitchen where they are just setting up the fires and he asks me what I would like to eat. Well, do you know that those wonderful people cooked just for me? And served me this marvelous meal in the main dining room, where I reigned all by myself? Ah, what a lovely memory I have of those people! It's something that could only have happened in Italy. Certainly not in New York! In Italy they have human warmth; Italians have a heart. If they see you have a problem, they will help you in any possible way. Give you anything you need. While in some other countries you can be sure they will help "remove" from you any possible thing. Oh yes, when I come to Italy it warms my heart. I am really sorry I did not mention Italy in my book, but it's not for lack of affection, it's more because my memory, my souvenirs, need to be held up by the memories of my friends. You know, I spend my life flying from one place to another, and in the end I have a hard time remembering."

"It's understandable. Now, have you ever been to Sicily?"

"Sure! That's where I got my collection of 'Jew's harps.' Do you know I used to play it as a kid? But when I listened to those Sicilian harps . . . wow! Boy, they were perfection, not like the American ones. So I got myself a whole box in Palermo, but now I have only four left. I've got to return to Sicily to get another box."

"The proper name in Italy is not Jew's harp but Marranzano."

"M-a-r-a-n-z-a-n-o?"

"Right, except it has two r's."

"Marranzano . . . I remember when I saw them in that little shop . . . and when I tried them . . . I said to myself 'Ah-ha! This is something else; this is the sound I need . . .' I think I'll make a whole record with the . . . marranzano . . . what do you think?"

"It would be very . . . interesting! But tell me, how come you played a Sicilian instrument while living in the Deep South? Have you ever lived near an Italian community?"

"Yes, but not as a kid. About fifteen years ago we lived in Corona, in New York State, where also Louis Armstrong used to live. I remember this little Italian shoemaker, on my street, with whom I had become friends. Every time I came home from my tours I would go look him up, sooner or later, and have a talk. Yeah, he hadn't the slightest idea of who I was. To him I was just a neighbor with whom to share a bottle of wine, homemade by him. And he would fix my shoes with his magic hands. One day I tell him I'm going to Europe and what would he like me to bring him back? 'A Borsalino hat!' When I got back to the States I gave it to him, but I would not take his money; we were just good friends. Anyway, one day I come home from a tour and find his shop is closed. So I ask his neighbor at the candy store: 'Where's Frank?'"

"'He has a bad heart, so he's shut his shop and gone to live with his daughter in the Bronx. Here's her phone number.' So I call her: 'Is Frank there, please?'"

"Yes, can I ask who is calling?"

"Dizzy Gillespie."

"She drops the receiver, amazed, and I hear her asking her father, 'What? You know Dizzy Gillespie?' He comes to the phone: 'Who's this? Dizzy who?' I explain to him who I am and in the end he says, 'Ah, sure! Gillespie, my next door neighbor. . . . So you are . . . YOU?' How we laughed! He'd never had any idea of who I was; we were simply good neighbors. Great old man. He was Sicilian."

"And when is it that you and Lorraine will come to Italy, simply as a couple of tourists?"

"Well . . . not as long as I'm playing . . . but I'll tell you something. I've bought a piece of land with Kenny Clarke on the French Riviera, and that's where Lorraine and I want to end up staying. It's close enough for us to come to Italy, visit our friends, and eat the food."

"But you still don't speak either French or Italian?"

"Ah, but do you know the first word I learned in Italy, over thirty years ago . . . ?"

"Is it something to do with food?"

"No, no. There were all these beautiful Italian girls who had me jump out of the car window, so guess what words my Italian friends taught me . . . to shout at the girls in Rome . . . ?"

Remembering our first TV meeting I mock-frowned at him, to his delight.

"Yeah! Bbona! Hah, hah . . . Aah Bbbooonaaah!"

The interview ended there.

ACT VIII—CUBANO!

Dizzy enjoyed traveling using the Venice airport. Driving there in time for us to sit down in the comfortable waiting section and sip one last "outgoing cappuccino" plus cigar, we would comment on the past events and the next meeting to come. This time I commented on his headgear, which was, as always, very particular.

"By the way, Giovanni; you have the widest variety of hats, caps, berets, African headdresses, et cetera—now where on earth did you get THAT cap? It looks just like the one Fidel Castro wears!"

He gave me an amused, clever, little smile and then an offhand reply: "Well, yes. Fidel gave me this cap himself, in exchange for my cowboy hat . . ."

"Sure. And that's one of his personal Cuban cigars you're smoking, of course?"

A long side-look at me, then he carefully drew some snapshots from his wallet and handed them to me, in silence. There they were, grinning and pointing at each other, each with a fat cigar in his hand. Fidel was wearing a Stetson and Dizzy donning the famous cap. He then handed me a cigar with a gold band, where I read "Dizzy," very briefly, for he put it jealously away in the special humidor portable case. Always silent, he puffed on his cigar with a satisfied smile.

"But how did you manage to get permission from the U.S. government to go to Cuba at all? I thought it was strictly forbidden for U.S. citizens to go there?"

"Right; but I've been going every year, invited by the Cuban Jazz Festival authorities, and by Castro himself. No problem."

"No, really now . . . wasn't there a total embargo to visit Cuba? I mean . . ."

He interrupted me, and for the first time I saw a very sober man.

"Sure there was, and they tried to stop me the first time. But I told the State Department that if Eisenhower had chosen me—and used me—in 1956, as the first jazz musician to lead an orchestra to go on goodwill tours in countries where America was not too popular . . ."

"You mean the famous State Department Cultural Mission all over the world?"

"That's right; we were to represent the 'democratic spirit' with a racially mixed big band. They sent us to Africa, the Near East, Middle East and Asia, including India . . ."

"And you were the very first artist to be chosen?"

"Right, it was Adam Powell in Washington who convinced Eisenhower that we could smooth things out through our music, if we played for the very crowds who were protesting and throwing stones at our embassies all over the world."

"And you did? I mean . . . smooth things out?"

"You bet, though at times it was scary . . . but mostly because they would have us play in the embassies or other U.S.-controlled venues, and the public would be made up of chosen guests while the little people were protesting outside. It was also because the organizers were selling tickets that were much too expensive. So you know what I did, in Karachi? I got a huge bunch of tickets from the impresario and just went outside and gave them away! And whenever possible we would go out to the parks, the markets, wherever, and we joked and started playing for the people, and it worked fine. We went to Persia, Lebanon, Syria, Pakistan, Turkey, and Greece."

"And did you hold press conferences, debates on jazz history, or talk about the American way of life?"

"They had Marshall Stearns for that. He lectured on jazz in the various schools and colleges. As for the American way of life. . . ." He shook in his silent laugh and nudged me: "You want to know? The State Department was worried as hell about my 'unpredictable' behavior, so they kept asking me to go to Washington, before the tour, in order to 'brief me.' But I was already on tour in Europe, so they got hold of Lorraine, asking her to convince me to come back for a few days. I told Lorraine to inform them I needed no briefing. I knew *all* about the American way of life and what it's done to us for hundreds of years! So if anyone asked me particular questions, I would give them an honest answer."

"However, I know the results were highly appreciated by Eisenhower. You were given a special plaque at a special dinner at the White House, weren't you?"

This time he laughed outright. "Yeah, and some of the guys still kid me. About when the President started giving around these plaques calling each one by name. I was away from the stand so I didn't hear him at first till he called my name real loud, so I went forward waving to him and calling out: 'Right over here, Pops!'"

"You didn't! Pops?!"

"Well, he didn't mind 'cause that was the start of a whole series of tours for the State Department; in fact we went to South America soon after."

"Was that when you went to Cuba for the first time?"

"No, Cuba was something else. I had always wanted to go there. I think Cuba became special to me because of Chano Pozo. He made me discover a whole new rhythmical world right there in New York. He knew nothing about jazz; he was really African with his congas, and he got us all standing there like dumb kids, watching and listening to him play. He taught us what multi-rhythm was all about with those Cuban chants, each one from a different African root. I learned about the Nañigo, the Santo, the Ararra, and that's when I learned to play the congas. Chano taught me. He didn't speak English, he didn't know anything about jazz rhythm, but he taught all of us, starting with Gil Fuller, when we all worked on 'Manteca.' And Chano worked also with George Russell for 'Cubana Be—Cubana Bop.' It was really magic; it was the birth of Afro-Cuban Jazz."

"But then what happened? Suddenly there was no Chano Pozo anymore?"

"Well, one day Chano went back to Cuba 'for some business,' he said. Seems he was involved in bad stuff with the wrong people. When he came back to New York, he got shot to death. It was a great loss for our music. In fact, I would like to be able to open a school in Cuba as a living monument to him."

"But you still haven't told me how you got permission to break the embargo rules?"

"Well . . . I told the guys in Washington that after all those Cultural Diplomatic tours for the State Department for all those years . . . after that service, the least they could do was give me a free exit and entry visa back to the U.S. from anywhere in the world! So they did, and after that I've been going to Cuba whenever possible."

"Good for you! It must be great to play in Cuba with all those musicians who look up to you from the time of Chano Pozo. I organized a concert last month with Arturo Sandoval and his incredible musicians, and there's no doubt as to who inspires him!"

"Arturo plays great trumpet. In fact, I've obtained for him to come and visit me in the States and play with me. And if I can, I'll get him a green card. He deserves it, and I'd love to have him in a future big band."

"Tell me: of the young emerging musicians in Cuba, who would you say impressed you the most?"

"Ah, I know! There's this very young cat playing piano . . . Gonzalo Rubalcaba. You keep his name in mind, he's sure to emerge worldwide."

"Gonzalo Rubalcaba. OK, noted."

An announcement brought our conversation to an end.

"Ah, there we are, they're calling your flight. Give my love to Lorraine. I'll send you the clippings soon as I have them all in hand."

We exchanged a hug as I continued: "So your Italian barber can read them to you . . . or you to him . . . you're practically an Italian by now . . ."

ACT IX—ANOTHER RADIO INTERVIEW

In 1982 Dizzy discovered Italian soccer through my son's enthusiasm for the Italian "Squadra Azzurra" and Paolo Rossi. It took place during the Jazz Festival at Lido degli Estensi, near Ravenna, on the very day of the Spanish World Cup finals, when Italy was to face Western Germany.

I spoke to Dizzy about the famous Italian football coach, Enzo Bearzot, a great jazz fan who tried to train the national football team to play together with the same "feeling" that links together a jazz band. He had also confessed to sneaking away to New York every year to "fill up with lots of good jazz."

Out of curiosity, Dizzy settled himself next to Francesco in the crowded hotel TV room, among the other excited fans, and before long he was caught up in the general enthusiasm and was rooting for Italy. To their great satisfaction Italy beat Germany 3 to 1, winning the World Cup.

In Ravenna I proposed a radio interview, and Dizzy accepted willingly. With a cappuccino warming his hands, we were off:

"Apart from your music, which other things really interest you? I mean, what do you do with your free time?"

"Well, I sleep a lot . . . sure, go ahead and smile; however, I've got fresh news for you. Maybe you don't know this, but they are building a Dizzy Gillespie Center, for the cost of two and a half million dollars . . ."

"And where is this taking place?"

"In Laurinburg, South Carolina."

"Wasn't that your old school?"

"Yeah, that's where I studied as a kid—and listen to the idea that they worked out in order to collect the money. It's rather original, I would say unique. It will be a Center for the Arts, Communication, and Teaching. With a theater and a permanent library that will gather all my papers and documents. Then there'll be a gallery of famous names."

"What about the money?"

"Wait now. Right on the front of the building they'll put a small bust of myself, placed right on top of a wall of bricks, and every single brick will have a number carved on it and inside the building there'll be a panel with the corresponding number and the name of anyone who wishes to become a founding associate . . . It will cost five thousand dollars for each brick."

"And you've already started gathering members?"

"Norman Granz was the first one and George Wein; then Quincy Jones, Lionel Hampton, Morris Levy, which makes five. Then Oscar Cohen of ABC Associated Agency, Willard Alexander . . ."

"Apart from Quincy and Lionel, they are mostly promoters, organizers, and agents, aren't they?"

"Yeah, and it won't be difficult to sell those bricks because I know I have that kind of friends with that kind of money. Another thing, always inside, for those who have less bread, like me, there will be bricks for twenty-five dollars . . . and everything will be computerized with an information center. You'll press a button and have your answer."

"And what'll be the objective of such an institute?"

"Well, when it's completed, all my friends will want to give part of their time to teach there."

"Now that's a beautiful idea; have you already started construction?"

"No, not yet; right now we are simply putting the money together."

"It will take a few years then . . . ?"

"Yeah, but I'll be hanging around, keeping busy. I'm not going anywhere else."

"What about your plan to retire to the south of France and build a house next to Klook?"

"Well, right now I have the land next to him; all I need is the money to build the house . . . and that will take some four or five more years, I think. Lorraine likes the idea; she likes France."

"Let's talk about Lorraine. There's always a great woman behind a great man, they say. And from your autobiography I get the impression that she has always been your backbone, providing the firm ground on which you've been able to skip and hop at will."

"Lorraine is the anchor and I am the sail . . ."

"And how long has it been since she last came abroad with you? I get the impression that she would rather stay home and enjoy the house, the privacy. But you, being always on tour . . . how much time would you say you spend at home?"

"Not enough, but next year I intend to shorten my activity."

"And what will you do?"

"I'll enjoy my house. I'll have lots of things to do."

"Talking of things to do . . . it's been a long time since you've composed any new music or written those arrangements for which you are famous. I mean, after all, there is a whole Dizzy Gillespie world of music. Why did you stop? Too lazy?"

"Well, that's one of the reasons, I guess, my laziness. But I do have something special in mind. You see, as you know, I belong to the Bahá'í faith, which preaches unity in all the aspects of the Universe. Unity in diversity. And this includes music. Well, in the music of the Western Hemisphere, the one I know best . . . and I'm talking of Cuba, Brazil, the West Indies, and the United States . . . this music has its own unity, and I mean to put it together in such a way that when it will be played, you won't be able to say this is Cuban and this is something else. Music has only one mother . . . and that's what I'll work on, during my free time. . . . Like a United Nations band."

"Have you started working on it, or is it just an intention?"

"Well, I know exactly what to do; all I need now is the time to do it."

"Tell us a little more about Lorraine."

"Lorraine is probably the most incorruptible person on the face of earth. For her there are only two solutions to a problem: the right one and the wrong one. There are no halfway solutions for her, and at times this is a positive fact . . . but at times it isn't."

A small wry smile as he goes on: "I'm not saying she has the answer to all the problems of humanity, but she's the one who comes closest to the solution of many human problems. You know what would be her favorite pastime? Honest? Her greatest joy would be to be a real multimillionaire . . . and then give away all her money in the best way according to her ideas. That's what she would like. She never wants anything for herself, nothing at all; she's extraordinary, you know? After over forty-one years of marriage—we celebrated our anniversary on May 9th . . ."

"And were you together for the occasion?"

"No, I was on tour . . . but she and I know that some things have to be done, there's no problem . . ."

"Did you get her an adequate present?"

"No, but I'll tell you . . . I was waiting to come here, close to the Vatican to get her something special. Maybe you could help me. She's a very fervent Catholic as you know . . . and I thought I might perhaps find something that Christ used to carry around in His pockets . . ."

I gave a gasp, then burst out laughing "Oh, Diz, come on!"

"Yes, yes, don't laugh . . . that would really be something . . ."

"Yes, something special and most uncommon and very precious, I'm sure! But I hardly think they would sell it, even if such an item existed . . ."

"You think He had no pockets?"

"If He did, whatever He was 'carrying around' in them would not be for sale!"

"Yeah . . . I guess not . . . ," he smiled wryly "Well, then I'll have to get her a gift really worthy of her. It's no good just going to a jeweler and bringing her a piece of jewelry . . ."

"No, I guess it would have to be something very special and personal."

"Once I brought her a rosary made up of gold pearls, eighteen-karat gold and every pearl had a different sculpture. . . . It was really a wonderful object."

"Is Lorraine a very religious woman?"

"Ah, yessir! She is Catholic and very active."

"And what does she think of the fact that you are Bahá'í?"

"She doesn't understand it, but she respects me and recognizes that each one must make his own decision regarding his relationship with God."

"By the way, you and Lorraine have never had any children, right? Have you any other person . . . like some youngster, a nephew, someone you might have adopted sentimentally?"

"We have two of them, which we adopted. Today they are adults, and we help them financially. It's easy to help your family, Lorraine says, but you need a kind heart to help a stranger."

"How very true. Now, let's get back to the Bahá'í philosophy. What attracted you to their doctrine?"

"It's the philosophy on the unity of human beings. Their teachings are based on the following theme: Humanity has gone through many generations, and three epochs have been fixed in the evolution of man. The first was the concept of Family, then came the linking of the Tribe, then came the Cities, the States, and the national Governments. All this was done. Now the next logical step is the unifying of all these various components, and this is the aim of the Bahá'í: a World Commonwealth where everybody would participate."

"Yes, but isn't it just a very beautiful Utopia? How do you make it come about concretely?"

"With an administrative organization, like the one the Bahá'í already have. It would be enough for the rest of the world to refer to it. It had been hard to create the Family, and then it was difficult to put together the Tribe. As for the Nations, we are still making a mess of it today. But we can still obtain the final goal, with God's grace, because what will happen is this: With the fact that most nations have nuclear power, nobody seems to be afraid of his neighbor, and they wouldn't think twice of throwing an atom bomb. The United States have already done so since 1945. So there really is no other way to save ourselves but to have unity among the people of the world."

"Yes, but how long will it take?"

"That's not what is important . . ."

"Maybe you and I will no longer be around?"

"Not necessarily—something could happen in the future that would force them all to reconsider. . . . The idea is to love humanity enough to realize this project. Whether you can directly participate or not is not what's important."

"But then wouldn't it be a political action?"

"No, no! We Bahá'í are not authorized to move politically, but we must give these ideas to the people, get them to think about it. We do not have a clerical hierarchy, or preachers, et cetera. . . . We are all equal; our way of acting is through the contact person to person."

"How many countries host Bahá'í groups?"

"There are about 200 countries in the world. [The Bahá'í] teach that all religions are really one. The difference is in the various epochs. There is the message Moses gave, then the one from Jesus and also the other religious leaders. The message is really the same. The difference is only in the social order, which goes with that *one* religion that is most appropriate for the times in which it appears. Each religion taught the best way to live in its time, and each time has its message."

"But do you have a leader, like we have the Pope, for instance?"

"We've had a Guardian of the Faith; he was the nephew of the First Prophet, but he died in 1959 and is buried in London. He decided that there would be no other Guardian after him. He simply left us the instructions that were given by the First Prophet."

"And the religion is spread worldwide?"

"Yes, we are a sort of huge world family. Wherever I go, like if I see some flowers in my hotel room? I know who sent them, before I read the card."

"That's right! There were those flowers at your hotel in Bari, from 'Gianni' and that nice family who came to the theater to say hullo . . ."

"Yes, the Bahá'í brothers always come to say hullo to me wherever I'm playing in the world. One large prefabricated family . . ."

"It's very interesting. And now let's talk of your future. Is there still something you would like to tackle in the time ahead? Or are you really thinking of retiring to the French countryside?"

"There's no time for peaceful retirement. . . . I guess as a last activity I'll take up teaching."

"Have you any plans? Will you write texts, print your own Method?"

"Well . . ." he mused. "You know, there's the video . . . could be a good means for the new generations. Yeah, but right now . . . I'll tell you, all I have in mind is to play!"

At that, he grabbed the case containing his trumpet and opened it, laid out a hand towel neatly on a side table on which he deposited the various cleaning items he needed. Then he proceeded to take his instrument totally apart.

ACT X—A SYMPHONIC GILLESPIE

One evening I asked if—after having done so much; having been acclaimed all over the world as a Jazz Ambassador for the State Department; having wined and dined with presidents from Eisenhower to practically the latest man in the White House—there was still a secret wish, hidden in a corner of his heart, which had not yet materialized?

He looked at me musingly with his head to one side, pulling at his lower lip, and then leaned over to answer confidentially: "You know one thing I've never been able to do? Play my music with a large, but laaarge, *real* symphonic orchestra right here in Europe."

"Wow! That's a tall order! You know how stuffy and longhaired they are . . ."

"I know, I know . . . they've been trying for years to approach one of these European outfits; I've got some symphonic arrangements ready, but nothing's happening."

His downcast musing touched me.

"Giovanni, I can't promise you anything, for it really is difficult to make a breach in their walls. Years ago I was asked to organize a concert at the Vatican where Ellington was to play his last Sacred Concert for the Pope. We almost made it, then something drastic, like "Famine in India," came up, and it all went down the drain. But the Italian RAI TV has three different symphonic orchestras, in Rome, Milano, and Torino. I'm not promising you anything yet, and it may take a year or two, but who knows . . . one day I might be Mistress of Ceremonies at your symphonic concert somewhere in Italy?"

Giving me his amused-evaluating look, he patted my hand: "You know something? You remind me so much of Lorraine, you could be her kid sister. When you girls talk, you can tell there's no bullshit. Do you knit?"

Taken aback, I replied, hesitatingly: "Well, yes, actually I do."

"You make dresses, sweaters, coats?"

"Yes . . ."

"And caps and berets?" I nodded and he was delighted: "Just like Lorraine, I knew it! Wait till I tell her. You two girls would get on like a house on fire. . . ." He hesitated; eyeing me, then shook his head: "Nah. . . . Better the two of you never got together . . . you'd gang up on me and I'd be in reeeeeal trouble!"

But when he went home, he did speak to Lorraine about this young woman in Rome who "took no bullshit from him." That was the beginning of a long-distance friendship between us, and through the years there would be many telephone conversations, and many were the points we had in common; from our Catholic religion to our various allergies, the knitting, the love for our house, and the look-out for Dizzy's feeding weaknesses—which would become ever more dangerous as his diabetes progressed. When we finally did meet in person, it was as matter of fact as if we had dined together the previous evening.

Dear Lorraine . . . I wonder if she ever realized how very important she has always been to Dizzy. There was not one single day, when Dizzy was away from home, that he would not phone her from any far corner of the world. If I was present he would dial her number and pass me the phone, immediately whispering, "Here, let's surprise her, you talk to her, say something in Arabic!" Whereupon I would say, darkly, "Al Salaam aleikum," and she would answer: "Oh hullo Lilian, how are you? Have you tried that allergy medicine yet?" and off we would start chatting, while Dizzy would raise his eyes to heaven. I was very impressed with the relationship between them. They seemed so different from each other as to be living proof that opposites can live together in harmony.

One aspect I most enjoyed in Lorraine was her humorously critical way of speaking about Dizzy. I would phone at 10 A.M. Englewood time, and she would inform me that he had already gone out on his "tour" of the village.

"He's worse than a streetwalker, the way he knows every man on the street. Takes him hours just to get from one block to the other! Lord knows what he has to say to them, but at least he's out of my hair, 'cause he's a real mess at home!"

Another time he had just returned home from an overseas tour and had already left for California. To my surprise she had commented:

"I tell you, Lilian, I see more of his ass going out the door than I see his face coming in!" It was always entertaining to speak to Lorraine. We would laugh at our mutual allergies, commiserating with each other and exchanging medical suggestions from our respective experience; then we would talk of the remodeling of their home, which seemed to be taking an incredible length of time. It went on through the years, and just when it seemed about done, some other part of the house would fall into urgent need of repair. This seemed to aggravate Lorraine as much as it amused Dizzy.

"Sure," she would say. "He's out the door the moment he gets back; he doesn't have to handle it!"

At times it would seem as if she were really annoyed at him, and I do imagine he was not always easy to have around, more like a turbulent offspring to heed, curb, and console. But in a world where couples meet and seem to get married for the pleasure of divorcing as soon as possible, it was a constant wonder and encouragement to see how the years had welded their union into something as solid as it seemed matter of fact. It was Lorraine and Dizzy—then, of course, the rest of the world.

Thankfully, after the disappointment caused by Mondadori cancelling the publication of his autobiography—and after more than two years of discussions—I was able to give him good news about another project just as important to him. He was probably grinning on the phone upon hearing that, with the help of Simona and Toni Lama, producers well placed in the Torino RAI TV network, we had obtained—after much discussion, long meetings, hesitations, and misgivings—that he should play with the famous RAI Symphonic Orchestra of Torino in a special concert to be aired both on national radio and TV.

Shortly afterward I joined him in Paris for his sixty-fifth birthday on October 21, 1982, and he firmly accepted the engagement and promised to compose—after twenty years of silence—a special suite for the occasion. It was agreed that he would come to Italy with his jazz quintet, which would play the second half of the concert while an experienced director, of his choice, would conduct the Symphonic-Orchestra-plus-Quintet during the first half.

So began a series of letters, asking for detailed information, essential to the network organizers, but which never arrived.

On June 9, 1982, I wrote:

> Giovanni, my dear; please let me know *soon* the following facts:
>
> The program and the formation of your quintet. Perhaps Klook, if his health is up to it, and Stitt or Moody? Eddie Daniels also sounded very good with you in Nice. Last month, in New York, you mentioned Tom MacIntosh to direct the orchestra. As for the symphonic arrangements, could I suggest one by Lalo Schifrin for the Gillespiana Suite? Or George Russell with Cubana Be Cubana Bop? Also, Kush with the symphonic brass would be excellent. These famous works are mostly unknown by the younger generations here. Of course, you could take some time off at the end of your European tour in July and be our guest, with Lorraine, at our country house near Venice, where we could be joined by Simona and Tony Lama to work out the final details.
>
> How is the Laurinburg project coming on? And are you really taking it easier this year, as you had planned to do? Take care of yourself and slow down the pace; it's worth it. Please answer soon so we can get on with the organization. We've been talking about this symphonic concert for

> almost three years now, and at last we have this Torino opening—let's fix it, OK? All the best to both of you from mother, myself, and Francesco, who is here from USC for the holidays with all sorts of electronic gadgets, just like you, so that music blares at us all day long from all over the house. Ah well. Ciao Gillespo.

I received no written reply from him, of course. From the tone of our phone conversations I suspected he still did not really believe this operation would finally come through. But things were indeed moving on. Foremost was the fact that the Torino RAI director-general, Emilio Pozzi, was a fan of Dizzy's. He had one formal request: Dizzy should compose a special suite for the occasion. Naughty Dizzy readily accepted and announced the creation of the "Bella Italia Suite 1983"—which, in the end, turned out to be a series of his most recent tunes that had not yet been played in Italy.

At one time I wrote to him, but particularly to Lorraine, begging her to see that he complied with the conditions of the contract. The letter requested, among other information:

> Last two points: as we have to give all details in advance, almost to the color of your socks, according to the stiff RAI regulations, I have given the names of the quintet as you mentioned, as well as the program, and—most important—I have told them you were already preparing a new suite dedicated to Italy, after all these many years of lazy absence from the writing table. So sit right down and start fiddling with your piano, capito? Incidentally, Polillo and other jazz critics, both in Italy and Europe, are extremely interested to hear your new work. "Why . . . does he still write? I thought he only played by now." So you'll "sock it to them!" Please?
>
> You will probably be contacted in the United States by Toni Lama, who will be taking care of all administrative problems regarding your contract, transfer of funds, working permits, etc. Please tell me if you are satisfied with all details?

Of course, he didn't write back but left a phone message with my mother: "Tell Lilian it is 'Yes' to everything."

Finally, he did meet Tony Lama in New York to sign the contract. So we proceeded with the overall organization. On April 1, 1983, he received a final letter with reiterated details and recommendations:

> The RAI Torino program and posters for the whole concert season have been published and they include your jazz concert as part of the official

Symphonic Concert Season 1983. Simona Lama will send you copies as soon as they are available. Your seats have been booked for May 9th. I'm off on a brief tour—yes, found the time to sing again—and will call you by mid-April. Ciao, Giovanni Cappuccino!

ACT XI—LIKE VON KARAJAN

On May 10, 1983, we went to pick up Dizzy and his musicians at the Milano Malpensa Airport, as well as my son Francesco, who had flown in from USC to put himself totally at his Maestro's disposal during this symphonic adventure. Taking advantage of the fact that RAI was paying all expenses, we surprised Dizzy. All our rooms were reserved in a good-range hotel, except for his VIP suite in *the* hotel, just across from us.

"For once you are going to be treated like royalty, Maestro Gillespo, and just as Ellington would have all the band, including Mercer, stay at a good hotel across from the Rome Excelsior, where he had the best suite, so will you wallow in luxurious service as if you were von Karajan. Aren't you happy?"

He made a face and sighed, "I guess so, but what about everybody being together? I'm going to be real lonely in this place . . ."

During the next four days in Torino, rehearsing and then playing the two concerts, Dizzy would sigh resignedly as we all accompanied him to the marble lobby of his hotel, wishing him a good night with ostentatious deference; and every morning he would appear at our table to have breakfast with us, escaping the rarefied atmosphere of his own hotel. However, looking back at those days, every time he would remember the Torino experience he would give me a little nudge and chuckle, "You sure took good care of me . . . von Karajan, hah!"

On Dizzy's first day in Torino the RAI TV Press Office had organized a very formal press conference with reporters and critics from both the jazz and classic music milieu. I sat on the dais, between Dizzy and Tom MacIntosh, to translate for both of them. It all went very smoothly while Tom described the suites that would be played with the RAI Symphonic Orchestra: they were "Con Alma," arrangements by Robert Farnon; "A Night in Tunisia," orchestrated by J. J. Johnson; and a symphonic metamorphosis on the theme of "Algo Bueno" by Tom McIntosh. With his quintet, Dizzy would then play the "Bella Italia Suite 1983," composed for the occasion. Tom was also patiently efficient in answering the veiled ironic questions that some "classic music" critic would put to him. On my left, aware of it all, sat a very bored Dizzy, expecting the usual trite old questions he had heard for too many years.

Familiar with his reactions, I gave each answer directly, the way we had agreed upon on past occasions until came the fatal question of why he used a "bent" trumpet, and unfortunately it was asked by the ironical classic music reporter mentioned above.

Before I could give the usual explanation, Dizzy clamped his hand on my arm and moved forward to his microphone:

"I'll tell you how it happened. Some smart-ass guy who kept bugging me with his smart-ass questions came too close to me on that day, so I just stuck my trumpet up his smart-ass and gave the bell a twist. That's how it happened!"

There was a loud gasp and giggles from those reporters who spoke English. A silence followed while Dizzy smiled broadly at me shifting his microphone toward me:

"Go on . . ."

Once again I smiled and explained that Dizzy had just given an improvised answer to a question that really bored him to tears; however, the real reason for the shape was . . . et cetera.

Another incident happened later, when—Dizzy having rehearsed with the quintet formed by pianist Bobby Rodriguez, drummer Bernard Purdy, bassist Michael Howell, and Big Black on the congas—came the time for Tom McIntosh to take matters in hand and insert the quintet with the full symphonic orchestra to rehearse the special arrangements created for the occasion. I was backstage when Francesco came to me and murmured:

"Ma, trouble ahead. . . . It seems Dizzy's pianist does not read music at all, so he can't play the symphonic arrangements . . ."

Speechless, I rushed out to face an aloof pianist, and a sheepish Dizzy who widened his arms in apologetic despair.

"Lil, he's a brilliant pianist, so I just didn't . . . I mean, he never said anything when I spoke of symphonic arrangements to be played . . ."

For once Dizzy was at a loss, though he tried a crack at how I was giving him the "Lorraine" look. Tom McIntosh, lowered eyes, just kept shuffling through the pages, asking the orchestra if everybody had his music. . . . The symphonic musicians were all young, a number of them American, and they all looked forward to playing a symphonic Gillespie. Spying their pianist seated idly at his instrument, I was blessed by an inspiration. Grabbing Dizzy, I led him over to the pianist:

"Maestro; Dizzy has a special request for you. He is so happy to be playing with this wonderful orchestra that he would like to keep it complete, as it is. He would like to substitute his own pianist with you. Would you accept his invitation?"

"Signora Terry, I am a fan of Maestro Gillespie, I'll be honored to play with him."

Dizzy laughed his relief, patted the young man's shoulder, and then demanded that we start rehearsals immediately! What were we waiting for?

". . . annow . . . laydees an' gennelmen . . ."

On Thursday, May 12, and Friday, May 13, 1983, at 6:00 P.M., Dizzy Gillespie's first and only concerts with a full European Symphonic Orchestra took place. On the second evening—which was announced as the "6th Concert of the Spring

Season"—while watching from the wings we were amused to see the Symphonic Auditorium filled with the habitual "classic music" season-ticket holders, mostly older ladies with pearls, sitting primly next to noisy jazz fans.

There was no reason to worry, though, for Dizzy was at his most brilliant, fascinating, scintillating self, and by the end of that concert both the "pearls" and the fans were calling for encores, which he conceded graciously. The concert ended with an improvised "Torino Mama Blues" with his quintet, where, clinging on the tip of his toes to the microphone—which was fixed up to the height of his trumpet bell—he sang at the top of his rough voice, informing all and sundry that this "Torino Mama Blues" was dedicated to the RAI director Emilio Pozzi (pronounced *Eemilio* by Dizzy), who had made his "symphonic concert in Europe" a dream come true. And then he closed singing: "And if it wasn't for Lilian Terry, I wouldn't be here at all . . . !"

The thundering and amused applause, alas, triggered his unpredictable nature. Having just left the stage with his musicians, he caught us all by surprise by springing back onto the stage. Calling me to join him, he drew from the pocket of his elegant Italian silk suit . . . his beloved Sicilian-marranzano-Jew's-harp and instructed me to inform the public that he would play, as a last solo encore, a "Sicilian Serenade" FOR them and WITH them. Yes, for at given moments during the performance he would wiggle his brows at them while making a music break, and I would lead them to sing out—and mind the rhythm—the phrase "Watch that Booty!" and he would then resume playing.

In disbelief I muttered, "Come now, Dizzy, you can't ask *this* public . . . ," but of course I had no option but to translate his presentation. He called for their attention and actually "rehearsed" them a few times. . . . To make it short: it was an amazing—and fortunately brief—performance where Dizzy would huff and puff rhythmically on his marranzano, then at a certain point he would wiggle at me, nodding in time, and I would lift my arm and "conduct" rhythmically the whole auditorium to sing out with him whatever they had understood of his phrase.

It struck one as typical of the man who, having brought to a close an excellent symphonic concert, would feel this impish urge to have a long-haired symphonic audience sing and laugh with him and his Sicilian marranzano. You can imagine the applause, laughter, and shouts while I ran away before he could think up some other prank.

That night Emilio Pozzi, with all the Italian officials involved in the musical effort, offered us an extraordinary dinner, and Dizzy's satisfaction shone on his face as compliments were lavished on him from all sides and all through the dinner. Yes, he was truly at the happiest peak of the evening, and as we hugged goodnight, later, in the icy marble hall of his hotel, he held me at arm's length and said: "Liliah-nah, you, I love!" and gave me a noisy kiss on the cheek.

The French Riviera

Considering it had rained every single day and night in Torino—with Dizzy wishing us goodnight, saying, "Tomorrow, I promise you the sunshine"—we were delighted to learn that we were expected at another RAI studio, this time on the sunny French Riviera. The next day we would be driving from Torino to Cannes, to the site of the film festival where Dizzy would be interviewed by Gianni Minà, jazz fan and TV personality.

At that time there were still frontier posts between Italy and France, at Ventimiglia. Our car, containing Dizzy, Emilio Pozzi, Tom McIntosh, Francesco, and myself, was rapidly waved through, with Dizzy receiving the usual smiles and waves of recognition by the frontier guards. We noticed, however, that the second car with the other musicians was not following. We could see there was some form of heated argument going on, so we drove back to the Italian post to discover that our jazz pianist had another surprise in store for us. His Philippine passport had just expired that very day. He was caught between the two nations and neither France nor Italy would let him pass either way. We could not help chuckling at the thought of the man navigating forever, like a Flying Dutchman, between the two frontier posts.

Fortunately, Emilio Pozzi made a few official phone calls, and eventually the pianist was allowed to enter France, briefly. Years later, remembering this incident, there was one scene that made Dizzy laugh right out. The pianist would be waving his passport in front of the Italian and French frontier post officials saying, with an exasperated voice, that he happened to be "Imelda Marcos's favorite pianist!" To which both nations reacted with French and Italian shoulder-and-hand mimicry signifying "So what?"

Of course it continued to rain, though it was now a gentle drizzle.

As we drove through the Moyenne Corniche, I sighed that one day I would live on the French Riviera, in Nice. Dizzy reminded me that he and Kenny Clarke had bought a piece of land at Draguignon and intended to build two houses, back to back, with a large sliding door shared by their two living rooms, which could become one huge music room, right there on the Côte d'Azur. . . . He then generously offered that we should make it three houses close together. He promised he would take me there someday.

He did, the next summer when, on a sunny morning during the Grande Parade du Jazz in Nice, he got somebody to drive us by car all the way to Draguignon. There, in the midst of nowhere, we were in front of an abandoned piece of land in urgent need of radical weeding, clearing, and upkeeping. Half was his and the other half Klook's. Asked when they intended to start building, Dizzy shrugged: "Sooner or later."

"I see. You're waiting for this land to turn into a nice thick jungle. . . . Won't take long now . . ."

"Then why don't YOU take care of it?! Klook said you've got a beautiful country pad in Italy. You could do the same here . . ."

"Yes, except that mine is two hundred years old and the upkeep of the house, the vineyard, and the garden are driving me bankrupt."

"Then why not consider moving here?"

"I told you. If I move to the Riviera it will be in an apartment with a terrace overlooking the Mediterranean, in Nice. But thanks for the offer anyway."

Back to May 1983. As we drove through the Promenade des Anglais, on the way to Cannes, Dizzy pointed to the nearby hills above the Hyatt Hotel (which later changed names three times and today is called the Radisson), saying he had some very nice French friends living "up there." I replied: how odd, so did I, a charming couple with two children; and the husband was a jazz buff. Well, Diz replied archly, so were *his* friends! I continued, ". . . and their names are Bernard . . ." ". . . and Colette Taride?" he interrupted me. Of the hundreds of jazz fans living in Nice, we had separately struck a close friendship with the same family.

Through the years, the welcoming home of the Tarides would gather us all together to enjoy their hospitality. That today I finally have my refuge in the western hills of Nice, overlooking the Mediterranean, a few yards from their home, is thanks to Colette and Bernard. Needless to say, with so many happy memories, Dizzy's presence is still here among us.

The show at Cannes was yet another success and that night Dizzy, Francesco, and I went strolling in high spirits through the "zone piétonne" in drizzling Nice. Dizzy spied a poster announcing the Grande Parade du Jazz, and he addressed bystanders, pointing at himself and at the poster, explaining, in approximate French, that the figure with the protruding stomach and the trumpet was he. The usual request for autographs followed.

We finally reached the flat offered by RAI at Le Copacabana, on the Promenade. We were all very happy, satisfied and full of ". . . and remember when . . . ?" regarding the past days, until we realized it was four in the morning.

Dizzy embraced the two of us together, looking from one to the other.

"I do love you guys, you know?"

"Yes, Giovanni, and 'ooh means we love ooh too' . . . but shall we get some sleep?"

"OK-OK. And tomorrow . . . I promise you the sunshine!"

"Don't you dare?! It means it will keep on raining!"

"Know what? If it rains, I'll write a song for you."

"Sure, like the special 'Bella Italia 1983 Suite' you did NOT compose for the Torino concert, right?"

A last chuckle.

The next morning it still rained, and he confirmed his promise. I would have his song to sing by the next meeting; meanwhile, I could write the lyrics and send them to him.

In the car I gave him a copy of my latest CD.

"Here, you've never heard me sing, have you? This is my very favorite; I recorded it in Milano last year with Tommy Flanagan, Ed Thigpen, and Jesper Lundgaard. When you find the time to listen to it, I'll be curious to have your opinion."

He examined it, mumbling the title. "Hmm . . . *Lilian Terry Meets Tommy Flanagan—A Dream Comes True*. You're in good company here."

"And how! You know why 'a dream comes true'? Because the only thing I truly envied Ella for . . . were the many years he accompanied her. I told him so one evening at a dinner in Rome and also that I had vowed to myself never to cut another record again unless it was with him. Know what he said? 'Ah, well now . . . and which date would you have in mind?' as he fingered through his agenda. And he meant it!"

"Yeah, he's a great guy, great musician. You've got some serious stuff here . . . 'I Remember Clifford,' 'Lush Life,' ''Round Midnight.' Hmmm. Interesting."

"Yes, but put it away before you lose it."

"OK-OK."

He snored in his corner the rest of the way to Milano airport. Barely time for his "outgoing cappuccino," hugs, and ciaos; then, as he walked away, he turned, pointing his finger at us:

"Hey, you guys. I'll never forget these days, you know?"

"Neither shall we, von Karajan! Now rush or you'll miss your plane . . ."

He hurried away, shaking his head.

A few days later I mailed him my lyrics for a ballad, and when we spoke on the phone, I asked him if he had received, approved, and begun writing the song as he had promised. Yes, he had received it. Yes, beautiful lyrics; in fact, he had folded the paper and now carried it in his wallet, right over his heart . . .

"Well, thank you but don't carry it too long in there! Remember, you promised me the sunshine or else a song to sing. And it rained!"

"Yeah, I know, OK-OK. I'll work on it, I promise."

ACT XII—ONCE AGAIN, NOW, EEMILIO!

Emilio Pozzi, the Torino RAI director, had so enjoyed the adventurous happenings with Dizzy that, just a few months later, he had felt the urge to renew the experience. Being on the panel of the famous "Maschera d'Argento" award, which took place every year in Campione d'Italia—in Swizerland—he had obtained that Dizzy be given the Award for a Life Career in Jazz Music. I was chosen officially to present it to him but above all to coordinate and ensure his presence in Campione. He would be flown in and out just for this occasion, with no musicians attached. Emilio would send Dizzy a formal invitation, while I would write to explain in minute detail what the invitation entailed.

Giovanni, my dear. You have received a cable informing you of the nomination to the Maschera d'Argento award with a formal letter detailing the festivities. If you accept the invitation, then you will receive a prepaid return ticket, Alitalia special class, New York–Milano–New York. You will leave on the evening of the 22nd of September, a Thursday, arriving in Milano on the morning of Friday the 23rd. I'll pick you up at the airport and we'll drive to Campione d'Italia, which is near Lugano. You'll be allowed your jetlag sleep till 8 P.M., when we'll be involved in various social happenings, a dinner, and a very fancy stage show at the municipal casino, Campione being a gambling resort.

Saturday the 24th in the morning we'll attend a big press meeting along with the various nominees from the fields of theater, sport, fashion, cinema, music, opera, and ballet, followed by a luncheon for the nominees, the members of the jury, and some chosen journalists. At 8 P.M. we have a gala dinner (tuxedo, please) in the Festival Hall of the casino in honor of the nominees. At 10 P.M. you'll get your Silver Mask award. Sunday the 25th we'll have a farewell luncheon, then I must leave for Bassano. Monday the 26th you'll be driven to Milano to catch your plane for New York, arriving in New York the same day with very nice memories. How about that for a well-deserved ego-trip? So please get your black book out and mark from the evening of September 22nd to Monday the 26th with "From Italy with Love." Now please cable RIGHT NOW your acceptance in the following manner . . .

Upon learning of this invitation extended by his good friend "Eemilio," Dizzy accepted immediately. I would pick him up at the Milano airport, and we would be driven to Campione in a limousine put at our disposal by the organization. Von Karajan service again.

At Malpensa Airport I began to worry when, more than an hour after having landed in the early morning, Dizzy was still nowhere to be seen. I finally asked a policeman if I could check inside customs to find out what had happened to my friend Gillespie.

"Ah, Dizzy?! He's OK, don't worry, he's just having a chat with us. There . . . see him?"

I peeked through the exit door and there he was indeed, seated on the table, with all his traveling paraphernalia spread around him, laughing and joking with a group of frontier guards complete with sniffing hounds. Everybody was having a great time while the limo driver was impatiently waiting outside, double parked.

I called, "Giovanni!" and he immediately looked up, surprised and then abashed as I pointed at my watch. With teasing laughs they helped him down from the table, handed him all the stuff he would hang around his neck on every trip, and with friendly "ciaos" they let him through the dividing door.

"Nice guys you know? Every time I fly into Milano there's always some guard I know from before. We were remembering when one of them had to rush me into town to a dentist, and it was a Sunday, can you imagine?"

I was looking at him: happy as a little boy and, hanging from his neck, a Leica camera, a portable CD player, a cassette player, and even a pair of binoculars! So I joined my palms and bowed Japanese style to him.

"Very happy you could finally emerge, Gillespo-san, you look like a Japanese tourist, with all those things hanging round your neck. . . . Unfortunately, at this point we have no time for your 'incoming cappuccino,' as the limo is impatiently waiting to go by the Milano railway station to pick up another distinguished guest."

Disappointed about the cappuccino but not daring to protest, he followed me with his luggage trolley until the driver took over and ushered us into the limousine.

We were shamefully late at the station, but the distinguished guest was Fulvio Roiter, a photographer friend of mine of international renown and a buoyant, vigorous hand shaker. He accepted our apologies good-naturedly. He and Dizzy sat at the back while I traveled practically turned around on my front seat, as neither of them spoke the other's language properly and I translated as they got acquainted.

Suddenly I heard shouts, laughter, and excitement, and there they were, each one showing off his Leica to the other. Fulvio asked if Dizzy was an experienced photographer and Dizzy tried to act like a pro, handling his camera. Then he suddenly gave up and, with great humility, confessed he was an "under-beginner" and the Leica was a recent gift. Would Fulvio explain a few technical things? Lilian, would you . . . ? And for the rest of the drive they chattered and giggled like a couple of schoolboys sharing similar toys.

We finally arrived in Campione at the beautiful Hotel Lago di Lugano, nestled in a tropical garden. We went up to our rooms and within minutes Dizzy was knocking hurriedly at my door.

"Hey, Lilian? My horn . . . you got it, right?"

"Diz, you never let anyone carry your horn. And I didn't see your trumpet case at the customs."

"No, I'm carrying it in a special leather cover, sort of like a handbag, easier to carry around . . ."

"Did you put it in one of your suitcases?"

"Nope, I was showing the new leather cover to some of the guys . . ."

"You mean at the airport customs?"

"Yeah . . . but I was sure I had it when we left . . . sure you don't have it here?"

I reached for the phone and asked if our driver was still there. He went looking carefully in the limousine. Sorry, no.

At that moment our host Emilio Pozzi called my room to welcome us. Informed of Dizzy's plight, "Eemilio" first laughed and then controlled himself saying he would call customs at Milano airport and call us back. A very subdued Dizzy sat in my room, motionless as he stared at his shoes, shaking his head, till Pozzi called back. Yes! Milano customs held the precious trumpet and our driver had been dispatched immediately to recuperate it. No problem. Have a good rest. See you that evening at the reception. Enjoy your stay.

From that moment Dizzy became buoyant, impatient to go, see, and do whatever the place offered. Never mind the jetlag! The car would be back only after two hours, so how about a cappuccino? Fulvio Roiter joined us at the bar; he wished to take some shots—would Dizzy like to bring his Leica? And I of course was invited along as interpreter. They must have shot every bush, monument, piazza . . . totally enthusiastic about each other's company . . . while Dizzy kept ordering me to stand there, sit here and, Lil, ask Fulvio how this thing here works . . .

Eventually we had "shot" our way to the Festival Hall. At a side entrance was the large RAI TV studio bus where the technical director and his crew hailed me. They were delighted to meet Dizzy and Fulvio in person, and when they saw the enthusiasm and pride with which Dizzy was telling them of the great pictures he was going to take back home, the director said, "Look here, we have a photo facility on the bus. If Dizzy likes, he can give me the film right now and we can let you have the copies by tonight."

I translated while Fulvio nodded his approval. Dizzy was touched and utterly eager to hand them his film, and there followed an unforgettable lightning scene:

There were anguished yells of "No! Stop! Wait!" from everybody while Dizzy flipped open his camera and then realized he had just exposed the film. Once again there was that familiar moment of disbelief, with six of us gasping, and when we breathed again, we all joined in consoling Dizzy who for once was truly speechless. Fulvio patted him on the shoulder and promised to give him some more coaching, maybe tomorrow morning in the hotel's luscious garden? The technical director gave him a roll of special film as a consolation gift, and I led him back to the hotel, reminding him that his trumpet was probably waiting for him. He shook his head:

"I've really done it this time . . ."

"So what else is new . . . ? Now, how about a cappuccino?"

Yes, his trumpet was there! While he unwrapped it to show it to the hotel concierge, I glanced at the list of personalities who were receiving the "Maschera d'Argento" the next evening. Very impressive: a ballerina from La Scala, a young concert pianist of renown, and various other guests; then, suddenly, a name emerged before my enthusiastic eyes. For film music I read Michel Legrand! Ah, I had admired his art and sung his songs for a lifetime, and now, finally, I would meet him in person! I told this to Dizzy as he joined me to read the awardees list.

"You don't know Michel? We just came back from a jazz cruise together, in the North Sea. I didn't know he was coming here. Bet he'll be surprised to see me! What's his room number? Let's go say hullo."

We walked up the stairs, and as we approached the door Dizzy drew out his horn, saying, "Wait a minute, let's surprise him!" and blew the first eight bars of "Night in Tunisia."

The surprise worked both ways.

From inside the room there was a yell of joyful recognition and WHAM! the door was flung open. Michel Legrand stood there, stark naked and dripping wet.

Once again there was a holding of amazed breaths by all concerned, till Dizzy let out a chuckle then soberly made the introductions:

"Michel, this is Lilian Terry; she's a jazz singer and a fan of yours. Lilian? I have the pleasure to present to you *all* of Michel Legrand!"

This was said with a wave of his hand comprising Michel from wet head to bare feet.

"How do you do?" I murmured most formally, looking directly in his eyes, as we shook hands.

Michel had recovered his cool by then. Very formally he invited us in, turning on his heels to lead us into the room. And with that final view I had really and totally met Michel Legrand.

In de evenin' . . . when de sun goes down . . .

According to the detailed invitation, the award festivities were to last two days. The first evening offered a gala dinner, complete with floor show and sexy dancing girls. Needless to say, my three companions—Michel Legrand having joined Dizzy and Fulvio—were rather interested. In fact, they were already in the hotel lobby, all dressed up, when the limousine arrived with Swiss punctuality.

So began the excellent dinner, interspersed with welcoming speeches from the various organizers and authorities. The speeches over, we were invited to enjoy the food and the cabaret show. And enjoy we did, for the show was full of beautiful blonde dancers, scantily clad and with bursting curves. But what fascinated me most were the athletic male dancers who grabbed the girls and swung them around, flinging them at each other like Frisbees. My three escorts sat there, enjoying every move, while I anticipated with great interest the moment when one of the ladies might be flung into our soup.

At one point Michel asked me point blank: "So you sing?"

Before I could answer, Dizzy intervened. "She's one hell of a good singer. You should hear her record with Tommy Flanagan." Then he nudged me. "Even if our New Jersey radio station bugs me 'cause it won't stop playing it from top to bottom every day."

I smiled, pleased. "I know, and I can't believe it. The other day Abbey Lincoln called me from New York to tease me with her complaint on the same line."

"Well, with those musicians and that repertoire you couldn't miss."

"Why, thank you Giovanni, you've never told me all this! I am really flattered. However, I bet you're just being nice. You'd never consider recording with me . . . ?" I teased him.

He passed his hand across his brow in a mock mopping gesture.

"Phew! I thought you'd never ask me!"

I turned to Michel.

"Now you are a witness to this. You heard him."

"Oh yes, I'd say he practically asked for it . . ."

Dizzy had already extracted his little black book and was going through the days and months, mumbling.

"Now let's see. . . . Humm, next year is pretty much taken up. . . . Let's see 1985. Here, I have about four days off in May, from the 13th. I'll be on my European tour with Wim Wigt. I'll tell him I want those days free and you can call him to make the necessary arrangements. Let's see now; I'll be coming down from Bern, so I'll just take the train to Milano. . . . What's wrong?"

I was staring at him.

"You amaze me! You're not only serious about this record, but suddenly you are taking matters in hand as efficiently as . . . Simone Ginibre with her Nice festival! Where is the absentminded 'oops-I've-done-it-again' character I've been looking after for all these years?"

With a sphinx-like smile he noted in the little black book, then asked: "So from May 13th to the 16th, 1985, I'm all yours. OK? You can't back out now. I am writing it down."

To his amusement, I was speechless.

At 3 A.M. the official party broke up, and on the way out of the building Michel, Dizzy, and I spied an empty bar with a grand piano. Inevitably and simultaneously Michel headed for the piano while Dizzy opened his trumpet's leather bag—which at this point never left his sight. Michel made room for me on the piano bench, and I asked him if he would sing "What Are You Doing the Rest of Your Life."

So the three of us had our private jam session, and finally, as a closing tune, came "My Funny Valentine," a ballad Dizzy would often play for me during the concerts I organized for his group. Having once told him teasingly that my favorite version was the one by Miles Davis of the "Kind of Blue" period, he had raised his brows and had begun an intro totally à la Miles, muted, squeezed sound and all. Of course after a few bars he had slid back to his own sound, and yet there remained a certain wistfulness that made his version very endearing. I guess our trio rendition of the ballad that night was rather introspective, for when the last note echoed away, there was a collective sigh.

We strolled back to the hotel, meeting Fulvio along the way, and parted with a late breakfast date, when Fulvio would take some special pictures of Dizzy in the hotel park. He asked: "By the way, Dizzy, can you wear something fancy, something African?"

"Oh yes . . ." Dizzy replied with a big smile, ". . . it was given to me last month in Ghana . . ."

"Perfect. Buonanotte."

While having breakfast the next morning, waiting for Fulvio, I reminded Dizzy that a car was coming to drive me back to Bassano the next day, while he would be accompanied to Milano airport by another driver on the following day. He seemed disappointed.

". . . and you'd leave me here by myself?"

"Of course not; tomorrow you have the farewell luncheon with your friends Eemilio and Fulvio and Michel and . . ."

"But what's the rush?"

"Well, tomorrow night in Bassano a very special event will take place."

I kept silent to tease his curiosity, till he said, "Well?"

"Well, after two years of cajoling and begging the mayor of Bassano, I have finally obtained the premises for a jazz school. It will be the first one of its kind in the whole Veneto region and one of four in all of Italy. I am terribly happy, and tomorrow evening we'll inaugurate the school with the authorities, radios, TV, newspapers, and all."

He had been listening intently, then shook his head.

"Now that's some project, and you never said a word about it. What will you call it?"

"We have agreed on 'The Popular School of Music,' as opposed to the classic music conservatories in the Veneto, where they don't even teach guitar, considering it a 'pop' instrument. The young people kept coming to see me after each of the jazz concerts I organized—especially when we had great guitarists like Jim Hall—and they kept asking me to help them study their instrument properly. So I asked the mayor, 'What if Bassano was to become the seat of an important jazz school nationwide?' Being young and ambitious, he considered it. I brought him about 150 student petitions, and in the end he said OK, but on condition that I take the entire responsibility as founder and director. You know our motto: 'Why not?' So I took a deep breath and plunged, and tomorrow night we inaugurate the Popular School of Music of Bassano del Grappa. Insha'Allah, may God help us and look kindly upon us."

Dizzy had been listening with a thoughtful expression on his face.

"OK. I've only one question. How about calling it 'The Dizzy Gillespie Popular School of Music'? It would be the only school in the world to carry my name legally. How's about that? And I come with you tomorrow for the inauguration?"

I stared at him, moved to the verge of tears, so he concluded hastily:

"At least this way I get to see this . . . town of yours, and I don't have to stay here all on my own!"

Laughing nervously, I embraced him and then hit him on the arm.

"Oh, you! You've been a constant source of surprise on this trip. And I thought I knew you by now. OK, let me call Bassano so as to organize your visit. They won't believe it. I still don't believe it myself!"

He called after me: "Just make sure I get some of that 'Baccalà' fish you told me about!"

Needless to say, in Bassano they were amazed and delighted, and immediately went about to inform the local radios and newspapers. Then they reserved the best suite at the Hotel Belvedere (which through the years was to become his home away from home) and contacted the best restaurant to provide his "Baccalà alla Vicentina." Of course, the normal car that would have picked me up was replaced by a large limousine.

In the meantime, Dizzy had been grabbed and hustled by an eager and energetic Fulvio carrying all sorts of photographic appendages around his neck, to Dizzy's great envy.

Wearing a pale apricot-and-brown African costume, Dizzy merged with the tropical garden where he posed for a series of shots while Fulvio laughed his pleasure for such an inventive model with so many amusing stances and expressions.

I joined them and went discreetly behind Dizzy to murmur the good news about Bassano, and he gave a huge, satisfied smile, which scene was instantly recorded by a wildly clicking Fulvio.

"Si, si, cosi'! Very good Lilian, flirt with him . . . make him smile that way . . ."

Once again I was involved in some of the poses. My favorite is the one where we lay on the grass under a huge flowering hydrangea bush. Dizzy's arm is pointed to the skies as—yet another surprise—he quotes appropriate words from *The Rubàiyàt of Omar Khayyàm.*

A year later producer Giovanni Bonandrini chose those two special pictures as the front and back cover of our Soul Note record.

It was evening time in Campione d'Italia, time to dress up for *the* event, the awards. The occasion was important, and Dizzy had brought along a very elegant Italian silk tuxedo. In the hotel foyer we joined Michel and Fulvio and once again the limousine dropped us off, this time at the festivities hall of the gambling casino.

"Eemilio" was there to give us a warm welcome. Winking, he inquired after Dizzy's trumpet; Dizzy thanked him again for his patience in solving yet another problem. Pozzi then pointed to a hall where Fulvio's photographs were already obtaining wide attention and our two "photographers" trotted off so Dizzy could study them under Fulvio's guidance. Our host then informed Michel that a tape with some of his Oscar-winning film scores was being aired and appreciated at that very moment, and that a grand piano stood on stage just in case, later . . .

In other words, it was a very pleasant reunion of artists, sportsmen, the inevitable politicians-cum-journalists, and high-fashion designers mingling easily in the various halls, introducing themselves with mutual admiration, drink in hand, until it was time to be seated for dinner; the four of us plus the young classic pianist Michele Campanella and a lovely ballerina from La Scala were invited to share a table.

When came the time for the awards, each recipient was called on stage where "Eemilio" announced the reason for the choice of each nominee, then a personality related to each field would come forward to hand the prize. It was customary that, when the nominee was an artist, he would offer an artistic "thank you." Needless to say, when I gave Dizzy his award . . . there was his trumpet, resting on the piano, and to everybody's pleasure Michel and Dizzy played together.

ACT XIII—"ON THE ROAD"

During the long ride to Bassano del Grappa the next morning, Dizzy listened to the history of this special town, with its very ancient castle and its historical wooden bridge built by the famous architect Andrea Palladio. Destroyed by the Austrian Army during World War I, it had been faithfully rebuilt in wood, according to the original Palladio plans, to be re-destroyed by the German Army during World War II. Rebuilt a second time, today it graced the town straddling the Brenta River. Incidentally, through the years that followed, Dizzy would always find the time, during his visits, to stroll across the bridge. He would stand on the lookout and gaze at the mountains with a peaceful smile on his face.

Dizzy had been listening carefully: "You know, I feel I'm going to like this 'Bazzano.'"

I asked him if he would accept becoming the honorary president of our school and—perhaps during the inauguration that evening—he could hold a speech about the importance of music, as a faithful companion, et cetera. He nodded his consent and immediately fell asleep.

Suddenly, he woke up and reached inside his pocket excitedly: "Hey, wait a minute, you've gotta see this!"

He proudly presented a hearing aid, declaring he had never worn one before. Congratulating him, I asked why he wasn't wearing it in his ear.

"Aaah, it's good enough that I carry it with me . . . ," he shrugged, and slipped it back into his pocket.

"It's not much use to your hearing if you keep it in your pocket, is it? You know, mother wears one too, and I often fix it for her. Would you like me to try? It's quite easy."

Grumbling, he fished again in his jacket and handed me the "thing."

There ensued a tragic-comic struggle between my efforts to find the correct volume and his negative attitude full of suspicion and resentment toward the small instrument till I finally gave up and handed back the hearing aid.

"OK, you win. Here, I'll just keep on sitting on the side of your good ear to be sure you hear me."

"Oh, I hear you all right, and I also listen to you . . . most of the time."

The car ride lasted just over three hours while he snored off and on. Each time he snapped awake, he would have some surprising question.

"Say, can you sing in Egyptian?" he asked me suddenly.

I offered an Arab love song to the best of my abilities, begging forgiveness to the great Om Khalsoum. He listened, nodding in pleasure, then asked me what it was all about.

"It's called 'Balash te busni fil anaya—Don't kiss me on the eyelids' because that's the kiss of goodbye."

"So you really are Egyptian after all?"

"Not Egyptian, as my parents were European, but I was the fourth generation born there . . ."

"Say . . . and did you guys do that special fasting . . . Ramadan?"

"No, only Muslims choose to do that, but how do you know about Ramadan?"

He gave me a mock supercilious look announcing, "I'll have you know that I did Ramadan myself, in Syria, many years ago!"

"Now *you* are putting me on!"

He nodded emphatically: "Yes, we did! We had this afternoon concert in Damascus, see? And they told us that at sundown the public could finally break the day's fast according to the rule of Ramadan. In fact, they had fixed up a huge banquet in the hall just behind the stage. So I decided to honor their religious custom, and all of us in the band played and waited on an empty stomach till I was signaled that it was exactly sundown, when I held up my arm and the guys came down with a loud, long chord. I told the public, 'Food! Let's go eat!' And just about everybody rushed to the feast. I remember they were very impressed that we had done the Ramadan with them when we didn't really have to."

"Then you're more Middle Eastern than I am!" I kidded him.

"Tell you something . . ." he hesitated, pulling at his lower lip, eyeing me sideways while I expected some incredible comment.

"How about you and I go to Egypt together . . . to Cairo? You could be my translator."

"Translator? Why? Are you going to hold a speech?" I was amused.

"That's right. You take me to that important religious school . . ."

"Al Azhar?! It's the most important Madrassa in the Arab world. But they wouldn't let us in; you, perhaps, but certainly not a European woman. But I thought you were Bahá'í?"

"That's exactly why. I want to go and talk with them and ask them to stop persecuting the Bahá'í faithful as they've been doing for years now, in Iran and all over the Muslim world."

Once again, he had me breathless.

"Sure! And why not try it from Mecca, during the yearly Hajj?"

"Yeah! Tell me about this Hajj . . . some sort of pilgrimage you've got to do every year, right?"

"Not every year but at least once in your lifetime. The Hajj is called 'the fifth pillar of Islam.'"

"Remind me about these pillars?" He was fully awake now and interested.

"Well, the first pillar is the 'shahada,' or the renewal of one's faith in Islam as being monotheistic and recognizing Muhammad's mission as envoy of God."

"Ah yes, wait . . . it's the one that mentions God's divinity . . . I remember that from when we traveled to Syria. And what's the second pillar?"

"It's the 'salat.' The rite of adoration of the only God, to be expressed five times a day."

"That's when they go to the mosque to pray together?"

"They can also pray privately, although it's preferable that they do so collectively."

"And they've got to pray at special times of the day, don't they?"

"Not really. The Koran says 'between the decline of the sun and the darkening of night,' while the psalms are recited at dawn."

"And every time, they have to wash up to purify themselves before prayer, right?"

"I say . . . ! You're quite an expert; did you learn all that when you did the Ramadan?"

"Yeah, I was very interested in the Ramadan, which is another one of the 'pillars,' right?

"The religious name of Ramadan is 'al-siyam,' and it takes place during the ninth month of the lunar year; it corresponds with the Jewish Feast of Expiation. Today it lasts thirty days during which, in the daytime, you cannot eat, or drink, or smoke . . ."

"Yeah, I know . . . and you can't have sex either!"

I cleared my throat.

"Right. Until the sun goes down when you can do . . . whatever you like, until dawn."

"Wow! Sounds like a loooong party . . . during thirty days!"

"Then the fourth pillar is the 'zakat,' the obligation of giving alms, and the Koran calls it a 'purifying withdrawal of money,' for God will not save a community where there lives even one man who goes hungry."

"Some sort of tax?"

"It's according to what you earn and what you've saved. Special officers are involved in gathering the money and distributing it to the needy."

"And now the fifth pillar! The Hajj!" he was extremely interested.

"It's the holy pilgrimage. In the old days they would organize long caravans from all over the Muslim world to cross the desert plain of Arafat and arrive at Mecca, in Saudi Arabia."

"That's that very special place . . ."

"Mecca is the most sacred place in Islam, together with Medina, and this pilgrimage, at least once in your lifetime, is a duty whereby you submit your life to the judgement of Allah, hoping to obtain the 'inner renewal.' It's practically the oldest rule."

". . . from the time of Adam and Eve, I bet?" He joked.

"You're not far wrong. . . . You see, for the Muslims, when Adam and Eve were chased from Paradise, they ended up in this deserted region, where today you have Mecca, where Adam built the House of God known as the Kaaba, which is now the very heart of the holy city."

". . . and then Muhammad came along and started the whole religious thing?"

"No. According to ancient history it was Abraham who started the cult at the Kaaba."

"But isn't Abraham in the Christian and Jewish traditions?"

"Actually, studying the origin of these three religions, one discovers that the Judeo-Christian-Islamic religions are intertwined. When Abraham was called upon to sacrifice his son to God . . ."

". . . Isaac, right?"

"Wrong, Ismael. For the Muslim world, contrary to the Judeo-Christian belief, the son that Abraham had been called upon to sacrifice to God was Ismael, born of his faithful servant Agar. Then God accepted that a lamb be sacrificed instead."

"Ahah! Which they sacrifice during Ramadan. . . . They eat lots of lamb . . ."

"Actually, the sacrifice of the lamb is evoked during nine stages in the ritual of the Hajj."

"When they go round and round that big black place?"

"Actually, the last stage takes place in the city of Medina, in the desert, a city founded by the Prophet shortly after he had been visited by the Archangel Gabriel, who announced that he had been chosen as the Messenger of God . . ."

"You mean the one who played trumpet?"

I looked at him in surprise, so he went on:

"Yeah . . . I mean Gabriel . . . who blew his horn . . ."

I kept a straight face.

"You're right. However, after the Prophet's death, this religious ritual at Medina is one of the strong moments for most Muslims."

"And are women allowed there too?"

"Yes, in fact it's the only time and place where men and women can mingle together. The men are all dressed in white, the women all in black."

"How do you know all this? You're a Catholic, ain't you? Did you go there too?"

I laughed at him: "Sure, every year! No, seriously, I'm just very interested in the history of all religions. By the way, I'd be interested in reading something on the Bahá'í faith, too."

"OK-OK. I'll have them send you something, either from the States or from Italy. But about Mecca . . . maybe we could go there next year so I could talk to them about the problems of the Bahá'í . . . ?"

"Why not? You could stand on the Arafat Mountain and preach to them! And get stoned to death by a few thousand infuriated faithful?"

For a second his eyes had lit up at the first part of my suggestion. He thought better of it and then shook his head.

"Nah, but I think the Cairo plan could work . . ."

I did not know whether to laugh or shake him.

"Giovanni, my dear. You are speaking of Al Azhar, a religious fortress open only to the high-level Muslim scholars and very close to the Egyptian Fundamentalists. They would never receive you."

"But we could try. . . . What if you were to talk to them, explain . . . ?"

"Dizzy, you're not listening to me! First of all, I wouldn't be allowed to reach the front door. Next, if they did let *you* through the front door, I don't know if and how you would be ejected out, once you declared your intentions. So let's forget the whole project and avoid having our heads chopped off, va bene? I don't see how you can even consider it. It's pure madness."

"Humph!" he snorted his disappointment and displeasure, then he shrugged his shoulders and muttered: "Bah, I bet you've never even *been* to Cairo, after all . . ."

And he mumbled himself to sleep in his corner.

ACT XIV—A SCHOOL IS BORN

We arrived at the handsome ancient building housing the Municipality of Bassano, where the leading officials were waiting for us in the mayor's imposing office. Dizzy was welcomed cordially, and we were offered a glass of excellent prosecco wine to toast the occasion. Then the future musical director of our school, Roberto Beggio, entered the room and saw Dizzy. He froze at the door, looking at his idol, who gave him a benign smile, and such was the emotion that poor Roberto burst into tears. Dizzy got up and went over to him as he stood by the door, and drew him inside to sit beside him. The Bassano administrators were nonplussed by so much emotion.

Dizzy was then invited to take possession of his suite at the Belvedere Hotel, and we were off for his baccalà luncheon.

In the afternoon he came home with me, met my mother, and within minutes had her laughing and promising to prepare "real minestrone" for him on his next visit. Shortly after, Roberto and the other young teachers of our future school filed in shyly to meet him. He greeted them with his wide smile, shaking hands while repeating each name correctly; he must have noticed their very shiny eyes from the emotion of meeting him.

They sat around him at the long kitchen table, gazing at him, listening carefully while the ones who spoke English plied him with questions.

Before long it was time to drive back to Bassano for the inauguration, which was to take place in a public school theater. The parking lot was filled with cars from faraway towns. I realized that the news and the word-of-mouth had reached quite a number of Gillespie fans, and this was confirmed when we entered the theater through the back door.

As soon as they spied his presence there was an "Ola" tidal wave of warm emotion expressed by calls of his name and enthusiastic applause. The impact of this loving welcome seemed to immobilize Dizzy for a second. Then he stepped forward along the aisle toward the bandstand, shaking proffered hands along the way and saying, "Ciao! Comee staee?"

Once Dizzy settled on the bandstand, the mayor greeted him officially, again, and made his speech announcing the new music school that would bear such a famous and unique name. He thanked Dizzy and hoped that this would be only the first of such visits. Other authorities came up to the microphone, and finally it was time for Dizzy to speak, while I stood beside him to translate.

He spoke of the importance of music in his life as a problem kid who was often getting into trouble. He spoke of the difficulty for most young people to have proper access to a musical education unless confined to conservatories and classic music institutes; he congratulated the mayor and the municipality for such a brilliant and useful decision. He encouraged the students to go on studying even if, at times, things would seem too difficult to cope with. He invited the teachers to share all their knowledge with patience, intelligence, and brotherly generosity. Finally, he put a hand on my shoulder and murmured:

"Now you translate every word I'm going to say!"

"What have I done until now?" I murmured back.

He continued talking to the public:

"However! The most important person in this new venture is Lilian here. If I am here tonight, it's because of her. If I give willingly my name to this school, it's because I trust her judgement. And here is one last thing. And this I say to all the students as well as the teachers: Do whatever Lilian tells you to do. You may not understand why . . . I often wonder about her decisions myself . . . but don't worry, do like me. Trust her. You may not know what the point is, but she does."

I finished translating hurriedly, with a certain roughness growing in my voice. Applause followed as he gave me an affectionate pat on the shoulder and then turned to the musicians.

"OK-OK now. So . . . Roberto, where's my trumpet? Let's go, guys!"

With an emotional confusion the teachers organized themselves, and the inauguration concert was soon going full swing.

Early the next morning the car arrived at the Belvedere Hotel to drive him to the Milano Malpensa airport. Saying goodbye at the hotel entrance, I told him I had no words . . . he interrupted me to say that he was coming back to Bassano for sure. To begin with, during May 1985 when he would be in Milano for our recording session, unless I had changed my mind? Maybe we could play a concert here in Bassano? And he would see how the school was coming on.

We checked if he had his trumpet safely in his luggage. He said to be sure to ask Fulvio Roiter to let him have a copy of the pictures taken at the hotel at Campione and to thank again "Eemilio" for a great weekend.

The driver pointed at his watch, opening the car door. Ooops—yes!

"Ciao Lil. I'll be sure to have them send you reading material about the Bahá'í."

". . . And next time we meet you'll question me to see if I've done my homework . . ."

"I won't kiss your eyelids!" as he smacked my cheek. "I'll call you from New York."

"Yes, but please not at three in the morning! And give my love to Lorraine."

As the car drove away, he was waving back with a large smile.

Some days later I dropped him a few lines to thank him.

> Giovanni, what a profound impression you have left on every single person who has met you here! Our music teachers say it's an experience that will influence all their lives. I watched you seated at the table, in our kitchen, and it looked like Leonardo da Vinci's *Last Supper*, for I really counted twelve musicians around you! I only hope you felt the warmth and the love that can express our "thank you" better than words. I do believe that the reason you are still with us—when so many great musicians of your generation have gone—is because you give so much at all levels, that the Lord keeps you here as "therapy" against the many evils of our society. You certainly worked wonders here with us. But enough or you'll become a conceited fat-head. . . . My very best to Lorraine, keep some for you."

Citizen of "Bazzano"

It should be added that from that day in September 1983 to the spring of 1991 he made sure that on all his European tours he would find the time to spend at least one day in Bassano, in a flash surprise visit to the school, flirting with the female students ("This school reeks with beautiful girls!") and encouraging everyone. Invariably the teachers would organize a musical welcome in our school auditorium, so as to show him the level reached by our students, and Dizzy enjoyed it all, often joining in.

On one such occasion, when all the students were seated in the hall and with the teachers asking him various technical questions, someone asked him what would be his basic advice to any student of any instrument. He puffed seriously on his Cuban cigar then said slowly, while I translated: "First of all, let me give you the basic concepts from the Bahá'í religion, which I follow . . . live a healthy life, in body and soul. No adultery, no alcohol, no violence, no smoking . . ." he looked at the huge cigar in his hand, mimicking amazement as the audience laughed out loud, delighted.

He went on: "Ah, well . . . human weakness. . . . But seriously, a healthy life is essential to your musical activity. Next and very important . . . everybody should learn to play the piano, no matter which instrument you decide to play. And learn it to perfection, with lots of practice, just as you practice your other instrument. Then listen a lot. Listen to the best musicians, learn their style, and then develop a style of your own. But I repeat, take it from the piano, so as to build in your mind the foundation of any instrumentation and improvisation."

The next day we made copies of this little lesson, which was then distributed religiously to all the students.

Every time he visited us I would try to surprise his taste buds, like the time the chef prepared a special "risotto alla fragola," that is, a "strawberry risotto." He stared at the pink concoction, amazed. Hesitating, he picked up a small forkful, tasted it delicately . . . and dived in.

Another time, during an official dinner with the Bassano authorities, who enjoyed watching his enthusiastic appetite, the owner of the restaurant invited Dizzy to visit his famous cellar.

"Ah, Lil, you know I don't drink wine . . ."

"You needn't drink it; just make the man happy by admiring his famous collection of unique wines. It's worth it."

Curiosity got the better of him, and we visited a wine collector's delight with special "millesimes" and rare bottles. At one point the owner winked and motioned to follow him around a corner, where stood a large, old-fashioned safe. He opened the door and extracted a bottle, where I read, to my delight, "PICCOLIT." The man explained that this was an extremely precious wine, perhaps the most expensive, as it came from tiny grapes in rare bunches on the vine and only in the region of the Friuli, near the Yugoslav border. The vintners had considered stopping production, as it entailed a lot of work for a very small amount of wine, but the motion had been fortunately vetoed, and here was one bottle that the owner was opening religiously . . . and getting out three goblets . . . and pouring most carefully the nectar before our eyes . . .

I said to Dizzy: "Ah, what a pity that you won't be able to drink this miracle of nature . . . but don't worry, I'll drink yours too . . ."

"Oh, yeah . . . ?"

He got hold of his glass most delicately and imitated the owner's actions. First, take a look at the golden liquid through the glass, then a first delicate sniff . . . ummm. A gentle swirl of the liquid in the glass and a second, stronger sniff . . . wow. With closed eyes, he took just a small mouthful and let it invade his palate before swallowing it. His eyes sprang open and he smiled at me.

"Boy! I promise from now on I'll never refuse a glass of wine from you!"

He proceeded to empty his glass, small sip by small sip to the last drop. On came a second glass. I was very discreet and promised never to mention the word Bahá'í when he was enjoying "God's gift to man."

ACT XV—THE CHILDREN

Once upon a time there lived a Pied Piper
Who would play over land and sea;
His music enchanted all children who heard him
And one of those children was me.

Dizzy enjoyed criticizing this convoluted limerick I had invented for him on the spur of the moment. We often argued about English grammar, kidding each other on the kind of education to be had at The English School in Heliopolis-Cairo, Egypt, as opposed to Cheraw, South Ca'linah! "You and me, or you and I?" or else his favorite showoff: "Give me just any word, Lil, in any language, and I'll spell it for you correctly down to the last letter, bet you a cappuccino?"

And most of the time he would win his cappuccino.

Of course, he was a natural clown, and a fascinating one, especially for the children he would meet in the street. He would squat to their level or sit on the ledge of a fountain in a piazza, gathering around him an array of all ages, often holding some amused grandpa by the hand. In the chatter and laughter of his mini audience he would call for their attention and, with his mimic, would ask them to put their finger vertically across their lips, as he was doing. OK? Now everybody blows against his own finger puffing out the cheeks like him.

"No possibile? Si, si, si! Come, come now, cosi' . . . try again, blow like this . . . cosi' . . . ah, there you go, see? Si!"

The children. Dizzy and Lorraine had none of their own, but he was father to all ages: from the music students seeking harmonic enlightenment to the babies who nestled peacefully in his arms. In his later years they had touched his heart in yet another way, so one day in 1985, as we sat outside a sunny café in Bassano del Grappa, drinking his favorite cappuccino, he suddenly sat up and nudged my arm: "Hey Lilian? Listen! I got something for you . . . I mean all those kids I see at my doctor's, even little kids, would you believe it? They've got it too, but it's much worse at their age and you've got to do something for the ones here in Italy. I'll help you, but you lay out the plan, I trust you."

While he sipped noisily on his hot cup, content to have parked his problem on me, I closed my eyes and searched rapidly for clues: His doctor? The only ailment I knew of was his diabetes. What did I know about diabetic children and the Italian medical involvement in their cure? For that matter, what did I know about diabetes itself, except that you had to watch your sugar intake and do something about your insulin? I had firm orders from Lorraine to watch out for Dizzy's sweet tooth, which often provoked mini-arguments and an underground battle mantled in courtesy.

"Oh, Liliah-nah, don't give up dessert just because I can't have it. Isn't that your favorite cake? The Sachersomething?"

"The Sachertorte, and I'm not fooled. The moment the waiter would set it on my plate you'd be digging into it. . . . But it's OK; I don't mind giving it up—it will show you how much I care . . ."

"But I know how much you care! You don't have to prove it by giving up something you love so much . . . humm . . . look at that chocolate crust . . ."

"Dizzy! Just the other day you were saying that I too would probably end up sitting next to you in your doctor's waiting room . . ."

"Humph! OK-OK . . . !"

This brought me back to his request that something be done for Italian juvenile diabetes.

"OK Diz, I'm willing to try but you must tell me more about it."

Still blissfully engrossed in his cup, he raised his eyebrows in surprise: "Huh?" So I turned soul sister: "Ah means like-a, ma-an, you'se got dis chile problem, right? So lay it on me, you know . . . Like . . . gimme some light, dig?"

My approximate Southern drawl startled him; he opened his mouth and threw back his head in the familiar laugh.

"Aaa . . . Hah! I know what! Remember that time in . . . was it Brescia? That was great, what you got for me. You could have it on a national scale for all diabetic kids, right?"

"Giovanni. . . . Just *what* did I get for you in Brescia that should be done on a national scale?"

"Don't you remember? You had that friend of yours at the restaurant make this special sugarless ice cream for me . . . hummm, it was *so* good . . . don't you remember?"

"Oh, but I do now, and *you* decided the ice cream was all for you and gobbled my portion as well *and* cleaned up the serving dish."

He cackled his satisfaction: "Yeh, yeh. . . . Well, don't you know any big ice cream factory that could, maybe, buy the formula from your friend and put it on the market for the kids? I mean, you know everybody . . . ?"

"I don't, but I know *you* . . . OK, I'll inquire and let you know as soon as I have something etched out . . ."

"Etched or sketched? Do you know the exact difference between those words?"

He asked with that gleam in his eyes and we were off again. What could a Mediterranean girl brought up on the banks of the Nile know about the English language? Always more than an urchin from Cheraw! Oh yeah?

Together Again

Some months later we were together again for a concert near Venice. As usual, I picked him up at Venice airport in my sturdy Peugeot, and, as usual, he commented on my sharing the same peculiar taste for broken-down cars with the TV sleuth "Columbo." At the suggestion that he ride with his musicians in the larger car, he emphatically declared that my "Roman way of driving" was too stimulating, and he wouldn't miss it for a Rolls. At that moment I caught sight, in my side rearview mirror, of a bright red miracle looming behind us.

"Ah, Giovanni . . . you can keep your Rolls . . . Here comes THE perfect BEAUTY . . ."

And the red Ferrari came abreast, purring, whining, then roaring past as I sighed audibly.

Followed a deep silence; then he nudged me. "Bet you'd love to drive one of them cars, huh?"

"Did I tell you that my ex-husband is what they call a 'gentleman racer'? He raced, but not professionally. With his pal Giannino Marzotto they won twice the famous road race called "Mille Miglia" with a Ferrari. Actually, I met the great Enzo Ferrari in person, a charming man, and when Marco and I got married he lent us his Ferrari Barchetta to use during our honeymoon."

"So you did get to drive a Ferrari?"

I sighed heavily, shaking my head.

"Nope, Marco would not let me drive it, alas . . ."

"Wise man," Dizzy commented.

"And what car do *you* drive in the States?"

"A beautiful limo . . . with driver . . . who comes to pick me up whenever I phone him . . ."

"Ah, that's why you criticize my driving . . . you're unable to drive yourself! Yet most jazz musicians I know own some kind of sports car . . ."

"Yeah. Like Miles. He's a Ferrari addict like you. He goes directly to the factory to pick it up. He's got at least three of them at home . . ."

"Ah, lucky guy!"

"Yep, but I never accepted to ride with him; though now, after riding around with you . . ."

I retorted that my speed did not seem to bother him if he could sprawl out and snore his head off the moment we left the curb!

This time, however, he was interested in the "working holiday" that had been organized for him. The producers of the concert at San Donà di Piave, a fishing town along the Venetian coast, had asked how they could show their appreciation for the visit of the "grande Gillespie." Learning that Dizzy doted on fish, one of the producers declared he would go to the harbor at dawn, as the boats came in, to pick the very best that the Adriatic Sea could offer. Maria, the wife who was an expert cook, would produce a menu fit for the Guide Michelin. Did Gillespie like baccalà? And the famous "granseole," Adriatic crabs?

So there we were in the car with Dizzy all ears, eyes, and smiles as he listened to the gourmet delight that awaited him.

"Ooooh . . . that sounds nice. . . . You know, Lorraine says she can always tell when I'm coming to Italy for your concerts . . ."

"I know. The other day on the phone she told me you were on your morning tour of Englewood spreading the news. She also told me that the moment you get back home you show all your friends, at your barber's, your Italian newspaper clippings."

"Yeah, that's right. And I read 'em out to them."

"But you don't read Italian . . . !"

He laughed and nudged me.

"I know, but I *sound* like I do. And my barber . . . he's Italian, so he knows I'm putting them on, but when they ask him he tells them, surprised: 'Don't you understand what he's reading?' 'No, do you?' And, poker faced, he says: 'Sure! It's Italian. Dizzy reads perfect Italian.'"

His big laugh again.

"Well, at least your barber can translate the articles for you."

"Why, you know what that 'mutha' does when I hand them to him? He reads them silently with grunts and smiles and ahahs, and when I ask him what they say, he puts away the clippings and shrugs: 'Aah . . . same old stuff, great concert, great artist, and the usual blah, blah, so what else is new?' . . . And that's all he'll tell me!"

Dizzy often mentioned his friend the Italian barber, and one day we went shopping in Rome for an original Borsalino hat to give him. Maybe one day I'll meet him and we'll speak of our friend. Of how much he loved Italy, and how much Italy loved him.

Back to San Donà, where the other members of the quintet had also been invited to this special luncheon. Soon we were all sitting in a private garden with a tasty "aperitivo e stuzzichini," an aperitif with choice morsels, while a bevy of nice ladies, young and old, were bustling about. Dizzy and his musicians were enjoying the occasion. Toasts were raised to Dizzy's health, and he rose to express his heartfelt thanks for being admitted into such a lovely home with such gracious hosts.

Finally, all were urged to enter the dining room—"E' pronto!"

Sitting at a huge square table, literally covered with various trays of hors d'oeuvres, Dizzy seemed mellowed by the patriarchal atmosphere: husbands, wives, grandparents, well-behaved children . . . all sitting around the most delicious food.

He squeezed my arm and shook his head. "This is unbelievable; Lorraine should see this."

"Next time you *must* bring her over with you; she's been promising to come for ages. . . . I've even spoken to a friend for an audience with the Pope."

"I know, and she's always telling her friends at church that she's coming over to meet the Pope. But then something urgent turns up—or breaks down in the house—and she has to stay home."

Suddenly, Dizzy's bass player, John Lee, sprang to his feet from the opposite side of the table. He held out his glass and, almost gruffly, said he spoke on behalf of all the musicians. They wished to express their appreciation for this special hospitality and to declare that they never enjoyed their gigs so much, or met such nice people, as they did with me. "So . . . well, thank you." And, just as suddenly, he sat down.

There was a pause of pleased surprise as I translated for our hosts while Dizzy smiled, approving, then clinked his glass to mine. Everybody beamed as the many entrées came in: spaghetti alle vongole veraci; farfalle ai gamberetti e piselli; risotto alla marinara . . .

Dizzy stuck the large napkin around his neck, as expectant as a little boy, with round, happy eyes.

We often organized his concert tours with one or two days off for him to discover a different Italy and genuine Italian hospitality. This time a surprise awaited him, so he was warned to ask no questions but be ready by nine the next morning and to bring a cardigan, as we were going to the mountains. He had raised his eyebrows, sizing me up shrewdly, and then nodded OK.

At a quarter to nine the next morning he was sitting at a hearty breakfast in his usual jovial spirits. He hailed me loudly across the dining room: "Buon-gee-ornow Liliah-nah. Comee stahee?"

"Buongiorno Giovanni Gillespo. Did you sleep well? Are you ready for a very special day?"

While sipping loudly on his cappuccino, he nodded and waited for me to continue.

"OK. So. A limo is coming to pick us up, and we'll drive out to the mountains."

He pointed out of the window: "You mean them peaks way out there? They look fa-aar away to me! We'll get back in time? OK-OK, if you say so, I know we will. So, where are we going?"

"To a small mountain village called Busche."

"Busche . . . Busche . . . you spell it b-u-s-k . . . no, no, wait a minute, the Italian way is b-u-s-c-h-e, right?"

"Don't know how you do it, but you have an extraordinary ear for spelling. Anyway, guess where we are going and what for?"

His one-track mind prompted: "Food?"

"What is it you like very much, apart from sweets, pasta, and fish?"

He mused very soberly on the question: "Hummm . . . Cheese?"

I nodded just as soberly. "Right. We are going to visit one of northern Italy's largest milk and cheese factories. You will hold a press meeting. You will be met by the president and the director general of this factory *and* they will give you a present I know you will appreciate, *and* . . ."

Pause for drama . . .

". . . The subject will be Italian juvenile diabetes."

A bear hug and a cappuccino kiss on my cheek:

"Aowww! I knew you'd think of something! What is it, tell me?"

The limo arrived in time to save me from disclosing the surprise.

As was to be expected, Dizzy was soon snoring noisily to one side, and one wondered if all this sleepiness at ten in the morning could not be a strong signal regarding his health.

Upon arrival Dizzy emerged from the car rested and buoyant to charm and entertain the authorities who were waiting at the factory entrance. He was given a formal welcome and was ushered into a conference room, where various journalists greeted him.

Dizzy was obviously in his favorite element: limelight, interviewers, compliments, photographers, pretty secretaries giggling at the cheeky way he would ogle them. Then the official presentation of the gift: a small, hand-wrought silver periscopic trumpet on a neck chain, made by a well-known artist who happened to be a Gillespie fan. Dizzy was truly touched by the beauty of the object. He gave me one of his mellow smiles and hung it around his neck, next to the Bahá'í stone from Mount Carmel.

The president and the director general were talking officially now, and Dizzy leaned his good ear toward me so I could translate. His face broke gradually into one of his largest smiles on learning that, having just bought an ice cream factory, the men had decided to study the scientific possibility of producing a special line of ice cream, fruit yogurts, and desserts for diabetic children to be distributed throughout Italy. All this had been brought about thanks to the personal concern of Maestro Gillespie, a diabetic himself, who was sensible to the plight of children whose illness prevented them from sharing the small joys afforded to their healthier companions. If feasible, then the line would be named "Dizzy."

It was a very happy day as Dizzy visited the factory, drank different types of milk, tried a dozen cheeses, poked his nose into the various proceedings, and finally emerged with the gift of a huge wheel of mountain cheese in its travelling cardboard box, which he held on to jealously with both arms. He then snored like a dragon during the two-hour drive back to San Donà.

The concert was a huge success ("So what else is new?" his barber would have said). The jazz musicians who taught at our music school in Bassano had come to greet him, and he entertained everybody with his good humor. The next day, driving him to the Venice airport, I promised to keep him informed regarding the ice cream factory. One last "outgoing cappuccino" at the airport café, then a hug of affection, and with a final crack we parted, laughing and waving farewell.

Unfortunately, a few months later the director of the dairy informed me that he was truly sorry but their experiments for glucose-less ice cream, to be produced on a large scale, had been scientifically and financially negative, so they were giving up.

Informed of the outcome, Dizzy heaved a big sigh and then consoled me: "Well, you sure gave it a good try, Lil; I appreciate it, honest."

ACT XVI—"OO-SHOO-BE-DOO-BE"

It was May 1985 and, Dizzy having confirmed his presence in the recording studio in Milano, a series of engagements were quickly organized. The main event was the recording session, from midday on Monday the 13th to midday of Wednesday the 15th. The trio that Dizzy had approved of comprised Kenny Drew, Ed Thigpen, and Swiss bassist Isla Eckinger. They would join us directly in Milano.

On the first evening the quartet would also appear at an important TV show in Milano. On the second evening we would appear at the Bobadilla, a plush jazz club in Dalmine, outside Milano. On the third evening we would play a concert in Bassano as part of the concert season we organized each year. Finally, on the last day, after his favorite "minestrone" lunch with my mother, he would pass by his music school in a flash visit on his way to Milano airport. Having arranged with Wim Wigt all the details regarding Dizzy's travel, all was finally set.

For this very special occasion our friends from Nice, Colette and Bernard Taride, had driven to Milano to join us. While we waited for Dizzy's arrival—someone had been dispatched to the railway station to look out for him—we went through a list of songs in order to make the final choice and then decided to go on with the sound check.

Kenny began playing "I'm in the Mood for Love," which was not on the list but we all joined in. Not bad, then Kenny asked me if I knew James Moody's version. I asked the technician to play back the song we had just recorded, and I sang Moody's "Mood for Love" over it. The technician had recorded also this double version, so we listened, approved, and decided to add it to the list just as it was. After all, Moody was very close to Dizzy's heart. . . .

Finally, Maestro Gillespo arrived from the station, sneezing and grumbling that Bern had been humid and the train cold. While he greeted and hugged everybody, I got out my homeopathic first-aid kit and instructed him to take the medication. He looked dubiously at me.

"Ah, you're on this stuff too? Just like Faddis: in fact, his wife is a homeopath and they are always telling me I should take this . . ."

"So there you are. Now this is miraculous—it's Oscillococcinum. Just open up your mouth like a good boy and let me pour the granules—come on, it won't kill you. I want you alive and well for the next few days . . ."

He obeyed, muttering about waiting till he told Jon about this. Eventually, his first cappuccino of the day arrived, and very soon the recording session was under way.

We had not really rehearsed any of the songs but simply distributed the various solos.

Of course the first song was my lucky charm, which was to give the title to the album: "Oo-shoo-be-doo-be. Oo-Oo!"

I was supposed to sing the song from the first chorus, as in the original recording. So we began with his famous trumpet intro, and just as I opened my mouth to sing, I heard his nasal/gravelly voice singing "One day while strolling . . ." and there he was, eyes closed, singing blissfully my part.

I waited and joined him on the "Ooo-shoo-be-doo-be," at which point he turned to look at me, surprised and then abashed, but I shook my head and motioned for him not to stop. We smiled and kept singing together. As I did not wish to alter the order of the choruses, I waited for Ed Thigpen's drum solo to join him with my singing.

Take one was approved, and we moved on to the rest of the repertoire.

"Con Alma" was first sung with the original lyrics and, upon Dizzy's suggestion, with a religious feeling. Then I surprised him in my second solo by singing the lyrics by my sister-of-the-soul Abbey Lincoln, dedicated to a "man of music, lover of beauty. . . ." He was pleased.

For "Body and Soul" I teased him, asking for a Miles Davis kind-of-blue feeling; he complied, and everybody joined in the mood he had set. At the very end, unrehearsed, Kenny and I went into the changes of the coda, nodding at each other while, in the very last chords, I omitted singing the line "body and soul" altogether but left a questioning "myself to you . . . ?" hanging there.

When came the time for "Night in Tunisia," I asked Dizzy to make it *very* "Arabian Nights," for I had a surprise for him. They went into a long oriental intro where he brought out his marranzano, shook his famous "Nndo stick" made up of clinking Coke caps, and then finally I started singing. I sang in Arabic, with lyrics written together with my Egyptian friend Leila Moustapha. He kept blowing but his eyebrows were raised to the ceiling in amazement. Everybody had fun with that tune, and I spoke words of ardent love in Egyptian during his solo, while he replied with the muted horn.

• • •

Allow me a digression: Practically a year after the CD had been issued also in the United States, I received a phone call.

"Pronto?"

"Prontow Liliah-nah! I've got to apologize to you . . ."

"You bet; it's three in the morning . . . again!"

"It is? Humph. Well anyway . . . I had to call you right this minute to apologize because, listen to this: I'm in this taxi, driving home from Manhattan, and the radio plays our "Night in Tunisia." The driver starts getting all excited, and he tells me it's the first time he hears jazz sung in Arabic. So I ask him if he can really understand the words, and he tells me, "Of course! It's in Egyptian, like me!" So the moment I got home I had to grab the phone to apologize."

"What for?"

"Well, you see . . . I never believed the lyrics were in real Arabic. I thought you were putting me on, in Milano, just blah-blahing."

"Well, grazie mille! So you wake me at dawn to tell me you thought I was a phony?"

"OK-OK. I'm sorry, but I did want to tell you. Now you go back to your beauty sleep . . ."

"I know, 'because I sure need it.' . . ." I listened to his cackle. "However, I'm glad you told me all this. Ciao, Giovanni, good night."

• • •

Back to the recording studio; came the moment for Dizzy to produce the song he had promised when it had rained so much in Torino and in Nice.

"Dizzy, where's my song? I know you got my lyrics . . ."

"Oh yes . . . I have them right here in my wallet, over my heart."

"But where's the music?! You promised! Remember?"

"Well . . . how about we work out a low-down blues instead? You work out the lyrics while I have this cappuccino . . ."

And that's how "The Sunshine Blues" was improvised by all.

The first line began: "You promised me the sunshine . . . and all I got from you was rain . . ."

On that last morning, during a break, I treated Dizzy to his cappuccino in the nearby café that had won his preference during those days. On the way back we strolled, window shopping, to the special menswear boutique where Dizzy kept ogling some Irish cotton cable-knit sweaters. Which one was nicer, the red one or the pale leaf green? The green was more elegant for a man, apart from the fact that red . . . considering his stomach . . . Oh, yeah?! Anyway, he shook his head and strolled off to the recording studio next door. I entered the shop and got three identical sweaters, two green ones for Dizzy and Francesco and a red one for me (which I still wear to this day).

In the studio we recorded and listened to the last song. OK, that's it; wrap it up. Off to the hotel to shower and change for lunch.

And what's this on his bed?

The note on the sweater read:

"From Cairo Lil to Diz the Wiz. Wear this in good health. Shukran."

"Hey, Leeleeahn . . ." he called out. "Honest now . . . you shouldn'a have . . . and what's 'shookrun'?"

"It's Egyptian to say 'Thank you.'"

He wore it instantly.

All the tunes had been recorded lazily during the three days, with lots of cappuccino breaks, some excellent lunches and dinners, and when also Bernard and Colette Taride joined in the final judgment, adding their positive vote, we finally decided to leave it at that.

The following day we headed for Bassano. During the concert sound check Roberto and the teachers of our school joined us, and then we all strolled down to

Dizzy's favorite promenade spot, the old Wooden Bridge from whence he would look at the Grappa Mountains with that special smile on his face.

The next day at my house he met a new addition to my household, a Giant Schnauzer puppy I had named Bebop. Dizzy smiled with raised eyebrows and I explained:

". . . 'cause he's a unique black phenomenon. Just like Bebop, no?"

"Yeah!" he grinned as he fondled the dog's ear.

Time to return to Bassano, where a limo was waiting to drive him to the Milano airport. We first went by the school, and he approved the attractive school sign by the front door, which he read aloud: "Scuola Popolare di Musica 'Dizzy Gillespie.'"

As we parted I asked the driver to take him over the old Wooden Bridge for a brief pause.

"Ciao, Giovanni! We have one last pleasant moment for you . . ."

"What is it?"

"Be patient. Ciaaao. . . ." I waved him off.

Eventually, he did remember his promise, and one day I received some publications on the Bahá'í faith, some in English and some in Italian. I applied myself dutifully, waiting for the time he would decide to give me my "exams."

ACT XVII—ODDS AND ENDS

Looking back at the many years of friendship, so many memories reach out to us, like flash anecdotes, that they must be mentioned just as they come to mind and as a single section.

A Family Man

One aspect about Dizzy Gillespie, perhaps lesser known, was his enjoyment of family life. When Francesco and Lisa were married in September 1985, they went to live in New Jersey, where my granddaughter Alice was born in April 1987. One day an enthusiastic letter told me of their visit at Dizzy's home in Englewood, enclosing snapshots of fatherly Dizzy with two-month-old Alice as he held her in his arms carefully while she smiled up at him. This grandfatherly attitude continued through the years. In 1988 Francesco, having moved to Los Angeles, wrote about Dizzy as "babysitter." Invited to join Dizzy for lunch, Francesco had explained that he was taking care of Alice for the day. No problem: Francesco was to drive by the back door of the hotel, and Dizzy would sneak out incognito—and Alice was welcome to go along with them. They had gone to Korea Town on Olympic Boulevard to Dizzy's favorite restaurant where, once seated with Alice perched in the baby seat between them, Francesco had realized he had forgotten her "in case" diapers. Dizzy had simply sent him off to the nearest drugstore while he would look after Alice, not to worry! An anxious Francesco had returned to the restaurant to a scene where Dizzy and Alice were making faces at each other, chuckling and having a great time.

Honolulu in 1991. Dizzy, arriving on a Hawaiian tour had brought four-year-old Alice a gift necklace. Picked up at the Prince Hotel, he had been driven around to enjoy Oahu's beauty spots in Lisa's car. Faithful to his motoring habits, he had slumbered off while sitting in the back seat next to Alice; both snoring away, leaning against each other like two drunks. However, in the picture they sent me, Alice is sitting on his knees, in the living room, both of them well awake and grinning.

Commencement Day

During mother's eightieth birthday and "farewell trip" through the United States, we arrived in Los Angeles for Francesco's commencement day as he was graduating from USC. Cherry on the cake, Dizzy was briefly in Los Angeles for a club engagement.

We were invited to join him at his hotel suite, where he paid special attention to mother, as usual. He invited us to the jazz club that same evening, and of course Francesco and I went like a shot. We took a cab and said, "Marla's Memory Lane, please?"

The cabbie turned around to look at us, amazed:

"You mean that club in South Central? That's in the Watts neighborhood, you know that?"

Our nod, his shrug, and off we went.

We soon realized why the driver had hesitated. It was a very black jazz club in a very black neighborhood, and Francesco and I stood out like two sore white thumbs. Dizzy must have informed the doorman to expect us, for he very grumpily let us through and led us to a tiny table right by the toilets. We sat perched uncomfortably and tried to smile at the frowning stares while Francesco, ever optimistic, assured me that the atmosphere would improve once Dizzy arrived and they saw our relationship with him. To use one of Dizzy's expressions, I said "Humph!"

The music was excellent, and we soon forgot the scene, the human perfume wafting from the nearby toilet, and the "friendly" service. At the end of the first set Dizzy sat with us and seemed amused by the negative effect we had on his public, but eventually he suggested we return downtown before the second set and provided us with a drive back to USC.

"Well, Giovanni, apart from the pleasure of your music and your impressive conga drumming, I must thank you for another experience. . . . You see, tonight I really understood what racial discrimination feels like, and rightly so."

Intimacy

One day in his hotel room in Brescia, while shaving in the bathroom, he called out to me.

"Hey, Leeleeyahn. . . . Notice my hair?"

I walked to the open door of the bathroom.

"What about it?"

"You DON'T notice any difference?"

At his disappointment I gave him a scrutinizing look and realized that in fact he had stopped coloring his hair. Acting puzzled, to tease him, I shook my head.

"Nope. The only difference I see in you . . ." (*pause*) . . . "is that you have turned into a very distinguished-looking gentleman with a becoming iron-grey head."

"Hah!" He was satisfied.

". . . And a notable paunch . . ."

"Huh?" less satisfied.

At that moment the room-service waiter knocked and brought in a cappuccino that he set on the small table by the bathroom door, against which I was leaning.

The man looked at Dizzy shaving in his underwear, gave me a long sly look as I stood there, then with a little smirk left the room.

"Ah, well, Giovanni. . . . That's it, there goes my reputation. In two minutes everyone will know that Gillespie has a female in his bathroom where he stands in a state of undress. They will all think I am your mistress or something."

He kept shaving, a little smile creeping up, and then shrugged: "Well, everybody thinks so anyway. The guys in the band, our friends . . . I don't mind . . ."

"They do? Your friends think . . ."

"Anyway . . . the whole 'mistress' scene . . . it gives us a certain glamor, don't you think?"

"Sure, why not? At least we have the glamor of an affair without the physical effort!"

There followed the fraction of a frown, taken aback, and then his laughter.

This is the answer to anyone who might have wondered about us, at one time or another, during our long years of friendship. Was there intimacy? Yes—of an affectionate nature but never physical. We had the glamor without the effort. He loved that phrase.

Happy Birthday Concert Party

Dizzy's seventieth birthday was on October 21, 1987, but all along that year there were celebrations all over the world, wherever he went.

While visiting Francesco in New York, we received an invitation to attend a special "birthday concert" at Carnegie Hall, where the JVC Jazz Festival of New York presented:

Tuesday Evening, June 23, 1987, at 8:00
Wynton Marsalis salutes Dizzy Gillespie
On his Seventieth Birthday
The Dizzy Gillespie Big Band

There followed the long and detailed list of the musicians involved. This Big Band was formed also by his faithful and historic sidemen, some of whom later became members of his United Nations Orchestra, his last dream come true.

At the theater we were conducted to the side entrance and ushered into an elevator and up into a drawing room with a grand piano, a birthday cake perched upon it. The place was crowded with VIPs, champagne flutes in hand, and everybody vied for his attention. He was sitting at the piano, chewing his Cuban cigar, a new cowboy hat perched rakishly, playing with one hand and chatting with everybody. Francesco approached him shyly to say hello. Dizzy greeted him, and soon they were discussing music, with Dizzy explaining to him, on the piano, "the importance of the diminished fifth in the Bebop evolution, conceptually, harmonically, and stylistically!"

On that occasion he introduced us to Walter Gil Fuller and asked him to take care of us when the organizers engulfed him and carried him away.

Some days later Fuller invited us to his favorite Sushi place in Fort Lee, New Jersey, and while chatting about jazz music and its place in European culture, we mentioned our admiration for his unique arrangements of Dizzy's music, especially the ones to be heard on the Verve collection and, of course, above all "Manteca." To our surprise he seemed irritated and finally explained that he had done "much more than just arrange those tunes" and gave us to understand that some of them had been his compositions to begin with. I soothed him by mentioning that in his autobiography, Dizzy had declared repeatedly how essential Fuller had been in putting together the famous big band in 1946 and what a great organizer and original arranger he was . . .

This brought back memories and anecdotes of that historic orchestra with the various famous soloists, and at that point, enthusiastically, Francesco mentioned the name of Charlie Parker. Fuller frowned again, and then explained. It had so happened that at one time Bird had come back to New York from California to rejoin the band. Dizzy had been watching over him like a warden, as the last thing they needed was for the new band to get all the bad press that Parker seemed to draw upon himself, implying that all beboppers were junkies. But soon it was starting all over again, so that Bird would reach the stage in such a state that he couldn't even blow his notes. And he would be nodding on the bandstand, and all the younger musicians who were looking up to him were beginning to imitate his habit. In the end Dizzy and Fuller were forced to take a drastic decision. They took him off the bandstand as a player and simply paid him for all the wonderful tunes he would compose for them.

I later thanked Dizzy for having introduced us to Gil Fuller, for he was a charming man and we remained in contact with him and his beautiful wife for a number of years.

Exams

So one day, during a long chauffeur-driven ride, instead of falling asleep in his corner he puffed on his "Cuban," and with a clever little smile Dizzy asked me point-blank:

"So . . . and where is the seat of the Bahá'í?!"

I gathered my wits . . . so this was it . . . the test. OK, Giovanni . . . I'll show you!

"The central seat of the Bahá'í is in Haifa, Israel, at the Mausoleum of the Founders, but actually the religion was founded in the nineteenth century in Iran. It tried to gather together the sense of all past religions, yet it was mainly inspired by Iranian Islamic practice, like with the fast and the forbidden alcohol."

After a first surprise he nodded approvingly at me, preparing his next question.

"Tell me about the original founder . . . ?"

"In 1844 the faith was founded by the Iranian Mirza Ali Mohammed, born in 1820, a Shiite and therefore convinced of the return of the Imam, the messenger of God. He declared he was the 'Bab,' the 'door' through which one would reach God. He died in 1850 in Tabriz, executed on the orders of the shah."

I grinned, for he was surprised by my command of dates and facts. He attacked again:

"Who succeeded him and what is he famous for?"

"Easy! Mizra Hussein Ali, born 1817, buried in London in 1892. He called himself the Bahá'u'lláh, which means 'Splendor of God,' and he broke with the Islamic influence, deciding that the Bahá'í be a modern and nonviolent religion dedicated to the reconciliation of all creeds around some strong common principles, based on God."

"That's very good! Of course, I've already told you about the various stages of humanity, the family, the tribe, and finally the family of Man. And about the main principle that God is unique, as is the human family, and that all religions have a common foundation and must find common grounds with science and reason. And that men and women must have the same rights . . ."

"Yes! That's what pleased me most, the fact that even then women had the same right to education and to accede to social power, just like the men. The early Bahá'ís were really fervent emancipators of women, rejecting polygamy and unfaithfulness in marriage and . . . Ahem . . . they forbid alcohol and smoke."

I cleared my throat noisily while looking pointedly at his cigar and remembering the Piccolit wine experience. But he ignored the open innuendo and picked up, unmoved:

"Yes, that's from the side of Islam, just as we have the nineteen days of fast, and we pray three times daily, morning, noon, and evening. But we have no clergy, no religious ceremonial. We have the local community or the local spiritual assembly and then the national one . . ."

I added my two cents, showing off:

". . . And when the spiritual assembly meets, you recite the prayers of the Bab, of Bahá'u'lláh, and then you take care of all the different questions, including material ones, regarding the life of the community. By the way, do you say your prayers too? Can you recite one? The first that comes to mind . . . ?"

He nodded with a smile and recited: "Blessed be the place and the house, and the city and the heart, and the mountain and the refuge, and the cavern and the valley, and the land and the sea, and the island and the prairie wherever a sign of God is made and where His praise is lifted high."

"Yes! And it was written by Bahá'u'lláh!"

"I see you've received all the publications I asked for you . . ."

"Yes, including the book by Shoghi Effendi, *The Promised Day Is Come*, and a beautiful folder with all those lovely pictures of the Mausoleum and the Gardens on Mount Carmel. I must say it gives a feeling of beauty and peace just looking at them."

"That's what the Bahá'í religion is all about, beauty and peace."

"Yes . . . however, I was impressed by some of the sentences by Bahá'u'lláh, written in the early twentieth century, where he speaks . . . about the destruction of the world and its people through a terrifying upheaval and dreadful tribulations that will shower upon all men. Because God will punish us for the evil we have done with our own hands. And the leaders of the world will call aloud for help, but because of their foolishness they will receive no answer. . . . It's practically the Apocalypse, no?"

"Yes; however, Bahá'u'lláh also says that in the end, all over the earth her most noble fruits will grow, and the tallest trees and the most beautiful flowers and the most exquisite gifts from heaven. And every creature will lay down its heavy load and grace will pervade all things, visible and invisible."

"That's all very well, but what about the oppression and violence we see today around us in all forms?"

"He says that these oppressions prepare the advent of Supreme Justice, which will be the advent of the Greater Peace, which will inaugurate the Supreme World Civilization, which will be forever united in His name."

"But, my dear Giovanni, from the way the world is going now, this Great Peace is not for tomorrow. If and when it does happen, we won't be around to enjoy it."

"That's not important. But the day will come."

"As you see, I have really done my homework . . ."

He nodded his approval, patting my hand, and I knew I had passed my exams.

ACT XVIII—WOODY 'N YOU

I was preparing a radio program dedicated to the famous recording ban during the Second World War, and the ensuing special Armed Forces production of V-discs. That series of records had just been reissued worldwide, and RAI had dispatched me to the United States to interview as many personalities of that era as were still available, to illustrate the actual facts that had taken place during those years. In New York I spoke with, among others, George Simon and good friend George Avakian. Then I moved to California for a pleasant, if loud-pitched, meeting with Red Norvo and then was welcomed by Woody Herman in his beautiful Hollywood home.

Next, I was off to Washington, where I visited the Library of Congress and finally had lunch with Willis Conover of the Voice of America.

To catch the shuttle back to New York I left Willis hurriedly and stepped toward a cab that was just parking by the curb. Dizzy emerged and we stared at each other, surprised.

"Hey Lil, I thought you were in New York with Abbey?"

". . . and Lorraine told me you were playing in LA?"

"The gig was postponed and this venue came next. You're staying on, ain't you? Let me show you the place, it's right around the corner in this alley . . ."

I decided to catch the next shuttle, to humor him, and soon we were entering the club. We sat at a table where he was immediately served what looked like an excellent soul food plate, which I declined, having just lunched with Conover. I then explained about my ". . . recherche du Jazz perdu . . ." with an amusing anecdote that concerned him.

During the interview with Woody Herman we had obviously spoken about his Herds, with special mention of the Four Brothers. At that point Woody had given a little laugh and touched my hand, saying:

"Here's a story you will appreciate, it's about Dizzy during the years of The Street, you know . . . in New York in the early forties. I had noticed that some of my soloists were playing some weird solos that didn't really fit with the band arrangements. So, when they spoke about this 'bebop' music, I told them to go ahead and get some special tune written specifically for the Herd. So we got something called 'Swing Shift,' and later one called 'Down Under," composed and arranged by someone called Gillespie. These tunes had a very special arrangement that really floored us, and I said to myself: 'This music is the beginning of an era!' To be honest, the guys had to work very hard to play those arrangements, and they would sneak away to listen to this bebop music—like everyone had begun to call it—every chance they got. So finally, must have been in 1942 or '43, they took me to this club on Fifty-Second Street to meet the composer and arranger of our tunes. I sat at the bar and listened to a cat playing a horn, and I did not like his style at all. Then up he comes to introduce himself, says he's glad the band liked his tunes, and we talk for a while. I ask him for some more stuff, but he tells me that his real work is with his trumpet, which takes a lot of his time. So I tell him, honestly and sincerely, that I did not really think he had a future as a trumpet player but should concentrate on writing and arranging his great music instead. This was Dizzy Gillespie I was talking to! You realize?! Fortunately, he paid no attention to my advice!"

Dizzy had been listening with a little smile as I related our conversation, nodding and puffing on his Cubano as I continued:

"He was amused and tickled to tell this story as one of his favorite memories about those war years . . . Gillespie or the Beginning of an Era! He also added something about you, Parker, and Monk and your other musicians, and how today the newcomers don't really realize that what they're hearing and playing now is something historic, something that revolutionized jazz from what it had been in the swing era. He was truly complimentary about you, said you were . . . ah yes, a giant!"

"Yeah, but it was really thanks to my association with Bird. He really gave me a huge inspiration, far above anything musical that I have ever done since."

"Would you mind telling me a little more about your relationship with Charlie Parker? Everybody has a different opinion, especially about the problems he caused you and your band through the years. Apart from the musical magic you two created together, he remains a mystery to many of us. What sort of human being was he? One only hears about his addiction. You probably knew him more deeply than any of those other cats who hung around him for the worst reason. Do you mind talking about him?"

"Well, for instance, he was much better read than I was. Used to read all the time and about all subjects, and we'd have these long talks and discussions about politics, religion, philosophy. . . . I remember his discovery of this French writer, Baudelaire; talked about him all the time. I learned a lot about life and the social order from Bird . . ."

"Which would you say was the highest moment in the music you created together, or was there a special one?"

"Oh yes. The highest height was at the Three Deuces with Bird, Max Roach, Bud Powell, and Curley Russell, who was later replaced by Ray Brown."

"Ah, yes . . . those special, creative years . . . and was Bird already . . . using, then?"

"I believe he started fooling around with drugs when he was fourteen, but he was very careful about it at the beginning. In fact, Bird and I were very close in a certain way but we didn't mix when he would hang around with those other guys. He was always very discreet about his habit, never using or smoking in front of me."

"But then something happened in California, didn't it? When he ended up in Camarillo Hospital and you were forced to leave him there to return to New York for your engagements?"

"That's right," he sighed.

"But still there remained this special bond of respect between the two of you. In your book, Al Haig said that you were perhaps the only one to understand the inner workings of Bird's mind. And Max Roach mentioned how you tried in every way to get him to take better care of himself, and that once he answered that "his notoriety was to show young people not to use dope and throw their life away like he was doing"—I mean, how do you help someone who gives you an answer like that?"

"Yet I never let him down, even if I couldn't take him back into my band anymore, at least not to play regularly. The last time I saw him was just before he died, in 1955. He came to where I was playing, and he looked terrible. We were talking when he suddenly said, "Diz, why don't you save me?" I asked him: "How?" "I don't know, just save me, man." I felt helpless and sad because I knew I couldn't save him from himself. But we remained closest friends until his death . . ."

"He passed away in Nica's home, didn't he?"

"She called me to say Yardbird had just died in her apartment. It broke me up, we were so very close. With all the problems he had caused everybody, and we all knew his life hung by a thread by his own making . . . still, I had this strong feeling toward him, so that the sudden loss just shocked me. I was at home when Nica called, so I told Lorraine what had happened and then went down to the basement to be on my own."

The look in his eyes made me search for a happy memory of their relationship.

"By the way, Diz, what was this story about you two guys kissing each other on stage at Carnegie Hall?"

The memory brought a smile back:

"Yeah . . . must have been in 1947 and we were finally playing Carnegie Hall. Our relationship was just perfect then. We were enjoying playing together and impressed the audience. Suddenly, after we close one of the numbers, Bird walks off in silence. Then he comes back and he holds this beautiful, expensive, long-stemmed red rose that he hands to me in silence. Then he kisses me noisily on the lips and leaves the stage!"

While he smiled at the memory, I stood up and gave him a brief hug.

"OK, Giovanni. I have no long-stemmed red rose to give you, but a kiss always! Here! I must really rush now. See you in New York! Ciao-ciao!"

ACT XIX—MONSIEUR DIZI' JILLEPSI'

There were the annual meetings at the Grande Parade du Jazz at Nice, every July. Dizzy would often join us for a special meal at the excellent table of Bernard and Colette Taride, after which he would burp his satisfaction and go off to the festival, ahead of us.

At other times he would meet me directly on the festival grounds and drag me for an afternoon meal at the Soul Food restaurant. I would tease him, remembering with a dreamy sigh the excellent soul food lunch offered me by Max Roach at the Boondocks in New York, and he would react with his invitation to take me to Cheraw and enjoy a *real* soul food meal prepared by his favorite aunt.

"She's a great cook, the greatest . . . ! The Boondocks . . . bah!"

There was one amusing aspect of his personality that seemed to emerge whenever he was on the festival grounds, often seated with a group of his older musician friends. His voice and his accent, as well as his English phrasing, would gradually become rougher and more Southern, as if he were back in his youth in South Ca'linah. I told him so once, how he spoke much more hurriedly on those occasions, almost stuttering at some points, and that he sounded as if he had "a hot potato" in his mouth.

He gave me a long, supercilious look, but I knew he was amused. Then he raised his brows and spoke with the most incredible posh-English accent:

"Oh, I say! Really now, *is* that so? Hmm . . . rather peculiar; what?!" Then he added, "Hah! Gotcha!"

And the times when we would meet directly in the festival grounds at Cimiez and exchange a "bisou" French style on both cheeks, speaking volubly in French, "Mon cher Maestro Dizi' Jilepsi'!" . . . "Ah, Madame Lili'!"

I would invariably sniff his cheek and try to guess his aftershave lotion. On one occasion I complimented him on a particularly refined and classic scent but he would not tell me the name of it. The next day he found me, backstage, and handed me a small package.

"Here, keep this preciously 'cause it's made especially for me by my friend the perfumer. This way you can close your eyes, sniff, and think of me."

Today I have it on my table, as I write, and I read the label on the cologne bottle: "Dizzy 930," made by Parfums Premiers—Compagnie de Argeville.

How he loved those festival days in the Arènes de Cimiez, in the brotherly atmosphere of all those famous jazzmen gathered together by George Wein and Simone Ginibre! Dizzy's laughing voice would be heard miles away, and he was a constant magnet for the crowds who migrated from one of the three stages to the next one, and then the last one, in search of his performances. Those magic days and nights, those great historical performers who enjoyed being there, together, to play their own program and then join their friends on some other stage. They would produce jam sessions of such quality and uniqueness that made one think: "When one day all this will come to an end, there will be thousands of people who will look back at all these magic, incredible years and feel a melancholy for the loss, but also very lucky for having lived them."

And Dizzy will remain one of the leading figures of those memories, as everyone will recall the unique poster publicizing the Grande Parade du Jazz for all those many years: a caricature of Dizzy in a knee-length bathing suit, from whence protruded his rounded stomach, playing a trumpet to the sun.

For any nostalgic who will take a stroll on the grounds of Cimiez today, he will read the names of famous jazz artists on the various Allées crossing the vast area. Barney Willem, Ellington, Armstrong, a bust of Hampton . . .

Then strolling along the Allée Miles Davis—toward the garden steps leading to the Saint Francis Church and Cemetery where Henri Matisse is buried—he will find on the righthand side, at the corner of that road, an angle with the two signs, nudging each other: Allée Dizzy Gillespie—Allée Miles Davis. He will notice that they passed away within two years of each other.

Sorting out my memories of "Dizzy and the Riviera," I believe the last time we met there was in July 1990. This time he was to play at the Antibes–Juan-les-Pins Jazz Festival, leading his great "dream come true," the United Nations Orchestra with musicians chosen from among the best from North and South America: along with James Moody were Mario Riviera, Paquito de Rivera, Claudio Roditi, Arturo Sandoval, Slide Hampton, Steve Turre, Danilo Perez, John Lee, Ed Cherry, Airto Moreira, Giovanni Hidalgo, and Ignacio Berroa.

Presently we were sitting in his hotel room, having just spoken on the phone with Lorraine, and I congratulated him: "So now you have succeeded in your Bahá'í project; you have united the various nations in a brotherhood of music. You must be satisfied, no?"

"Yeah, they're great guys, but that's just one step in the right direction. I just hope they will carry on after I've gone . . ."

"After you've gone . . . and left me crying . . . ," I sang sobbingly to him to break the melancholy mood that seemed about to creep on him. He smiled and asked when I was going to cook the same pasta I had prepared for him in New York, when he had joined us for lunch at Abbey Lincoln's place on the day of Count Basie's funeral. It had been a concoction that had won his enthusiastic approval.

I had been Abbey's guest at the time. Calling Dizzy on the phone, we had made a date for the next day at the Abyssinian Church in Harlem and, after the funeral, he had come to Abbey's home for his special pasta.

At lunch we had spoken of various things, remembered some friends who had gone ahead, and it had been a very relaxed, thoughtful afternoon with a Dizzy mellowed by the day's occasion. However, just before leaving, he had grabbed the phone, dialed a number and exclaimed, "Hey . . . Longo! Here's a real Italian for you; let's see if you really speak it!" and handed me the phone, telling me to speak Italian. Of course, I was familiar with the name of Mike Longo, the pianist who had stood by Dizzy in the critical 1960s and had taken care of him during his alcoholic sprees, including the time Dizzy had ended up in hospital as a DOA case in 1973.

I picked up the phone, and Mike Longo proved to be a very pleasant person indeed. Dizzy had meanwhile sneaked away from the apartment, chuckling.

So now we were back in Nice with Dizzy's pasta request. Very well; with Robert and Lydia Amoyel as well as Bernard and Colette Taride it was agreed, on the spot, to organize a special dinner in Antibes, at the Amoyel home, where each one of the ladies involved would offer a special dish to satisfy Dizzy's gourmet weakness. How about the next evening, early, before the performance? Yes! Bernard would pick him up at the hotel and drive him to the Amoyel home.

By now the intimate dinner had become a reunion of a large number of Dizzy's French friends and admirers: men, women, and children. Simone Ginibre had also been kidnapped from Nice to join us. Dizzy enjoyed the food and the affection bestowed upon him, so much so that in the end, his assistant-manager had to drag him away in time for the concert. Standing in front of his United Nations Orchestra that night, he looked truly satisfied with life.

"Signor Giovanni Gillespo"

Later that same summer we met in Verona. The summer jazz festival held at the impressive Arena amphitheater—which hosted also an exceptional opera season—on that particular evening offered a program that jazz fans would remember all their lives. On that magic evening they would enjoy three groups: the one with Miles Davis; then Dizzy Gillespie with his United Nations Orchestra; and the Max Roach percussion group plus the Maxine Roach strings.

When I joined Dizzy in Verona, he had first dragged me on a guided tour of that beautiful city. Upon finally entering the Arena from the artists' entrance, he had stepped out onto the stage to stand, motionless, gazing at the ancient golden stones in the afternoon sun. Shaking his head, he had returned to his dressing room and commented with Max on the beauty of the scene. I had told them to wait till nightfall, during the concert, when thousands of people crowding all the space available would light up the candles furnished by the organization.

Dizzy was a happy, mellow man that day, and when Miles Davis arrived as well, passing by Dizzy's dressing room with just a glance and a nod, Dizzy was gracious enough to join Davis in his room and chat with him.

As the concert unfolded, one couldn't help considering that here were two famous artists: Max Roach and Miles Davis, who truly owed a huge debt of gratitude to Dizzy, who had welcomed them as young kids in his newly created jazz world, teaching Miles his instrumental secrets and nurturing Max out of a dangerous addiction when he was just sixteen. It also warmed one's heart to watch Dizzy directing his "dream come true" orchestra.

ACT XX—DIZZY'S DAY

Thinking back along those many years, it gives us a warm feeling of satisfaction to remember the two special events we had been able to offer him.

Of course, one of them had been the unforgettable adventure of his one-and-only European concert with the full symphonic orchestra of RAI Torino. The other was "Dizzy's Day" in September 1987, when we organized—with the City of Bassano's blessing—a huge "concert-party" for Dizzy's seventieth birthday. It was decreed that on that occasion he would be given official Honorary Citizenship by the Administration of Bassano del Grappa, and we were also announcing a new section, for blind students, in our music school. This decision had come about when we were approached by two young men during one of the concerts we produced for the City of Bassano. They were blind and had asked if we could teach them jazz in braille.

We discovered that in Italy there were hardly any institutes for the blind who taught music at all, let alone jazz. Dizzy was touched by the request and as usual expressed his total faith in my abilities to "go ahead and do something about it" . . . so I began by investigating what was being done in the United States, and this time he took an active part in our project. He handed me a letter dutifully signed by him, to be sent to a list of people who could help us in obtaining some musical material in braille typescript.

I have the original letter underhand, and here is his message:

> Dear Interested Philanthropist. (*This heading is in his handwriting.*)
>
> The "Dizzy Gillespie" Popular School of Music was founded in September 1983, in Bassano del Grappa, Italy, mainly as a means of bringing today's youth closer to music and off the streets. In September 1987 the School enlarged its scope to include non-seeing students. Many problems arise on this project and a major one is the scarce jazz material available in Braille print. It would seem that this is a general lack throughout the world.
>
> We intend to organize a "Bank" of such jazz material, and, once transcribed from normal print into Braille, it will be put at the disposal of any blind student or musical institute in need of it.
>
> If you feel that such an endeavor has merit, please participate by making available any of your music, methods, exercises, etc., with a written authorization to transcribe it into Braille print and to make free use of it.
>
> I shall personally be very happy to see you join us in our effort, and ask you to contact our Director and Co-founder, Lilian Terry, at the address printed above, who will follow up in detail.
>
> Thank you. Sincerely, Dizzy Gillespie (*hand signed*).
>
> John B. Gillespie, Founder and Honorary President.

It was decided that on the occasion of Dizzy's Day we would inform the press and all institutes concerned.

Obviously, the organization of the event began a year ahead. I will not go into the harrowing details that such a huge task entailed. I'll just mention that the "happening" took place in the Bassano Velodrome, which seated five thousand people, and that about eighty jazz musicians had been invited. The press, radio, and TV media were attracted from various parts of Europe, and a large, handsome, and colorful poster was soon to become a collector's piece.

Here is the last letter of recommendations sent to Dizzy, just before his departure for Italy.

28 August 1987,

My dear Giovanni Cappuccino. Thirteen days to D-Day and I am a sleepless, foodless robot wondering how on earth I got myself involved in this huge project. It's your fault because you backed us on the Bassano jazz school and so we want to thank you publicly with all the honors and affection you deserve.

Now the latest news: I have gone back to working directly for the Municipality with a new office in the Town Hall and two girls to assist me; plus some students from our school as "gofers." Incidentally, you should see the huge posters that our graphic artist Franco Barbon has drawn up. I'll send you some copies at home for your collection.

Now here is the program and please take note:

Leave NY by ALITALIA on Wednesday 09/09. Please be at Kennedy airport by 5.30pm, at the ticket office of Alitalia where a charming lady, Clara Chernin, will take good care of you. Departure is at 7.30pm.

Arrive at MILANO Malpensa in the morning. Yes, you'll have time for your "incoming cappuccino" then you will be driven to Bassano to the Hotel Belvedere, to your usual suite.

Rest until 5 pm when I shall pick you up to go to the Town Hall. There you shall witness the official Meeting of the Council (40 aldermen) who will vote on your Honorary Citizenship. Then the Mayor will confer upon you the official Citizenship, probably with some gold key, and everybody will kiss you. Then we'll go to dinner and possibly a party at the Sporting Club to celebrate the affair.

Incidentally, you will travel with Max Roach and Sandra Jackson while Milt will fly in the next morning from Los Angeles, just for that concert night and then fly back again . . . Also Randy Brecker will fly in and out on the 11th just to play with you. Johnny Griffin and Madame will come from France, Tete Montoliou from Barcelona and Eric Peters from Switzerland, and that's your band. There will also be another 70 musicians who will play in your honor.

On the morning of the 11th you will be interviewed and televiewed. At the Town Hall the Mayor of Bassano will give you your honorary citizenship. At lunchtime you will elope with me to go home where mother will fix you some gourmet surprises, the farmwoman will pick your fresh figs and we shall have a bucolic luncheon with lots of goodies cooked by different guests who want to honor you through your taste buds. One of them is thinking up some fig desserts for "diabetic trumpet players" for you to enjoy at this lunch.

Of course also Max and Bags and the other musicians of your group will be there. Some VIPs from Bassano will also be there and, while you relax in your favorite garden easy chair, everybody will tell you how great you are and what you mean to them. Another ego-trip, in other words.

At 5pm we'll go over to the Velodrome for a sound check and brief rehearsal with your group then you are off to rest until 9pm.

The concert starts at 6pm with all the young jazz musicians who are coming from various parts of Italy to join in the party. However, you will be brought back to the Velodrome around 9pm when the festivities will get into high gear until well after midnight.

I seem to remember your weakness for a certain pistachio cake? Well, who knows what surprises we have up our sleeve? An "after midnight" gourmet dinner in a lovely home will close the whole works and the next morning you will be driven to Venice airport to fly to Paris and be met by Wim Wigt.

Ah, my dear Giovanni! For the first time in my life I am organizing a maxi event with 70 musicians, over six hours of music non-stop with people flying in from everywhere at different times, hotels, car rides, radio and TV, and sponsors who back out . . . Mother looks at me and shakes her head in silence . . . At night I wake with a start at 4am and kick myself for having brought all this upon myself. Then I think of our school, and I am grateful that you let me use your charismatic name to bring it all about. So I go back to sleep saying to myself that it's OK, it will all work out beautifully. I am so tired, physically and mentally, but I must send this to you before the Monday morning rush.

I'll phone you in a week's time. Regards to Lorraine, is the house all fixed up by now? How is her health? Are you quite sure she won't change her mind and come after all? Love to both of you."

For once, to my great wonder, there were no unusual problems to solve. Everybody arrived from everywhere at the right time, everybody was happy to be part of the festivities. Everybody did his best for a smooth and successful unwinding of the concert. Everybody succeeded in doing so.

But the first important step took place in the morning at the town hall. Dressed in his Armani suit, Dizzy entered the hall very soberly and joined the mayor and leading aldermen on the dais. He listened attentively to my translation of the motivation for this occasion, and the mayor handed him the Keys to the City, pronouncing John Birks Gillespie an Honorary Citizen of Bassano del Grappa. Next, he was asked to sign the Special Illustrious Guest Book. He did so, very soberly, and then realized that the signature just before his own was that of the Queen Mother of England on a previous visit. That did it. His irrepressible sense of humor sent him rushing to seat himself in the mayor's seat with a look of royal importance. The solemn atmosphere dissolved in smiles and amused shaking of heads.

The rest of the day—at lunch at our house and later in town for the sound check—was a concentrated series of sober discussions that would dissolve in a burst of general laughter. His highest peak was when, while waiting for his cappuccino in his favorite bar, he smiled at all the bystanders who ogled him and then burst out singing "O Sole Mio!"

We were finally able to send him off for a nap at his hotel.

At 9:30 P.M., when the concert had been underway since 6:00 P.M., Dizzy's limousine arrived behind the huge circular bandstand covered by a large circus tent, set in the very center of the Velodrome. They led him almost secretly to his caravan "for his privacy," unaware of his huge curiosity. He was soon sneaking around, embracing old friends—and pretty assistants—and finally he arrived at the corner edge of the bandstand, where, leaning lazily against it, he looked around at the multitude gathered for him. In the tropical heat of the night he saw a crowd made of young and old, with restless children running about while the older fans were happy to witness a live concert by the idol of their youth. The atmosphere was of friendly expectation, and Dizzy took it all in.

He was holding his periscopic trumpet by his side, and in no time somebody recognized him; soon, there was a huge roar calling him: "Ciao Dizzy!" "Hey Dizzy!" "Dizzy!"

Before we could guess what was on his mind, he had walked straight out toward the public, waving his trumpet and grinning as he crossed the field. When he climbed the flight of steps to the low barrier that separated the public from the field and started shaking hands, there was a large downward wave of movement from the very far upper end of the seats as well as the wings, all reaching out to him. Finally, the police and firemen had to rush to him and practically lift him off his feet to escort him safely backstage, where I scolded him.

"You realize that a crowd of five thousand fans was about to break down the safety barrier in order to get to you? And that the musicians on stage had to stop their performance?"

"Gee guys, I'm sorry . . ."—then an impish smile: "I only wanted to say ciao to the guys who had noticed me . . . I didn't think that the whole crowd would . . ."

"Lorraine would say you just don't think. But it's OK, I'm glad you were able to feel this huge wave of love . . ."

"Yeah, incredible . . . I'm sorry I couldn't shake everybody's hand . . ."

"Yes, and after five thousand handshakes, then play with your feet?"

"Gee, look at that! It's beautiful . . ."

He was looking at the huge scoreboard high above the field where the technicians had designed a periscopic trumpet with stars and flowers flashing out and changing into "Dizzy's Day." This was followed by "Happy birthday Dizzy," "Felice compleanno Maestro," and "Auguri Dizzy," interspersed with electronic fireworks. Like a small boy, he watched the whole exhibition with joyful wonder, turning to shake his head at me from time to time.

The various groups invited to "play their good wishes" were giving their best to an appreciative audience when came another most unexpected moment during the evening that really took everybody by surprise—the public, the sound technicians, and myself.

During a pause—while one group was leaving the stage and the following one was starting to set up—our irrepressible Dizzy had managed to sneak onstage, quietly. He had sat himself at the piano and started playing "'Round Midnight."

One of the technicians passing by had turned on the piano microphones, and when we looked to see who was playing . . . there he was! He had motioned to the same man to set up a voice microphone, and suddenly we had the most unexpected performance of Dizzy as pianist and blues singer! He sang-shouted his joy at being there, and as a finale he fiddled around with the keys, hummed, and closed his performance right there.

He rose and bowed from the waist very formally, like a classic concert pianist, and walked off in dignity amid the roar of the crowd.

And finally, at long last, our stars were climbing onstage: from Spain, pianist Tete Montoliu, from Switzerland Eric Peter on bass, and then the young American trumpet player Randy Brecker. And **now!** Here were the historic names: on saxophone Johnny Griffin, the MJQ vibraphonist Milt Jackson, and the giant of percussion Max Roach. And, finally, the long-awaited guest star Dizzy Gillespie! After many years, Dizzy was surrounded by his—now famous—ex-students, who had willingly come to Italy just for two days in order to wish him a musical "happy birthday."

What followed was a series of musical fireworks, acclaimed with a true ovation by the enthusiastic public. But the occasion that floored Dizzy was when—having been led off to his secluded caravan car to meet the press—we quickly set on the grounds, almost in front of the stage and with the assistance of five strong stage hands, a truly enormous seven-tiered pistachio cake that rose well over three meters above. The revolving base tier was about two meters in diameter, while the top one was at least fifty centimeters and carried a very large, candied, golden periscopic trumpet held by a chocolate hand. Seventy gold candles shone around the seven tiers, and a tall folding ladder was opened for him to climb gradually to the top so he could blow out all the candles, with three stagehands standing by to assist him in his climb while the cake was turned around on its pivot, within his reach.

When all was set, we informed the public that we were going to surprise Dizzy, and would they please keep very quiet until he came forward and saw the cake. Then all would sing "Happy Birthday" to him.

I went backstage to call him and, walking and talking arm in arm, we turned the corner and he stopped short, one leg lifted forward, gasping and looking way up to the top of the lit up cake.

"Here's your pistachio goodie, Giovanni Gillespo."

As I leaned over to kiss his cheek, there began the huge wave of five thousand voices singing together: "Happy birthday to you . . . ," in English and Italian, followed by all kinds of good wishes shouted in various languages. He closed his eyes tightly, shook his head, and heaved a sigh; then he turned to the cake.

He started blowing the candles one by one, gradually climbing onto the ladder, steadily assisted, while every tier was spun around on its special base. By the time he reached the seventh cake on top, he was clowning a heart attack, blowing his cheeks in the Gillespie fashion, and rolling his eyes. He finally grabbed the chocolate hand and golden periscopic trumpet and came gingerly down the ladder. A large silver knife appeared, and he gave two cuts on the bottom cake. *Applause!* The staff moved the cake to the side and started cutting small parts for as many people as possible in the public. Just before moving away, Dizzy put out his hand and grabbed a lump from the cake and stuffed it in his mouth. He shook his head: "Oh, my God, I can't believe it's so good!"

"Happy birthday, von Karajan . . ."

"Yeah . . . now I have two gifts from you that I won't forget, long as I live."

"We'll have another "Dizzy's Day" to celebrate your seventy-fifth. In October '92."

"Yeah . . . that would be nice."

"But only on condition that you bring Lorraine with you."

"Well, I'll try to convince her. She might!"

But, of course, by October 1992 he was not "in good enough shape" to accept our invitation.

CODA

John Birks Gillespie passed away in New Jersey on January 6, 1993. Fatefully, it was Lorraine Gillespie's birthday.

Just two days earlier, she had informed us that Dizzy was again in hospital but should be coming home soon. She had given us his direct phone number that we might call him and cheer him up, as he had sounded depressed when she had last spoken to him.

I called the hospital, gave my name to the nurse, and then was speaking to him. He had a small, weary voice that touched my heart as we exchanged the usual Italian greetings. I told him I was calling from Francesco's home in Hawaii and that we all sent our love, including a collection of well-wishing messages from the students of our music school. They hoped to see him soon, during one of his surprise visits while on tour in Europe, and were preparing a special concert in his honor. He sounded pleased, but his voice was weakening by the minute.

"Giovanni, my dear, I'll let you rest now. We just wanted to give you all our love. We'll call again tomorrow or the next day, OK?"

Almost a whisper: "Yeah, ciao bella . . ."

Two mornings later Seth Markow, a Honolulu radio reporter, called to say that Dizzy had just passed away. Would we care to go to the radio station to commemorate him?

Sorry, not then nor for a long while would we be able to open the memories of a friendship as unusual as it had been special for our family.

Today we do so, trusting it might be of interest to the general reader to discover a most stimulating and unusual hero of the Afro-American cultural inheritance for which the United States of America are admired and appreciated the world over.

You have been offered a special look at particular moments concerning Dizzy Gillespie's later years, and we hope we have informed and amused you, whether you were familiar with his personality or not.

We realize that, having collected our happiest memories of those years, this narrative might seem written with a constant smile, for such was Dizzy's attitude toward life and probably the way he would wish to be remembered: with a smile.

However, he was not a "Santa Claus" kind of man. At given times his laughter could be ironical, though never sarcastic, and he was not constantly well disposed. His life's experience as a black man and a jazz musician—even after fame had blessed him—had been ruthless enough to give him a good dose of tempered distrust toward some of his fellowmen. Also, his energetic curiosity, his love of clowning, and his keen sense of human nature's ridicule had led him to behaviors not always in the best of taste. But his love of life and devotion to his music had raised him well above his shortcomings.

He had reflected one day that God must have decided that his role in the world was not to be just a musician. The fact that most of his contemporaries had departed long ago, while he was still around, made him consider that his role on earth had to go beyond his music. So he applied himself to being a humanitarian, reaching out in many ways—many unknown to the general public—especially toward the young people.

What is certain is the fact that he has never really left us. To quote Jon Hendricks, in Benny Golson's moving ballad "I Remember Clifford," we might say: ". . . for those who heard, they repeat him yet. So those who hear won't forget . . ."

At least as long as some trumpet player, anywhere on this planet, will raise his horn to the skies to play "A Night in Tunisia."

Way up above, be assured that Dizzy will be there, listening with a pleased smile and explaining the bebop chords to Archangel Gabriel, or probably—while slip-slapping his hands—he'll be illustrating one of Chano Pozo's special rhythm inventions. He might even be teaching Gabe to play his periscopic trumpet. They might be "chasing" and "exchanging fours" right now.

Why not?

But, of course, there is one truly perfect picture that comes to mind. Dizzy is finally reunited with Bird, the being he called "the other side of my heartbeat," and, as long ago, the heavens become alive with their music.

Pistoia, Italy, 1981—Laughing at the rain.
Courtesy of Carlo Ruberti

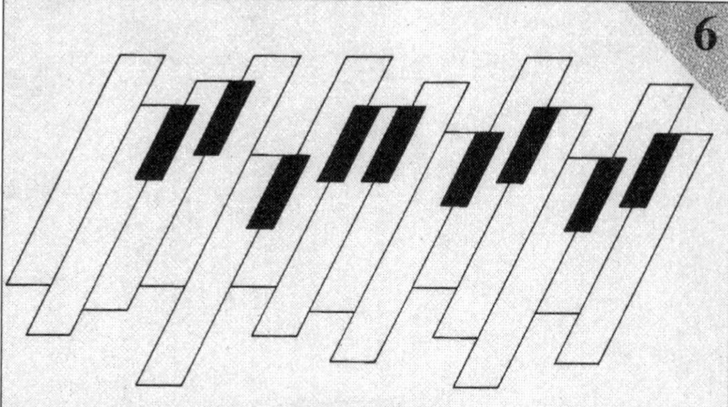

AUDITORIUM • I CONCERTI DI TORINO

Concerto Straordinario
Giovedì 12 maggio 1983 • ore 21.00

6° Concerto stagione di primavera
Venerdì 13 maggio 1983 • ore 21.00

Quintetto Dizzy Gillespie

ORCHESTRA SINFONICA DI TORINO
DELLA RADIOTELEVISIONE ITALIANA

Direttore
Tom Mc Intosh

Gillespie
Con Alma, suite
(Arrangiamento di Robert Farnon)
A night in Tunisia
(Arrangiamento e orchestrazione di J. J. Johnson)

Mc Intosh
Metamorfosi sinfoniche sul tema «Algo bueno» di Dizzy Gillespie
(1ª esecuzione delle versioni con orchestra sinfonica)

Dizzy Gillespie in Quintetto

Gillespie
Bella Italia Suite 1983
(1ª esecuzione assoluta)

Dizzy Gillespie
tromba
Roberto Enriquez
pianoforte
Michael Kent Howell
contrabbasso
Bernard Purdy
batteria
Big Black
conghe

Il concerto sarà trasmesso da Radio Uno in collegamento diretto.

A concerto iniziato non sarà consentito l'ingresso in Sala.

Turin, 1983—Poster for Dizzy's symphonic concert in Italy.

Campione d'Italia, in Switzerland, 1983. This photo becomes the cover photo of our LP together. Dizzy (in African dress) and Lilian Terry.
Courtesy of Fulvio Roiter.

September 1987—He is most officially named Honorary Citizen of Bazzano at the Municipality.

His lunch birthday party at our home.

The poster of the huge concert to celebrate "Dizzy's Day" (September 1987).

Crosses the field to go up to shake hands with the yelling public.

Cutting the cake, assisted by strong hands.

Hawaii 1991—Last visit with Francesco and little Alice.

1917–2017 Historic Centennial

February to November 1917

Birth of Communism through the Russian Revolution
that was to spread across the decades
from Petrograd the world over,
influencing nations to this very day.

October 21, 1917

Birth of John Birks "Dizzy" Gillespie, main creator of the Bebop revolution,
transforming jazz from "dancehall" to
"concert hall" music respected the world over,
influencing musicians to this very day.

LILIAN TERRY has been active in the European jazz field since the late 1950s as a singer, journalist, producer, Italian radio and TV personality, and concert organizer.

The University of Illinois Press
is a founding member of the
Association of American University Presses.

University of Illinois Press
1325 South Oak Street
Champaign, IL 61820-6903
www.press.uillinois.edu

Made in the USA
Middletown, DE
11 November 2022